Legends of Sambar

Child of Rydos

by James Willis

Legends of Sambar

Child of Rydos

First Edition: November 2017

ISBN: 9781973330004

This is a work of fiction. Names, characters, places, and incidents either are the product of the author's imagination or are used fictitiously, and any resemblance to actual persons, living or dead, business establishments, events, or locales is entirely coincidental.

Copyright © 2017 by James Willis
All rights reserved.

www.jameswillisauthor.com
www.legendsofsambar.com

For Allison

Contents

Map	iii
Prologue	1
Chapter I – Death of a Messenger	6
Chapter II – Death of a King	16
Chapter III – Conclave	30
Chapter IV – To the point	43
Chapter V – Unexpected Direction	58
Chapter VI – Little Thieves	69
Chapter VII – Frozen Delight	76
Chapter VIII – Children's Games	84
Chapter IX – Jewel of the Desert	93
Chapter X – Cartwheels and Cabbages	101
Chapter XI – Horsemeet	110
Chapter XII – Desert Deserters	116
Chapter XIII – Wizard's Wrath	131
Chapter XIV – Army Ambulation	140
Chapter XV – Servitude is an Option	150
Chapter XVI – Rope Tricks	160
Chapter XVII – Unwelcome Guests	168
Chapter XVIII – Swift Sails	179
Chapter XIX – Reunion	192
Chapter XX – Gorilla Warfare	202
Chapter XXI – Northern Run	212
Chapter XXII – Serfdom is not an Option	224
Chapter XXIII – Foothold	236
Chapter XXIV – Ptanga put down	244
Chapter XXV – Mountain Mystics	252
Chapter XXVI – Mystical Assembly	263

Chapter XXVII – Northern Support	272
Chapter XXVIII – Nars Opens	280
Epilogue	289

Map

The Kingdoms of Sambar

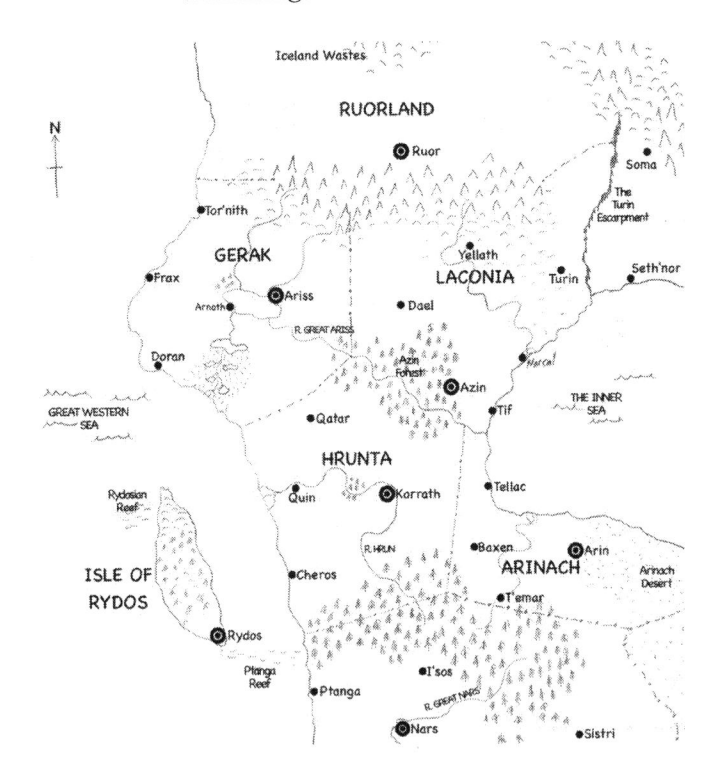

Prologue

Liliana could not remember how she had gotten here, nor was she certain of where 'here' was. Under her bare feet she could feel dried mud, leaf mulch and twigs. Trees loomed all around her, casting sinister shadows in the moonlight. A cold wind slid icy fingers over her skin and thin night shift. She was breathing heavily, she must have run here, but from where? She felt a sense of panic and foreboding. Her mind did not feel as if it were her own, almost as if some other force were trying to direct it, suggest ideas to it. In the distance, she thought she could hear someone calling her name and the sound of someone approaching through the forest. All she could think of was the fact she had to keep moving deeper into the forest. She picked up the hem of her night shift and ran onwards through the trees and into the depth of the night.

Liliana had lost track of time and direction as she continued to stumble on through the forest, branches from low trees and bushes scratching and slapping her as she forced her way through the undergrowth and away from the sounds of pursuers. She could not even remember what she was running from and who was chasing her. The experience had a nightmarish quality, but pain in her feet and from the scratches on her skin told her this could not be a dream. Still she knew the desperate need to continue onwards, hopefully towards salvation.

"Elerin, preserve me." She offered up quietly in

prayer, between her panting breaths, as she paused again briefly to catch her breath. There was no point trying to get her bearings, she did not recognise this forest at all. *Odd*, a small thought niggled on the edge of her subconscious, *I thought I knew all forests of my homeland.*

The moon was high overhead now, its gentle light piercing through the trees, which were thinning out slightly. Liliana was on the edge of utter exhaustion. She had already fallen completely flat to the ground, tripping over tree roots, or even just her own feet a number of times during her flight. Mud masked her pale complexion and dirtied her blonde hair, but her bright blue eyes still glittered in the moonlight through it all. She could not continue much longer. To be honest, she was surprised that she had not been caught yet. Her pursuers presumably knew this stretch of forest better than she did, but though she had heard them nearby several times, she did not think they had set eyes on her since her escape.

The quality of the air seemed different here, lighter, easier to breath, though perhaps that was just because she had stopped moving for too long and was regaining her breath. Liliana noted that the lightness and airiness of the forest seemed to increase in the direction off to her left, suggesting there might be some sort of clearing close by. Then she thought she heard a strange sound filtering through the trees. Not the sound of her pursuers, but more like a muffled cry. Rather than increase her fear, the sound filled her with curiosity. She moved slowly towards it, too exhausted now that she had paused and her body had begun to catch up with her to move any faster.

Prologue

Ahead was a glade in the trees, covered with long grass and moss, taking advantage of the opening to the sky. In the moonlight and with a gentle breeze that rustled the leaves, the spot seemed peaceful, except for the noise coming from what appeared to be a parcel of rags in the centre of the glade. Liliana moved quickly again now, reaching the rags and picking up the small bundle, which had stopped making any noise. As she straightened herself up, Liliana sensed that one of her pursuers had finally caught up with her. She turned around slowly to face her assailant, who was standing still at the edge of the clearing, peering from the gloom into the moonlit glade.

"My Lady?" Asked the man who stood there, dressed in hunting leathers and, an insignia blazoned on his sleeve. As she held the bundle – no simple bundle, but in fact a baby – and as she heard the voice of the man who had pursued her to this glade, the haze and confusion around her thoughts seemed to lift from her and she began to think more clearly. She recalled a name,

"… Beran?"

"Yes, my Lady?" Beran responded, growing confused himself, by this chase and his Lady's mood.

"Isn't it beautiful, Beran?" Liliana asked. It was then than Beran realised that she had found a child in this clearing, only adding to his confusion. What was an unattended baby doing in the middle of the forest? And what part of the forest were they in exactly as he could not recognise it? He was worried, but when he looked at the child everything seemed all right.

"My Lady," Beran sought to find the correct words, "The king woke to find you gone in the middle of the

Child of Rydos

night. He was concerned and so raised the entire hunting party to go out searching for you. You've had us on a merry pursuit half the night." As Beran spoke, Liliana came more and more to herself. She remembered now that it was the occasion of the annual royal hunt. An event she did not particularly have any taste for, but was an important part of Rydosian culture and something her husband, King Lysan, enjoyed greatly. It was not that she objected to the hunting of wild game. It was the less wild, and much less interesting, company amongst the ladies of the court that she had to keep at the royal hunting lodge whilst the men of the court were out having a gay time that she objected to. The day had been typically boring. The ladies of the court had bantered about nonsense and compared their husbands' prowess at the hunt based on the catches they brought back to the lodge. She had forced a smile on her face throughout the evening's banqueting and had retired for the night as soon as it was seemly for her to do so.

She remembered tossing and turning a lot as she tried to sleep. It was later in the evening that her memories became hazy. She did not remember leaving her bedroom, nor how she got herself into the forest and into the confused state of believing she was being chased. Even now those memories which had seemed so vivid of the night's chase through the forest had begun to fade. She would have though the whole thing a bizarre dream, if it were not for the small child she now held in her arms. Looking down at the child again she felt a fresh sense of calmness and rightness with the world.

"Perhaps we should be getting back to the king?"

Prologue

Beran broke the queen's reverie.

"Yes." Liliana responded, "Do you know your way back from here? I don't seem to recognise this part of the forest."

"Neither do I, my Lady," Beran admitted, much do his concern, "But, I'm fairly confident I can retrace my steps and get us back to the hunting lodge... I assume we're taking the child with us?"

"Well we certainly can't leave it here!" Liliana replied, shock entering into her voice. Beran quickly gave a gesture to indicate that he had not considered such to be an option.

"Won't my husband be in for a surprise?" Liliana remarked, almost too cheerfully, given the night's peculiar events, as they headed back into the forest.

Beran tried many times, over the years, to find that glade again, but no matter how hard he searched he never managed to come upon its location as he and the queen had that night.

Chapter I – Death of a Messenger

The guard watched as the ragged shell of a man staggered towards the southern gate of the city where he was on watch. The man's clothes were muddy and torn and his shoes were worn through. Eventually the man reached the gate and fell at the guard's feet.

"Please…please…" He rasped, "You must help me. I have an urgent message for the palace." The man lifted his hand, revealing his palm to the guard before collapsing in a heap at his feet. On the man's hand the guard saw, tattooed, three concentric circles, the symbol of Circular Ariss.

"Fetch a healer, quickly!" The guard shouted back inside the gate to one of his fellows in the guardhouse positioned behind the gate. He then knelt to see if he could help the man lying in the dirt. Looking over the man, it was obvious his condition was not due to physical injury as there were no marks of this. The guard assumed it was sickness of some sort, which made him reticent to do too much more in case it was contagious. Best to wait for the healers to arrive.

The guild of healers works across Sambar though their headquarters are based in Circular Ariss in Gerak. They do not discriminate, but try to help everyone who is in need of aid. The guild is therefore a charitable organisation and is funded mainly by donations from wealthy landowners and merchants as well as having governmental support and the support of various temples throughout Sambar. They have a great knowledge of herb lore and some specialise in chirurgy. The healers themselves are instantaneously recognisable by the blue robes they wear as a sign of their profession. Chief Healer Hatha was the head of the guild, a position he had gained by virtue of his knowledge of healing and his aptitude for politics. Despite his position, he still took a very active role in the day-to-day workings of the healers and it was he who went to attend the man who had fallen at the southern gate.

By the time Hatha reached the gate the guards on duty had manage to straighten out the man who had collapsed, though he was still unconscious.

"You have moved him." Hatha reprimanded the guard, "That was not necessarily a good idea at this stage." Hatha went and knelt next to the self-proclaimed messenger, placing a hand upon his forehead, then opening his mouth and examining his gums before smelling his breath.

"He has been poisoned. We must get him to the nearest healing house so I can properly minister to his needs." At a signal from the healer, the attendants he had brought with him laid a litter next to the man and lifted him onto it to bear him gently into the city. There were many healing houses in Ariss so they did not have to travel far. They passed through the southern gate and headed up the main paved concourse into the merchants' district of the city. Onlookers peered to see if they could catch whom it was that Chief Healer Hatha was escorting. It was only a few minutes before they arrived at the healing house, a large brick building with a covered courtyard on the main concourse. There was a queue leading out of the main building and a little way down the street of people with various minor maladies,

Child of Rydos

but they parted as soon as they saw the Chief Healer and the litter bearers, to allow them easier access to the complex. This healing house was one of the oldest in the city, being on the main route from the southern gate up to the palace in the centre of the city and it still retained most of its original features from when it was built nearly five hundred years before when the healers first began to operate as a guild. The main entrance had a pair of carved oak doors, worn from years of use. They were thrown open now to allow the litter access to the building. Hatha led the procession to a part of the building that was dark, yet well aired, as bright light would only serve to irritate the patient in his current state. They entered a small room which contained a cot with a horsehair mattress and the bearers gently lifted the still unconscious man onto the bed. Hatha asked everyone to leave the room whilst he bent over the ailing man to tend him.

The carriage drew to a stop, the driver got down and opened the carriage door. Gethas stepped out of the carriage,

"Wait here." He told the driver, before hurrying into the healing house, without waiting for a reply to see if his orders were being obeyed. A young healer met him at the entrance,

"This way, Your Majesty." He said, leading the king deeper into the healing house. Eventually they reached their destination and the young healer knocked quietly on the door.

"Enter." Called Hatha's distinctive voice from inside the room. The healer opened the door and let the king into the room, then leaving them he returned to his regular duties. As the king entered Hatha stood to face him, bowing deeply.

"Your Majesty, this is the man who requested your presence. He says he has urgent news. He is very near to death your Majesty, it appears he was shot with an arrow tipped with Querien, one of the most potent poisons available in Sambar. You should speak to him now, whilst he remains at least partially lucid." King Gethas walked over to the man lying on the cot in the middle of the room.

"Kino, you have served us valiantly. I'm sure you know that Hatha has been unable to do much more than ease your pain, there is no known cure for the poison you received. What news have you from your mission?"

"Your Majesty, thank you. I have terrible news. Everything we feared, it is true… I have seen it with my own eyes. We must be ready when the time comes. Their efforts are already well underway." Kino gasped for some air, "Also I think there is something wrong in the desert… I am not sure we can trust…" The poison was working fast now; a bluish tinge was evident under Kino's skin. His breathing became increasingly laboured, "…Your Majesty… I…" With that Kino took his final breath, his body started to convulse and suddenly it stopped, his body stiffening into a contorted posture.

"May Ranek watch over his soul in Aternium." Intoned Gethas, whilst simultaneously making the symbol of a diamond in the air, "Hatha, see if you can do something to make him more presentable, for his family's sake. I must go now; there is much to prepare for. Come to the palace once you have finished here."

"Yes, Your Majesty." Hatha bowed as the king left

the room.

Gerak was a prosperous nation because their trading interests did not lie in just one area, but they spread their resources across many areas, particularly focusing on trade with other nations. Their trade networks naturally led to an ability to establish extensive 'diplomatic' networks that made them the most well-informed nation in Sambar. This knowledge granted them great international powers, thus they were generally regarded as the leading nation of Sambar, despite not being as rich as Rydos. At the centre of Gerak was its capital, 'Circular' Ariss, which itself had been designed as a series of concentric circles, mimicking the feeling of most Gerakans that they were the centre of the world. The ordering to the ring-shaped districts of Ariss mirrored the social structure of the country as a whole. The poor were the most well represented, owning houses in the outermost, largest ring-district in the city, followed by the merchants, then the rich and noble. The centre of government, the king's and queen's palace, stood at the centre of all this, set in scenic gardens from which the whole city could be observed.

The city of Ariss had once been the capital of the historic kingdom of Sambar during the reign of Am Bære, over five hundred years ago. Am Bære had been the one who had spent his life uniting the once warring tribes and cities between the Inner Sea and the Great Western Sea. After the reign of Am Bære the kingdom had been split into six different nations, ruled over by Am Bære's children, and Ariss had at that point become the capital of the nation of Gerak. Construction on the palace had begun even before Am Bære had made the city his own as part of his conquests across the lands. The palace was a fairy tale-like conglomeration of mismatched towers, each built in the architectural style of its period. Siege had never been laid against its spirals and minarets; so much history could be traced by studying the awe-inspiring buildings. The only low-lying buildings in the palace complex were the royal stables, barracks and library.

The afternoon sun was already beginning its descent towards evening before the king was ready to discuss his plans with his advisors. He had called the gathering in his personal study in the east tower. The study was a large room with great, arched windows in a semicircle on the east side, which opened to allow access to a balcony. The vista looked out upon the Great Plains, stretching from Gerak, well into Laconia. Usually the room was filled with a few chairs and a couple of large oak desks. Today additional chairs had been added to the room to seat all those present. The walls of the study were the lined with bookshelves, historic tapestries and assorted maps.

Present were his most trusted advisors; his wife and co-ruler, Queen Gerta; his son, Koran; field general Kiesan, head of Gerak's armies; Gerakan Intelligence officer, Flint; King's Council Junta and Chief Healer Hatha. The healer wore his usual blue robes. Flint's clothing made him look suspiciously like a local merchant, with a colourful doublet and hose offsetting his lacklustre mousy hair. Both Koran and Keisen were dressed in army uniform, though both currently had set aside their armour. Gerakan military uniform consisted of woollen grey trousers and tunic worn over a white linen shirt. Golden coloured stitch work on their shirtsleeves and breasts indicated their ranking. Today the queen was wearing a modest, deep blue, empire line, silk dress, which came down to her ankles. An intricately woven silk shawl offset the plainly patterned dress. Gethas, himself, wore his robes of office, a bright-coloured affair worked with gold with long sleeves, obviously designed by someone with no sense of practicality. His attire signified to all in the room that this was a formal occasion.

"As you are all aware," Began Gethas, fixing his eyes on each person in the room in turn, to add weight to his speech, "Early this morning one of our field agents, Kino, returned to the city. He had been fatally poisoned in the line of duty and Hatha could do little but ease his suffering before he passed away. Before Kino died he passed some important information on to me, which I will relate to you now." Gethas drew a deep breath and looked around the chamber, "Some months ago, our agents began to hear rumours of strange occurrences in northern Narsos. Flint increased our agents working in the region, to get to the root of the rumours. Kino was the first of our agents to bring back any information, the others we sent are missing in action. There is a strong possibility that the Narsians are once again preparing for war, mobilising large numbers of troops. Our current intelligence is rather flaky though and we cannot risk acting without due cause; the situation is too volatile. I would have your thoughts on the action we should take at this stage." There was a heavy silence in the room as each member of the council weighed their thoughts, preparing to furnish the king with their ideas. Advisor Junta was the first to draw breath to speak. He stood to address the room as he did so, waiting for the king to be seated.

"This is momentous news. We cannot deal with this by ourselves, we need the cooperation of the other nations of Sambar." Noted Junta, "We must call Conclave to really discuss this issue. Furthermore, if the intelligence is proved true then it is our duty to inform the other nations, who will undoubtedly be affected by any war."

"Yes, I agree." Added Koran, "Though it is an awkward time internationally, I am not sure which nations will come, but Conclave must be called. We cannot make full preparations without the backing of the other nations of Sambar. I think most should come to a call of Conclave, though the Rydosians may stay away, due to the inopportune timing and Arinach has grown increasingly distant from us over the past two years…"

"You both are correct, my son, Junta." The king nodded to each as he replied, "Kino intimated that there may be some link between Arinach's behaviour and the news we have from Narsos. Even though we must wait for Conclave, there is still much we can discuss; the nation of Gerak can make their own surreptitious arrangements for the future whilst we wait to hear from others. It may also be useful to make some plans about how to proceed with Conclave."

"It would not hurt to start planning supply routes towards the south of the country." Suggested General Keisen, "We could even start moving some supplies surreptitiously." He glanced towards Flint with a raised eyebrow as he said this.

"Yes, we can probably manage something along those lines," Flint put in, "An increased number of trade wagons heading southwards may be surreptitious enough if we're careful. Then we'll be in a better position to support an army heading towards Narsos quickly if it is indeed required." The queen now decided to add her thoughts to the debate,

"We need to call and convene Conclave as expediently as possible. Carrier pigeons would be the quickest option, but they are more easily waylaid and this is a sensitive issue. It would be better, at least, for Rydos to hear the message directly. I suggest we send the messages by rider relay instead. Hopefully this will also prevent our correspondence from failing to reach their targets. If Narsos is planning war they undoubtedly have their own network of spies and agents working in Sambar. We had better make sure that we encrypt our messages. Narsos still has not managed to crack the technique we have used since Am Bære's time… Though if these rumours relating to Arinach are true, it may be that those secrets have been given away."

"I think we would know if Arinach had betrayed the rest of Sambar to that extent. Obviously, I keep regular checks on all suspected foreign agents working in Gerak." Commented Flint, "There are definitely a few Narsian agents at work, but nothing out of the ordinary as far as I can judge. It's easier to feed misinformation if we know who they are. It is feasible that there are some sleeper agents we have not yet discovered. I'll assign more operatives to look into it, given the circumstances."

"I think it might be time to have a reshuffle of the healers' guild. I'll attempt to make sure that those with expertise in battlefield medicine happen to be relocated to where they might be useful if it comes to war." Hatha added to the discussion.

"Good. I don't think there is much more we need to discuss right away. Each of you knows your duties. Make sure everything that can be done is done. You are dismissed." The king finished, waving towards the door, and so the preparations for Conclave began. Everyone except the queen and king filed out of his study. The two of them put their heads together and worked late into the evening, discussing how best to lay plans for the future. They huddled near the fireplace for light and warmth, in the cool autumn night-time, and it was not until the embers were glowing lightly and the dawn birds started to herald the morning that they retired to their chambers to get some rest.

Chapter II – Death of a King

Teran woke up with a start. Today was not a day he was looking forward to and consequently he had not slept at all well last night. He was sure that his mother and siblings had also slept unsoundly, for today they were to bury their father. To make matters worse, it would be a public funeral since their father was king and they would have to walk through the city with their father's bier, facing the crowds of Rydos who would no doubt want to catch a glimpse of their sovereign's funeral. Teran felt sorry for his elder brother as he would have to take on the responsibilities of ruling the small, yet prosperous, Isle of Rydos. It was probably time to get up soon so, rubbing sleep out of his eyes, he sat up letting the silk sheets fall away. He swung his legs round and got out of bed, walking over to the chair where his purple mourning robes had been laid out the night before in preparation for this morning.

Teran was a handsome young man, well tanned and muscular from years of weapons training in the sunny courtyards and gardens of the palace complex. His short brown hair had tinges of red and it was always ill-kempt. Like his mother, he had bright blue eyes, which on occasion could seem to pierce the very depths of your soul.

There was a knock at the door, so he quickly slipped his undergarments on and walked over to the door. The old maid, Gertha, who usually attended his brother was standing there.

"Your brother was wondering if you would like to take breakfast with him this morning, your highness." She told him.

"Is he ready to receive me right now?" He asked her.

"Yes, he has been up for some time, pacing about his rooms I think."

"Tell him I will be there soon."

"Yes, your highness." She bowed and scurried back to his brother's rooms. Teran closed the door and finished getting dressed. He then walked over to his mirror and made a short, unsuccessful attempt at trying to tame his hair.

"Well at least I tried." He sighed to himself and turned to walk out the door.

His brother's rooms were just a little further down the corridor from his own, though they were a bit more expansive and luxurious, since he was first in line to the throne. He would not officially be king until after their father's funeral, so he had kept his old rooms until then. He would be moving into his new apartments this evening. Teran knocked on the door.

"Enter!" A familiar voice called from inside. Teran opened the door slowly and entered the room. His brother, a good foot taller than him, with mousy brown hair and green eyes, but otherwise very similarly featured, was standing by a window, gazing out of it, across the palace grounds and down the royal avenue, which eventually led to the royal docks. Teran walked over to stand beside him.

"How are you feeling, Seban?" He asked him gently.

"I haven't had much sleep really, I've just been tossing and turning all night. I don't know how I'm going to cope with today. It wouldn't be so bad if we could grieve in private, but we have to go and parade in front of all of Rydos!" Seban started quietly sobbing, a luxury he could not afford in public, but which was possible with just his brother to witness. Teran put his arm around his brother to try and comfort him.

"I know. I've been restless all night as well. But just think of it this way, we're not the only ones who are grieving, the whole nation shares our loss and they want to show us, and especially you, their support. You're going to be their king. This is their chance to see you enter your birth rite as well. It is a happy occasion as well as a sad one." He said softly.

"I know you're right, and I am trying to focus on that, but it doesn't help much. Thank you for your support though, Teran. That does help."

"No charge this time, my brother." He grinned and a smile broke across Seban's face too.

"Sometimes, quite often actually, I wish you'd been first in line to the throne Teran."

"Oh no, not me!" He replied shaking his head, "I would make a terrible king, much too interested in exploring the world around me to be able to run a country. You've always been more interested in politics than I have as well. Rydos had much good fortune the day you were born and therefore became heir to the throne."

"I'm not going to win this argument, I can see, so why don't we go into the next room where our breakfast is waiting?"

"I was wondering when you'd get around to suggesting that, I'm famished!"

"I couldn't agree more!" Seban answered, leading his brother through into his dining room, where they sat down to take breakfast. Servants brought them unleavened breads, cheeses and cold meats to choose from, the traditional Rydosian breakfast foods.

"I've never understood how our Laconian cousins can stand to eat porridge for breakfast." Said Teran, his mouth half full, with a chunk of bread." The brothers rarely behaved formally when alone together.

"Neither have I." Replied Seban, his mouth equally full. After they had both eaten enough they went to meet their mother and sister who were probably already at the royal chapel in the southernmost wind of the palace.

It was a long walk from the brothers' rooms, through the vaulted marble corridors of the palace, to the chapel. Years of monopoly over the pearl fishing industry meant that, whilst the Isle of Rydos was very small, it could easily afford to have an independent state from the other kingdoms of Sambar. In fact, Rydos was the wealthiest of the Sambarian kingdoms and it also had the greatest navy. This was all made possible by the reefs that surrounded Rydos, which were the source of their pearl industry and whose navigation were a secret belonging only to the Rydosians. Many ships have been wrecked on the reefs of Rydos, and only the foolhardy captain with nothing to lose tries to pass through them without Rydosian assistance. The nation of Rydos had grown very wealthy selling their pearls to their neighbours, as the glistening pebbles were greatly sort after as decorations for ladies' ornaments and for works of art in temples and wealthy homes around Sambar and beyond.

Finally, the brothers approached the royal chapel. Dedicated to Elerin, goddess of the sea tide, its ceilings were high and vaulted and sheaved in marble and pearl. There were many paintings and tapestries, depicting ships being held aloft from raging seas, by the love of Elerin. There were also many statues of the goddess, usually showing her to be half fish and half woman.

At this moment, there were many purple drapes hanging from the walls and columns of the chapel, the Rydosian colour of mourning. In the centre of the chapel was King Lysan's bier, draped in purple and surrounded by white lilies. The king's body was fully wrapped in white cloth bandages and he lay in the centre of the bier his hands clasped in his lap. The Rydosian crown adorned his bandaged head. At the foot of his bier stood two ladies, clad in purple robes. One was in her mid-forties, the other was just 16, but they were otherwise almost identical in every way. Teran and Seban walked side by side up the chapel aisle to join their mother, Queen Liliana, and their sister, Loren.

"Are you both ready?" Seban asked them quietly.

"Yes, we are, let us begin so that soon this may be over." Replied their mother. Seban nodded to the elderly high priest of Elerin, who, as always, was dressed in white bleeched linen robes, though today he was also adorned with a purple mantle over his robes.

"Let us commend our king to Elerin and commit him to the sea!" Intoned the high priest, Corsan. Royal guardsmen, dressed in full ceremonial armour and wearing purples sashes across their chests, stepped forward to lift the bier up onto their shoulders to carry it out of the chapel. Corsan led the procession, followed by the two brothers, side by side, then Liliana and Loren. After them came King Lysan's bier, borne by a select few of the royal guardsmen and behind the bier came the king's honour guard led by Swordmaster Beran.

The procession left the chapel and entered the ornamental palace gardens. Cultivated over many years the gardens were covered in many varieties of tree, bush and flower. The path that led from the chapel into the city was banked on both sides by flowers of blue and yellow. Lining that ancient pathway were all the palace servants and guards, every one of them wearing purple sashes as a sign of respect to King Lysan. Only the close family of the deceased were allowed to wear the full robes of mourning, under Rydosian law, so it was customary for those who were not members of the close family, but wished to mourn, to wear purple sashes instead. The mourners had white lilies, which they threw in front of the procession, creating a white carpet, which was crushed under the feet of the royal family, those carrying the bier and the honour guard which followed.

All Rydosians were buried at sea, in honour of their deity, Elerin, and as a mark of their seaborne life. Upon their death, members of the royal family were paraded down from the palace through the streets of Rydos to the royal docks, where they would board a vessel for the final time, to be buried at sea. The road they took was one of the oldest in the city, the Royal Avenue, leading directly from the palace through the nobles' and merchants' quarters of the city, into the city plaza. The plaza was a wide cobbled area with substantial buildings surrounding it on all sides; some were residences, others were merchants' shops. The buildings here were uniformly painted white and gilded with gold. Substantial trees lined the edges of the square. Today, like most days, the plaza was thronged with people, but today the crowd was silent, apart from the odd sob, as the populace mourned King Lysan's passing.

The Royal Avenue departs from the south-east side of the plaza, heading through the pearl fishers' district, the industrial source of wealth for the country, finally leading to the very gates of the royal dockyards. Here the royal navy stood, prepared for the royal visitors. A purple carpet had been laid from the gates, leading all the way to *The Dolphin*, the royal flagship. The navy men silently lined the pathway, saluting the procession as they passed them and led up to the ship. They halted on the main deck and as Corsan turned to face the bier, the honour guard broke into two ranks and walked up to stand either side of the bier. The bearers then carefully rested their load to the ground and stepped backwards. The crew of the ship silently filed on and took their positions and, with a silent gesture from the captain, they began to prepare to sail. Beran blew a sharp note from a hunting horn and the crew cast off, directing the ship out of the great walled docks and into the open sea, north of the Ptanga reef.

The Ptanga reef was named for the city in Narsos, a little further down the coast. The reef itself stretched from mainland Sambar to the Isle of Rydos had been a great asset in the last war with Narsos, a little over five hundred years ago. The Narsians had been unable to navigate safely through the reef, and so had not been able to sail troops into Hrunta and cut off the supplies for Am Bære's army campaigning in northern Narsos. Am Bære's corsairs, under the cover of darkness, would navigate the reef using their secret and hard-won knowledge and wreak havoc upon the invading force's navy, whenever they made such an attempt. It was this that eventually allowed the Sambarians to beat back the Narsian invaders and restore peace to the region. The Ptanga reef was also one of the ocean beds around the Isle of Rydos favoured by pearl oysters, which had made the Rydosians so wealthy over the past centuries through pearl fishing.

Once the ship had reached the deepest part of the sea in the strait between the Isle of Rydos and the mainland, the burial ceremony continued,

"We have come here today to witness the passing of a great man, husband, father and king." Called Corsan, above the sea winds, "Great Elerin, we ask you look after your servant Lysan, as we send him into your deep embrace, do not forsake him in his hour of greatest need." The high priest genuflected and raised his staff of office over the body of the dead king. "Elerin, genova, imprecio mart'ja!" He shouted in the old Sambarian tongue. Roughly translated it meant *gentle Elerin, receive our prayer*. "Now let us commit our lord to the sea." Requested Corsan, indicating that it was time for the king to be prepared for committal to the ocean's waves. Swordsmaster Beran came forward and lifted the crown from Lysan's head, placing it upon a cushion, he then stepped to one side to allow the bearers to resume their duty. A ball and chain was clamped around the feet of the dead king to aid his journey to the bottom of the ocean.

Liliana began to cry loudly and she hugged her eldest son, Seban, for support. Seeing tears forming in her eyes Teran put his arm around Loren as well. The bearers came forward and lifted the dead body of the king off the bier and bore it toward the edge of the ship. An extra wide gangplank was at the side of the ship and

Child of Rydos

they carried the body onto it. The royal family walked up to the side of the gangplank and paid their final respects.

"Goodbye father." Cried Loren, her siblings and mother echoed her. "We love you dearly; watch over us until we join you." Added Liliana. Beran once again blew his horn and the body of Lysan was thrown into the sea and the waves came up to greet him and pull him into the deeps.

"The king is dead." Proclaimed Corsan, "Now let us crown our new king, with the permission of Mother Sea, Elerin of the tide." Seban approached the high priest, wiping tears from his eyes and trying his best to look regal in this time of grief. He had decided that though it was tradition he would try and change this tradition of burial of the old king and crowning of the new king on the same day, it was just too traumatic. Then he sighed, it was unlikely to change, he had noticed that people liked to cling to tradition, as it gave them comfort. Teran came up behind his brother carrying the king's robe of office. He placed the robe upon his brother's shoulders, over his mourning robes. Teran stood to his brother's right-hand side. Beran came, bearing the crown, to stand at Seban's left-hand side. Corsan lifted his staff above his head, "Mother Sea, we stand before you, facing your eternal judgement. We are here to crown Seban, son of Lysan, king over Rydos." He looked up into the sky, "Do you accept our offering of Seban, to be our sovereign, over your nation?" To the side of the ship, dolphins broke the surface and robe upon the waves, squeaking in their private language. Dolphins were the favoured animals of Elerin, and their appearing was a sure sign of her pleasure at Seban's crowning. "Elerin has shown us her sure sign, let us obey her command!"

Corsan took the crown from Beran and lifted it above Seban's head. "Elerin genova, tue Empre Seban!" And with those words, Corsan placed the crown upon his head.

"Long live King Seban!" Shouted Teran, a large smile breaking upon his face, despite the sombre occasion that had brought them here.

"Long live the king!" Everyone else responded in unison. At the aft of the deck, several sailors started playing the royal march on their lutes and horns, to welcome the new king.

"Your majesty, a ship has been sighted off our starboard bow." One of the sailors told King Seban.

"Is it approaching us?" He asked.

"No, it appears to be keeping its distance, looks like a Gerakan galleon to me, you can recognise them from a mile away. They're right tubs." Then recalling to whom he was speaking he added, with a slightly embarrassed look, "Your Majesty."

"They know why we're here then. They will not approach us and they will wait for us to dock before they do." Seban surmised, "Well then, I had better order my first royal command. Take us back to town, Captain!"

"Of course, Your Majesty." Admiral Ahram, Captain of *The Dolphin*, replied, "All hands to deck, man the sails! Get to it!" The sailors all got to work and soon the ship was underway again, sailing back towards the high walled city of Rydos.

Rydos was a well-defended city; the wealth they had gained through pearl fishing had not been spent idly. The city proper and the docks were completely walled in thick, smooth stone, several stories high, making it almost impossible to scale. The only gates into the city were at the northern and southern sides. The northern gate led to the rest of the small Isle of Rydos, whilst the southern gate was built out to sea to allow the ships and boats to enter into the city docks. The city had not existed during the previous war with Narsos, but had been built by Am Bære's son Rydan not long afterwards and he had made sure that the city would be defensible as a precaution against future attacks from their fleets. Since that time, however, Sambar had been at peace and the walls of the city had not yet been tested.

As the flagship sailed into port her sails were shortened to slow her approach. The crew knew her very well and the ship came to gently to rest, just next to the pier in the royal docks, ready for her passengers to disembark. The royal procession now had to return, via the same route, back through the city and once again into the palace so that King Seban could begin his rule. Though the populace were still mourning the death of King Lysan, they nonetheless cheered Seban as he passed, walking beside his mother and supporting her by the arm. Loren and Teran followed closely behind and the, now extended, honour guard, since the bearers no longer needed to carry the bier, brought up the rear of the procession.

"It doesn't seem right that the people should cheer me. Have they forgotten so quickly what my father meant to them?" Seban asked his mother, disgruntled.

"You have to understand, my son, that they are as happy to see you made monarch as they were sad over your father's death. And, it is expected of them to cheer you on your return, it is Rydosian tradition. The king has gone to sea dead, but come back alive, there is much to celebrate." Replied his mother, understandingly.

"As always mother, you are correct. I am glad that I still have you to guide me, especially through these beginning years of my reign."

"You have us all, Seban, your brother, sister and I, to guide you. We shall aid you as much as we can."

"I know mother," Seban smiled, "And I love you all."

The procession finally returned to the palace grounds, where the servants had already got to work preparing the palace for the arrival of the new king. Most of them had been involved in moving all Seban's possessions from his old rooms to the royal apartments. Gertha met them at the palace gates.

"Your Majesty, please allow me to direct you to your new apartments." She requested of him.

"Of course, dear Gertha, lead the way." Gertha walked ahead of them, leading them through the main palace doors. The king's apartments were on the first floor, so Gertha led them through the grand, marble entrance hall, up the broad oak stairs and down a grandly decorated corridor, finally reaching two great oak doors, with a marble mantle.

"Here we are Your Majesty, your apartments." She said, with an extravagant wave of her hand towards the door. Seban stepped forward and reached out towards the silver door handles. Slowly opening the door, he entered the room. The entrance hall of his apartments had a wooden floor and cool stone columns, with opulent tapestries and paintings adorning the walls. To the left was his principle reception room and this was where he led his family, to retire, after the taxing events of the day.

Child of Rydos

There was a knocking at the door. Seban looked around from his chair, where he had been sitting, talking to his mother.

"Enter." He said. The door opened and Beran entered, he was no longer wearing his ceremonial armour, but was still wearing his sash and the sword of his office hung at his side.

"My liege," Beran knelt before Seban, "King Gethas and the people of Gerak send their condolences at this time."

"Is that the reason for the arrival of the Gerakan galleon? So near to the time of our father's burial?"

"No sire, as you must well know, Gethas would not disturb you so close to King Lysan's funeral unless the need was indeed urgent. Here is the message the envoy was carrying." Beran said passing a sealed note to Seban. Seban broke the seal and opened the letter, reading it intently. After a few moments he spoke,

"Gethas has called a Conclave of Sambar. This is certainly unusual, so near to a royal death. He has not imparted any reason for the calling of Conclave so soon, but it must be important… very well." He sighed.

"Where is this Conclave to be held, sire?" Beran asked his king.

"In Ariss." Seban responded, "Would you make the necessary arrangements for our absence please?"

"As you wish, sire." Replied Beran, rising from the floor, he took his leave and went to do the king's bidding. Teran looked thoughtfully into the distance for a while before turning to his brother and saying,

"I think I shall be accompanying you on this journey. This cannot be a simple matter that Gethas wishes to discuss; his intelligence service must have discovered something that needs our attention."

"I think you are right. I would be grateful for your company Teran." Replied Seban in a relieved manner. He had not wanted to make this journey on his own, especially at this time and Teran had an unusual way of looking at things which had on occasion turned out to be very useful.

The Gerakan Intelligence service was renowned across Sambar. It was said that even a simple peasant in Arinach could not relieve himself without Gethas hearing about it through his spy network. Whilst this was almost certainly an exaggeration, it was possibly not too far from the truth as the Gerakan spies were very good at their jobs and seldom were discovered. Therefore, it was not unreasonable for Teran to make the assumption that Gerakan Intelligence had unearthed something major that required the attention of all the kingdoms of Sambar, hence the call to Conclave. Soon, more would be revealed.

Chapter III – Conclave

Seban and Teran made their way through the draughty stone corridors of the palace of Ariss and up the stairway of the central tower to reach King Gethas' conference room where they were to meet the other representatives from across Sambar. An entire floor of the central tower was devoted to the king's conference room and it commanded views in every direction from Ariss, from the mountainous northern wilds of Ruorland and the broad farmlands of Laconia, to the southern reaches of Hrunta and the Great Western Sea beyond Frax. Today, a great amount of noise and commotion filled the room as representatives from across Sambar discussed why they thought Gethas might have called a meeting of Conclave so soon after Lysan's death. It was quite irregular.

Seban looked around the room. Almost all the kingdoms were represented; in fact, only one representative was not yet in attendance this morning. Apart from himself and Teran there were also Gethas and Gerta, king and queen of Gerak, and their son Koran, who was a high-ranking member of the Gerakan Intelligence services as well as a decorated member of their army. No doubt he would be speaking later. Orin, Rhan of Ruorland and his son Olin were also present. The Ruors were a nomadic people who lived in the frozen ice lands north of the mountains; they had but one city, Ruor, which was more for the benefit of traders and diplomats than themselves. Such a life had made them a harsh people, resilient to the cold and very strong, as they fought the monsters that lived in the wilds with them. From Hrunta came the Horselords, Teslas and his brother Temac; from Laconia, King Tlanic and his nephew Teloran, they had forgone their traditional Laconian plate mail in favour of clothing a little more comfortable for the long conference ahead.

"If everybody could take their seats around the table then we can begin this Conclave of Sambar." Gethas requested, raising his voice above the general din.

"Gethas, Arran has not yet joined us; we have no representative of the Kingdom of Arinach. Law states Conclave cannot begin." Replied Orin in a surprised voice.

"We have reason to believe that there will be no representative from Arinach. It is one of the items we wish to discuss." Answered Koran, softly.

"I see… this is irregular, but if what you say is true, we have little choice but to get started then." He replied, taking his seat. The others in the room followed suit and sat themselves around the great oak table in the centre of the room. As was customary, Gethas sat at the head of the table as the chair of the discussion.

"As must be apparent, I would not have called this meeting of Conclave so soon, had not the reasons for it been so urgent. Thank you very much for travelling here and joining us at this delicate time Seban and Teran." Begun Gethas, nodding to each of them. He then cleared his throat, shuffled some papers on the table in front on him before proceeding.

Seban and Teran had set out ten days earlier, with a small guard led by Beran, though truthfully they did not

Child of Rydos

expect trouble within the borders of the nations of Sambar, the guard was more for propriety than need. They had responded as soon as they had received the call to Conclave, making it in good time to Circular Ariss. It had been difficult for them to leave so quickly after their father's funeral and it was not the simplest of journeys. The sea leg of the journey had taken four days, Rydosian ships being the fastest in the sea they quickly outran their Gerakan messengers. The weather had been calm and the voyage thankfully boring, giving Seban and Teran time to clear their heads to come to terms with their father's death and to ponder what news was so important for King Gethas to call Conclave at this time. They thus arrived at the port of Frax with little difficulty.

At Frax, a coach awaited them, but instead they chose to ride on horseback, procuring new mounts whenever possible to speed them on their journey across land. Thankfully they stayed at inns along the way, rather than having to camp rough, which made each day's hard ride bearable. The days passed as uneventfully as their sea voyage. Northern Sambar was a safe part of the world and Gerak was a tamed country. King Gethas kept a large standing army to keep peace throughout the land and patrol the major highways. In any case, the Gerakans took the novel step of having their intelligence service employ the shadier members of Gerakan society and send them abroad where their skills could be put to better use. Seban and Teran arrived in Circular Ariss after six days, having made their way around the northern edge of the great lake. At the west gate an honour guard from the palace joined them in an escort through the layers of the city to the palace and its grounds at the very centre. Here the royal family, Gethas, Gerta and Koran greeted them.

"Dear cousins, welcome." Said Gethas. It was tradition long held in Sambar that the royal families from each nation referred to each other as cousin, a reflection of the early history of Sambar, which was one nation under Am Bære until his death when he apportioned various smaller kingdoms to each of his children and their descendants. "Come inside and take some refreshments. The servants will see to your horses and your belongings." Gethas offered, as Seban and Teran each clasped hands with him and Koran in turn and also kissed Gerta on the cheek, before entering the palace with them.

The palace at Circular Ariss was a grand affair, though not as opulent as the castle at Rydos. It had been extended many times over the years and was now a sprawling mass of towers and wings, very confusing to navigate without intimate knowledge of its layout. The brothers were placed in a twin suite in the westernmost wing of the palace. Gethas and Gerta had taken their leave, but Koran stayed with them well into the night for they had been childhood friends and had not seen each other for many years. Koran was of a stocky, but muscular build. He had mousy hair and brown eyes with a slight squint, which made him look shrewd, betraying his high intelligence. After their friendship had been renewed they all turned in for the night, to be ready for the long day ahead of them on the morrow.

The early autumn sunlight streamed into the conference room through the eastern windows of the tower as Gethas spoke.

Child of Rydos

"We have been receiving some disturbing reports from Narsos and the surrounding regions through our people stationed there." He paused briefly to let everyone absorb the news, "There are rumours of an army gathering below Nars. An army with its eyes set northward towards Sambar." He looked around as he expected them to want to question him at this point. Perhaps surprisingly, everyone had their eyes fixed on him silently, almost in disbelief, waiting for his next word. "However, we have not been able to gather any definite proof as all our agents, bar one, have either not returned or worse, returned with no recollection of who they are or what they were sent to do."

"Hah! There has not been war with Narsos for over five hundred years. I do not think they wish to start one with us now. They know we are much more unified than they are and will react quickly and harshly. It sounds to me as if you need to get yourself some more reliable spies, Gethas!" Scoffed Tlanic.

"You have grown soft living by the protection of the Ruors from above and by the protection of the Hruntans and Arinachians from below, Tlanic." Snorted Teslas, "We Hruntans have not become so soft! The peace with Narsos is not so easy as you think and I have had reports of some of our horses and a few of our people going missing near the border with Narsos."

"Run-of-the-mill bandits I should think. Too much is being made of too little evidence!" Retorted Tlanic.

"What you say is true, Tlanic, but I do not think we have been made privy to all the evidence that Gethas wishes us to know yet." Teran added at this point, his voice much calmer than the other two, "Why is Arinach not present I ask you? There was also mention of one spy who *did* return, so what of him? Gethas is about to tell us I think."

"Yes, thank you Teran, you are absolutely correct of course." Gethas took control of the meeting again at this point, "We have been having the same problem with agents in Arinach as in Narsos. They come wandering back without a clue as to who they are or what is happening. Furthermore, Arinach did not respond to our call to Conclave. War is brewing in Narsos and there is a strong possibility it has already taken Arinach." Gethas looked around apologetically, "This was more-or-less confirmed by our agent who returned. Unfortunately, he did not give me any definite proof before he died from poisoning." He paused for a moment for dramatic effect, "In short gentlemen I am asking you to prepare for war. Not overtly, we will have the advantage if we can take them by surprise, but I think there can be little doubt that war is what they plan."

"What is happening to your agents sounds suspiciously magical, I am not sure that any other form of conditioning could make them forget so much, nor so completely." Seban postulated.

"If magic is involved we could be in more trouble than we originally thought. We have little-to-no magical talent in Sambar. We may have to rely on the gods to help protect us. There are, of course, the mystics of Laconia, but I am not sure of the extent of their power and they have remained aloof from us for many centuries now." Said Tlanic.

"We can cross that bridge if and when we need to. But more importantly I feel we must decide what to do about Arinach. We must know if they are on our side or not as it will make a great difference as to how we must fight this war." Added Koran sagely.

"I suggest we send a group of trusted men covertly to Arinach, so they may uncover what is occurring there. A group will have strength that the individual agent does not have and so may succeed where your agents, so far, have not been able to." Seban threw into the conversation.

"It is a good idea and has the merit of being an unusual approach, but I am not sure who we can trust at the moment." Koran replied, a pensive look upon his face, mirroring the mood of the room. The gathered kings, lords and advisors started arguing amongst themselves as to the best course of action.

"Send me." Said Teran, his voice low and quiet, yet somehow penetrating the entire room. "Send me," He repeated, his voice gaining strength, "And one other representative from each country here. That will make us a group of five. If we cannot be trusted nor discover the cause of the problems in Arinach and confirm the rumours in Narsos, then no one will be able to. Those remaining can begin your preparations for war, slowly moving troops and supplies into position."

"It is done then," Gethas proclaimed in a satisfied manner, "You shall go Teran along with Koran, Temac, Olin and Teloran." They nodded in turn as their names were called, each wearing a grim expression. "You can all be trusted and are great amongst your peoples, known for your skills with the sword and with your cunning. It is then left to the kings to make the necessary preparations for the coming war."

"Which brings us neatly up to lunch time I should think." Added Orin with a hearty laugh, thus signifying the end of Conclave for that morning. The assembled company made their way down the tower to the great hall where a veritable banquet had been prepared for them by the palace cooks, who always seemed to need little encouragement for a chance to show off their culinary skills.

After they had all taken lunch, Conclave continued. This time, however, they talked about their preparations for the coming war and how they were to marshal their forces in secret. There was a strong reason for the secrecy, as they did not want Narsos to know that the marshalling of their army had been discovered by the Sambarians. Furthermore, in the unlikely event that the rumours proved false, they would not want to harm their relations with Narsos. Between them the kings decided that it was best to disguise the armies heading southward with supplies as merchants and spread them out through Hrunta and the southernmost tip of Laconia. Forces would not be sent into Arinach until it was clear what was happening them to avoid arousing more suspicion than was absolutely necessary.

Teran and his companions did not re-join the meeting of Conclave for the afternoon. They had their own preparations to make and it would be best if they knew as little as possible about the war preparations. That way if they were captured they could not leak any information to the enemy if tortured. The companions discussed the best way for them to move unnoticed towards Arin, the capital of Arinach, and then down into Narsos. Their meeting was held in an informal lounge below the conference room. Gethas had supplied them with copies of his best maps of Sambar and Narsos to

Child of Rydos

assist their planning.

The first difficulty that the group faced was that they considered themselves equals, making it difficult for them decide who best should lead them. They were all sensible enough to realise that a leader must be chosen as in the field sometimes quick decisions were required to save lives. Although this journey had been Seban's and Teran's idea there was difficulty in deciding which country ranked most senior amongst them, who was the eldest and so on and so forth. Such disagreement was not the best beginning and resolution was only reached when it was agreed decisions could be made and problems addressed democratically. It was not the best way to make quick progress it must be said, but it was the best way to quieten dissent.

"We will want the quickest route to Arinach from Ariss, that means heading towards Qatar in Hrunta, then striking out southwest towards Baxen." Suggested Temac to the others.

"It would be safer to go east through Laconia, then south past Tellac and on to Arin if you ask my opinion. It avoids more major cities and it is less likely that Narsians have infiltrated spies that far north." Replied Teloran.

"There are farmers spread through all of Laconia, we'd never pass unnoticed through there. Northern Hrunta is much less populated as the herders will have begun to move their herds southwards as autumn progresses and winter arrives to find the best weather."

"They're serfs and peasants, no one important. They hardly count as people." Answered Teloran, causing the rest of the group to look at him in stunned silence for more than a moment.

"I cannot believe that you agree with the out-dated beliefs of the rest of Laconia, Teloran. I was hoping that when you ascend to the throne after your uncle dies that you would put a stop to the slavery of serfdom and give your people some rights," Said Olin in disbelief, "However, I agree with you that the best route is through Laconia, following the northern bank of Great Ariss through the country, then heading southward into Arinach. We'll hardly see any of your farmers using that route anyhow." Olin was the eldest of the companions. His father had shown amazing longevity for one who lives in the iceland wastes of Ruorland and so Olin was still not Rhan, despite being almost sixty years of age. He was a large man, built of layer upon layer of muscle, tall and battle scarred from many fights with the ice-land and mountain creatures. His complexion was pale due to the weak sun in northernmost Sambar, even in the summer. He had pale blue eyes and long blond hair which was braided. Many of the more southern Sambarians assumed that the Ruors were uncilivised and barbaric. This was, of course, not true, but they were a stoic people, made hardy by the challenges of living in such a climate.

"I wasn't suggesting we go through Azin forest! That would be madness; few people who enter that place ever come out. I meant to pass around the northern edge of the forest." Exclaimed Teloran. He then continued in a confused tone of voice, "I don't understand what you mean about Laconia. The people have plenty of rights and much freedom. Having serfs allows them to spend most of the day in idle pursuits such as practicing their jousting." Thus, he managed to completely miss the point being made by his peers.

"Yes, going through Azin forest is a bad idea, that is why I suggested passing through Hrunta toward Arinach." Temac added, in defence of his earlier idea.

"I can't believe that you're both scared of the Rangers of Azin. They are not a bad people; they just don't like us destroying their forest, I think. If we mean them no harm I am sure they will let us pass. They can little want Narsos to expand its borders up through Sambar either. We should take Olin's suggested path." Teran decided to speak up at this point. He had remained remarkably quiet until now, watching the others and listening to their ideas.

"Yes, listen to Teran and Olin. This should be our path, it will be the quickest and safest route to Arinach and time is an issue for us." Koran added his support.

"I don't know about safest route, but it seems we are outnumbered, Teloran. We will have to follow their lead. It is good there are five of us, if there were an even number it would take us even longer to reach majority decisions." Temac conceded at this point, ending the argument.

"Temac raises a good point. We really should have a leader, somebody who is able to make quick decisions at times when we need them. Teran is the most intelligent amongst us and it was his idea that it should be us who go, let it be him who leads us." Koran suggested, hoping to make the journey easier.

"Teran hardly says a word. I am the most senior and therefore most experienced amongst us, it should be me who makes the quick decisions." Olin answered in an angry voice.

"Yes, Olin is the eldest, let him lead. I'll just continue to suggest things when I think they'll help and we have time to discuss them, of course!" Teran said quietly, mollifying Olin somewhat. Koran did not look very happy about this decision, but since no one else seemed to be arguing about it, he let it lie for the moment. He had known Teran from a young age and thus knew him to be a natural born leader, just like his brother Seban. The problem was sometimes he was too reluctant to assert himself above others, though not much could be done about that for now.

"Getting to Arinach safely is only part of our problems. We will most likely need to travel into Narsos itself to confirm the rumours about the army massing there and whether they are using magic or not to aid them. It is likely that we will have trouble getting out of Narsos and may not be able to travel back across land into Hrunta without being captured. It will be hard enough getting into Narsos safely in the first place if the invasion is planned to take place soon. We need to think of some alternative routes in and, more importantly, out of Narsos." Olin led the discussion onwards to new areas, trying to show Koran that he was perfectly intelligent enough to lead the group of companions.

"I do not think we should have too much trouble travelling from Arin, through the forests of Narsos, to I'sos. Then afterwards, perhaps on to Nars if it is required of us. But, as for routes out of the country, if we cannot manage a border crossing back to Hrunta or Arinach, then I would suggest using the port of Ptanga." Teran glanced at Koran as he said this, "As I am sure Gerakan Intelligence is aware, my father, Lysan, set up several contacts in Ptanga who were sympathetic to the Sambarian way of life who would be more than happy to ferry us secretly out of port to the safety of a Rydosian patrol ship."

"This sounds like a most sensible plan of action. I do not think we can plan much more of the journey now and it is always bad to set things too securely in stone, as circumstances sometimes change. Let us all get an early night and plenty of rest. We'll meet before dawn tomorrow in the stables to begin our journey." Concluded Olin, stifling a large yawn. The others agreed and so they rolled up the maps they had been using and Koran stored them away, promising to bring them with him on the morrow. They then took leave of each other and went their own ways for the night. Seban was not yet back when Teran returned to their apartments, so he left his brother a note about their plans and hoped he could talk to him in the morning before he left. He stripped down to his undergarments and lay on his bed, slowly drifting off to sleep. Perhaps he would have a bath in the morning before their trek as he always found that long journeys usually meant few baths and smelly companions.

Chapter IV – To the point

When Teran woke in the morning his brother was still asleep. Although he wanted nothing more than to wake his brother to say goodbye he also did not want to disturb his rest. None of his family had slept well recently and it did not seem right to deprive him of what little sleep he could get. Instead Teran quietly rose and dressed himself, then grabbing a bag of things he had prepared before going to sleep, he left their rooms and headed straight towards the stables as he had risen too late to have the bath he had promised to himself. The others were just arriving at the same time he reached the stables. Almost everything had been prepared for them already, their horses had been harnessed and saddled by stable hands and a packhorse and supplies had been arranged to accompany them. The kitchen staff had made sure they were well provisioned so they would not have to stop so often for supplies, particularly early in their journey. The horses were Hruntan roans, a gift from King Teslas to speed them on their journey. Today they would try and make a few miles of their journey before they even stopped to breakfast.

Teloran was the last companion to arrive and he entered the stable wearing full plate mail. Teran looked up at him and sighed, he finished tightening a strap on his saddle and walked over to Teloran, quietly saying,

"You might not want to bring your armour on this journey, cousin. Leave it here and let your uncle take care of it for you. You shouldn't need it anyway."

"Not take my armour?" Teloran exclaimed loudly, quite shocked at the idea, "But I would feel quite undressed on the road without it. What if we run into danger?"

"I'm not suggesting you don't have any armour, but maybe something a little less conspicuous, like the chain mail Olin, Koran and I are wearing. People in the southern lands are not used to seeing fully equipped Laconian Knights and whilst I am sure you'll strike terror into their hearts, I am worried it will make you a little too memorable."

"I understand, Teran, I had not thought of that. I will leave my armour with my uncle, but I will need some other mail then."

"Of course, prepare your horse, Teloran. I'll see if I can find some chain mail that fits you from Gethas' armoury, I'm sure he will not mind you borrowing it." Replied Teran, heading for the door. As he went to leave, Temac approached him and said,

"Thanks for sorting that out, it can be a delicate situation trying to deal with Laconians and their need for plate mail." Teran grinned and, in response, went in pursuit of the armoury.

It was nearing dawn, the sun just rising of the eastern hills as the companions finally set out on their journey. The city of Ariss was quiet at this time in the morning. All those who had set to enjoying themselves in inns and taverns last night having already cleared the streets, but few people yet risen to start their day's work. Some people worked cleaning the streets and the smell of bakers hard at work, despite the early hour, drifted towards them as they headed towards the eastern gate of the city. No one paid them much attention, it was not that unusual to see early risers intent on getting a head start when travelling the long distances between countries. The companions were silent as they rode, each absorbed in their own thoughts. They managed to pass through the eastern gate unchallenged by any guards, something Koran or his father must have organised to keep their journey as quiet as possible.

Once out in the open country they made good time, despite heading across country towards Azin forest and the River Great Ariss, rather than keeping to the well-maintained roads. At what must have been around nine o'clock in the morning, by the angle the sun set in the sky, they decided to stop for breakfast.

"Now is as good a time as any to stop and eat. I'm getting decidedly hungry!" Exclaimed Olin.

"Yes, we have to make sure we're keeping you well fed so you don't lose any of your girth, Olin." Replied Koran, somewhat cheekily, as he dismounted his horse. The others followed suit and made sure they had brushed down their mounts, dealing with their horses' needs before attending to their own.

They did not bother with any ceremony, deciding to just sit on the grass to eat their food. They could have eaten in the saddle to save time, but the journey had just begun and they needed to discuss a little of their plans and examine some maps, which is much more difficult on horseback.

"It will take us three days hard riding to reach the edge of Azin forest. Longer, if we follow the course of Great Ariss exactly." Commented Koran.

"We'll have to find ourselves some entertainment whilst in the saddle then." Said Temac, "Are we likely to meet many settlements along the way?"

"Only if we stick to the river bank." Replied Koran, "Another good reason to keep a slightly straighter route away from the river, unless we need to get more supplies."

"We have enough food for a week, but I don't know how long it will take us to pass through Azin forest. The dense trees will definitely slow the horses, so it is probably best to restock as much as we can before entering." Volunteered Olin before biting off and chunk of bread and chewing on it.

They finished their food and discussion in quick order and cleared the camp, remounting and continuing their journey. They did not put special effort into making it look like they had not stopped there or to hide their tracks as they made their way towards Azin forest. They did not have any reason to expect anyone would be tracking them at this early stage in the journey, particularly whilst they were still so far from Arinach or Narsos and their travel time would have been slowed by such endeavours. They did not stop again that day until the sun was beginning to set over the western sea, having lunched in the saddle. They had made good time, but it would still be another couple of days before they reached the forest.

On the second night, they decided to stay in a town to restock their supplies. The only settlements nearer to the forest inside Gerak were the occasional small farmstead, and it would have been a gamble as to whether the individual farmsteads had food to sell at this time of year; most of their excess supply would have already been sold at market and they would have kept back only what they needed for themselves as autumn progressed and winter approached. Whilst they had been riding the companions had developed a cover story for their travels which they could tell anyone they met. They decided that their names were common enough that they did not need to choose new ones. Apart from Olin, who was obviously not Gerakan, the others could all pass for Gerakans. Thus, they decided that they would be a group of cousins from near the northern border of Gerak, with Ruor. Teran's brother, 'Joss' had been murdered by his wife in a passionate argument. When realizing what she had done she had run away. The cousins had travelled across Gerak in search of her. They suspected she was trying to reach the Rangers and hide with them in Azin forest, so they needed to catch up with her before she reached the forest. It probably was not necessary for them to have such an elaborate back story for their journey, but inventing it gave them something to do whilst riding through the countryside.

Koran informed them that the small town they were entering was called Forth. There was a small inn there called *The Forth and Forge,* which very rarely had guests and was more often used as a simple public house. 'Uncle' Olin arranged for their horses to be stabled and for bedrooms to be arranged for them. They would share the only two guestrooms the inn had between them. After placing their things in their rooms, they all came down into the common room to get some food and have a drink. The locals all stared at them as they re-entered the common room, their talk dying to a quiet hush. Strangers really were not usual here, though the occasional merchant passed through, particularly near harvest time when the local farmers had goods to trade.

Slowly the noise in the common room rose to its usual din, as the local townspeople grew used to the company of the strangers. The companions quickly ate the stew, bread and ale they were served, all the time talking about inconsequential things, or about their 'woman hunt'. They retired to their rooms as soon as possible, using the excuse that they would have to leave early the next morning in the hope of catching up with their quarry.

In fact, they all gathered in one of the rooms upstairs, which was quite a tight fit, to have a discussion about their real journey.

"Did you all notice the quiet, cloaked man in the corner of the common room downstairs?" Asked Teran, "The locals must know him because they paid him no heed, but I could swear he was watching us the entire time we were in the room."

"I think your mind must be playing tricks on you, Teran" Replied Teloran, "I think we all saw the man you're speaking of, but he cannot have had any interest in us. No one can know who we are; that would have required word of our journey to travel faster than we have ourselves."

"I know you are right, Teloran, but I just have a peculiar feeling. Well, we will be out of here early tomorrow, so there is probably no need to worry." Concluded Teran after Teloran had finished speaking. Olin then chose to speak about the next part of their journey,

"What do we know of the Rangers of Azin? Not the wild rumours, but the facts." He asked.

"Not much sadly. They are very secretive, which I guess tells us something at least." Sighed Koran, "As far as we know they don't recognise any sovereignty in

Sambar except their own. Azin belongs to them and they do not tolerate strangers to enter."

"The old records do mention tales of rangers who used to travel about Sambar, aiding others when required, but they may not necessarily be related to the Rangers of Azin." Comment Teran, "However, I don't think we have much choice but to hope they are the same rangers, otherwise our trip may be a lot shorter than we were expecting when we reach the forest."

"This is a foolish route to take, we should have travelled south through Hrunta." Said Temac, scornfully, "We do not know what we are heading in to. We are taking needless danger."

"We have discussed this already; time is of the essence. This route amongst the shorter ones available to us and has the advantage of the cover of the forest to hid our movements; the gain outweighs the risk. It would be stupid to lengthen our journey based on unfounded and vague rumours." Said Olin.

"Rumours are often based on truth though, like an oft repeated whisper, the truth is usually lost in a distant, unrecognisable past." Teran spoke sagely, "I don't think the Rangers should be our worry, though I cannot tell you why for sure." The conversation continued along similar themes until their candles ran low, then they retired for the night for another early start on the morrow.

It had been another quiet day of travel for the companions, despite Teran's worry about the watcher from the Inn. The sun was still a few hours from setting when they reached the western edge of Azin forest, where they stopped momentarily.

Child of Rydos

"Though we could make a few more hours of travel, I think we should rest here for the night." Temac suggested, looking around uneasily.

"It is a good suggestion, it will give the Rangers time to realise what we intend and give them the opportunity to prevent us from entering, hopefully in a peaceful manner, if that is what they wish. At least they will know we do not mean to invade their land." Added Koran, brushing his hands through his hair as he glanced into the nearby forest.

"There is something strange about this place." Commented Teran, almost to himself, "I cannot say for sure what, but a feeling of unease certainly. Staying here a night might put us at ease with our surroundings." Teran appeared to be the only member of the group who did not look concerned by the encroaching trees, but merely curious. Olin leapt from his horse, all the while fingering his axe loop.

"Let us set up camp here for the night then. Light a fire, but not too near the trees, we do not want to give the wrong impression to any Rangers who may already be watching us." He declared to the group. Teloran got to work kindling the fire whilst the others cleaned down the horses, started to prepare some food and also raise some rudimentary tents by tying waxed sheets between a few of the trees on the edge of the forest. The sky was very grey and seemed to reflect the companions' moods, it would likely rain, possibly even storm, tonight. It was a small, fitful fire which did not last long before the rain began to fall. At first it was a trickle, but slowly it became more torrential. The companions huddled under their makeshift tents, the group was very reticent and they spoke little before deciding to sleep; they would start their journey into Azin forest as soon as morning twilight began, the rest was certainly needed. Teran and Koran took the first watch of the evening, one staring into the forest, the other away, talking quietly together of long forgotten memories in an attempt to keep each other alert. Teran had a strong feeling that eyes were watching them, not just from the forest, but all around. It had gradually grown from a tiny seed to this inescapable thought as their journey had progressed towards the infamous forest. After a few hours, the watch changed and Temac and Olin took watch instead. Teran tried his best to sleep, but it quite easily evaded him and he had only managed a shallow doze by the time they had to rise again to take their first steps into the unknown.

It was nearing midday. The companions had followed the course of Great Ariss into Azin forest. At first, they had all been reticent, but slowly after no encounters with any Rangers and after realising that the forest teamed with life, like any other, they began to relax and chatting resumed. Along the bank of the river it was still possible for them to ride on horseback. If they had been trying to strike more directly through the forest the tightly wound trees and thick roots would have slowed them to a walking pace, whether on horseback or not. Bright rays of light pierced through the arching boughs of the clustered trees, spotlighting patches of mossy rocks or undergrowth reaching triumphantly toward the sky. The forest itself seemed peacefully at ease, but Teran was feeling increasingly edgy. He had a tingling feeling racing down the back of his neck, but he could not work out why. Suddenly he drew his horse to a stop,

"Something is wrong." He said simply.

"Wha..." Temac began, but then he suddenly found himself at sword point. From behind trees and bushes suddenly and swiftly out stepped men dressed completely in black with headscarves wrapped around their heads so all you could see were their eyes. They moved silently, but Teran became aware of them more fully now, he knew there must be near fifty, stretched out into the trees surrounding them. None of the companions dared to even breathe heavily in case it spelled their doom. There was little which could be done against so large a force. One of the men robed in black, as indistinguishable as the rest, stepped forward and a space cleared around him, in front of the companions. He slowly unwound part of his headscarf, revealing part of his forehead, nose, mouth and chin. His skin was as rich as ebony, his eyes piercing black orbs and his teeth pearly white as he spoke to them.

"You have been marked for death." He stated quite simply, "What is yours shall be ours. What you have, what you are, is no more." The words had a ritualistic tone to them, particularly in the rich, rolling accent that the stranger had. He took a step backwards and raised his hand, showing a flat palm. The bandits holding the companions at sword point released the pressure a little drawing back their swords, as if waiting. The stranger slowly curled his fingers down onto the palm of his hand. The meaning was clear, a slow death.

Two things happened at that point. Firstly, the robed swordsmen slowly advanced their swords towards the companions' flesh. Secondly, something streaked through the air, knocking one swordsman's arm away.

Suddenly the air seemed thick with arrows, a maelstrom of wood and fletching flying from all directions. A breath later the companions looked around. Only one man remained standing, the one who had spoken. The bodies of his comrades lay piled around him and the companions.

"Nu Imred du Cha ne." He said, in what sounded a stunned manner, before crumpling to the ground. The companions looked around in stunned silence themselves, too scared to comment or move.

"He should not have died; our arrows did not touch him." Said a disembodied voice. There was a flurry of movement as somebody jumped down from a tree to stand in front of the companions. Dressed in a mottled brown-green cloak, which almost seemed to take on the colour of its surroundings and holding a half-nocked bow, it was obviously a Ranger who stood before them. It was said no one saw a Ranger in their natural habitat unless they wanted to reveal themselves.

"I am Xantila." She said, drawing back her hood to reveal fair skin and pale green eyes, framed by straw blonde hair, which was cut short. "Who are you and why do you bring such as these to our forest?" She said bluntly, indicating the dead bodies littering the forest floor. Emboldened by the fact they were still alive, Teloran stepped forward and answered,

"These opportunistic bandits are none of our doing." He replied, "I am Teloran, nephew to King Tlanic, prince of Laconia. My companions are Olin, son of Rhan Orin, heir apparent to Ruorland, Temac brother to King Teslas, horselord of Hrunta, Koran, son of King Gethas, prince of Gerak, and Teran, brother to King Seban, prince of Rydos." He said, indicating each of them in turn as he spoke their names. Olin quickly took over at this point, asserting his seniority over the other,

"Rumours say war is brewing again in Narsos. Arinach has become estranged from Sambar. We have been sent to ascertain the truth of these matters so that Sambar may prepare itself not to be overrun. We knew secrecy, as well as expediency, was of the utmost importance and so decided we had to pass through Azin forest. We graciously ask your permission to pass through your lands." He rolled off his tongue, with a flourish.

"These men we have killed did not enter our forest." Xantila replied cryptically, an accusing air to her voice.

"What do you mean?" Asked Olin, in a confused manner, reflecting the thoughts of the rest of the companions.

"We notice all who pass the borders of our lands." Xantila responded, "These did not." She waved her hand indicating the dead bodies again.

"But they are here. They must have entered your realm." Emphasized Temac. Xantila looked angry at his response.

"We do not lie. We do not miss." There was more than one meaning to Xantila's words.

"They do not belong here," Said Teran, suddenly, "They did not cross the borders of Azin forest, but they are here. It is not our doing." Xantila looked at him for a long time. It was impossible to say what she was thinking as her eyes rested upon his.

"They are not bandits, they had purpose in their attack. Their appearance was your doing, for they would not have appeared in our realm if you had not entered it. Of this I am certain." Xantila knelt down beside one of the dead men and pulled back the sleeve of his robe, revealing a tattoo on the underside of his forearm, depicting a sword with a snake entwined around it.

"They all bear this sign," Responded Teran, perceptively, "But we do not know its meaning."

"Enough!" Shouted Olin suddenly, "What do you plan with us? You know that we have no knowledge of what has occurred here. Make your peace and leave us be!" He said agitatedly. Xantila took one look at him,

"You will come with us," She said, "Now." With that, many more Rangers leapt from the trees and appeared from the surrounding undergrowth, surrounding the companions. They were dressed much the same as Xantila and were thus difficult to see if they did not move. Barely a sound escaped the Rangers and certainly no word of what was happening. As they were led away, deeper into the forest, surrounded by their guard, Teran noticed that a good number of Rangers had also stayed behind and were beginning the process of burying the bodies, to satiate the forest.

They had been walking for a long time through the forest, leading their horses by the reigns, and Teran had the distinct impression that they had been going in circles, as he was sure he recognised parts of the forest after a while. He was thinking about mentioning this fact, but suddenly decided to keep it to himself. He realised that everyone in the group was being much more reticent in conversation than usual and as he glanced around at them he noticed that they all were in a trance-like state, not paying attention to their surroundings, but happily being led by the Rangers. Teran had a strange tingling sensation at the back of his head and it dawned on him that the Rangers must be using some sort of innate power of the forest to confuse the companions so they would not remember their way. Few people these days believed in magic and though Teran was not opposed to the idea, he was not exactly sure that was what was happening now. Perhaps the deep forest was just a confusing place to those not used to it.

It was difficult to track the movement of the sun through the sky in the depths of the forest and Teran really was not sure how long they had been walking, though he felt quite tired and so assumed they must have been travelling most of the day. This thought seemed corroborated by Xantila as she called a halt in a small clearing.

"We will rest here for the night." Xantila said simply, and as she spoke, Teran noticed the others break out of their reverie and take notice of the environment around them. The Rangers set up camp quickly and fed the group using simple travel rations that they had brought with them. Teran and his companions were left to deal with the needs of their horses, which they picketed at the edge of the clearing. The next morning, they broke their fast at as soon as the sun had risen and set off again. Teran noticed how a trance quickly fell on the group again as they walked with the Rangers. The second day of travel was the same as the first. It gave Teran plenty of time to consider the Rangers and this forest of theirs. It seemed most likely that it was some sort of ability akin to magic, if not magic, which was enabling the Rangers to keep his company subdued as they travelled into the heart of the forest.

On the third day, the forest began to change

imperceptibly. The air grew slowly less heavy and the light filtering through the trees slowly grew stronger. Ahead it looked like there might be a partial clearing in the trees. When they drew close to the edge of the treeline horns blew and everyone seemed to come to a little and none of them could believe what they saw,

"Horns blow to greet us. Welcome to Azin Heart." Said Xantila, simply. Before the companions, in the clearing was a living city built into the boughs of the ancient trees. They just looked on in awe, unable to speak.

Chapter V – Unexpected Direction

"Come," Xantila continued, "You must see Mother." With that she continued into the city of the Rangers, expecting everyone to follow her. She led them to the centre of the city, where the largest tree grew. Many of the roots of the tree were exposed and ran over the ground, gnarled and twisted. There was an opening the size of a door in these giant roots on the north side of the tree and into this Xantila led them. It was dark inside the tree and the companions could not see very well. A soft glow was coming from the other side of the interior and as their eyes adjusted the companions could see that there the roots from the tree rose up forming a throne-like seat upon which sat an old, wizened woman dressed in white.

"Few come to the heart of the forest," The woman said in a quiet, but firm voice, "Teran, you and your traveling companions are welcome here. I can sense that you mean us no harm and your quest is also of interest to us." Teran bowed and his companions followed suit, so as not to appear disrespectful.

"What do you know of our journey? It is meant to be a secret." Teran asked the woman.

"I am Xera, wise one and guide to the Rangers," Xera answered, "Here I see and hear many things if the forest wishes to tell me them. We live in harmony with its majestic boughs and fertile floors."

"The Rangers have long remained apart from the rest of Sambar," Teran stated, "Why do you have an interest in us now?"

"Nature stirs, it is unhappy. Something towards the south upsets its balance. Your quest is leading you in that direction and I think that your purpose shall overlap with ours." Xera replied.

"You had planned to send some of your own people to the south?" Koran asked, perceptively.

"Mmm, yes. There is much for us to discuss I think, but let us do so over dinner. You must all be hungry." With that, Xera stood and climbed down from the throne. Though her form was diminutive and shrivelled with age she could still move sprightly and glided quickly past her guests, leading them out of the confines of the tree's base and towards an outdoor marquee where the Rangers had prepared dinner for them.

The Rangers were not used to much ceremony, or entertaining for that matter. Rather than being seated at long banquet tables, they naturally split up into groups and sat cross-legged in small circles on the floor around the marquee to eat.

In the background a few younger, enterprising Rangers had set up a small band and were playing soft music on lutes and pipes which seemed to blend with and enhance the natural sounds of the forest around them. Rather than being served, all the food was laid out on tables around the edge of the marquee and groups just helped themselves to the fare before sitting down. There was a vast array of food from woodland berries and leaves and mushrooms to stuffed birds and wild stag and boar. Certainly enough to cater for most people's tastes.

Xantila sat with her mother, Xera, in a small group

with the travellers and they discussed their journey.

"We mean to make across land to Tellac, then down to Baxen, to use the fords across to Arin and simultaneously pick up any intelligence we can on what is going on in Arinach." Koran was informing their hosts.

"A wise choice to avoid the Inland Sea," Replied Xera, "It always seems to give newcomers an unwelcome reception, almost as if it had a will of its own."

"Yes," Replied Koran, "So many of the inland sailors have informed me on previous travels, hence our decision to avoid it now."

"I can fault your plans in only one respect," Continued Xera, "You will need our help to safely pass through the wilds of the forest of Narsos undetected. My daughter Xantila will accompany you."

"Our company was decided by Conclave, in which you have no part." Responded Olin, "What makes you think we should take you on board now?"

"Conclave rarely discusses things of interest to us, but you are wrong to think we are not part of it." Xera replied calmly, "You should check your historic records. Xantila will accompany you as our representative." Olin went to respond again, but Teran put a hand to his should and interrupted,

"It would seem we have little choice in the matter and we are grateful for your help. One more in our company will not slow us down, especially a Ranger as skilled as Xantila."

They enjoyed the Rangers' hospitality for the rest of that day and continued their journey the following morning. Their group enlarged and their supplies replenished they forged onwards along the banks of Great Ariss, then veered southwards, through the northern parts of Hrunta and Arinach, towards Tellac. As they passed through Hrunta, they came across a herd of horses tended by a small group of Hruntan horseherds. Whilst they still had their original mounts, they had been walking them, treating them more like pack animals than mounts, because Xantila did not have one. The Rangers did not make a habit of keeping horses, preferring instead the flexibility of taking to the trees. Temac being familiar with his own people's ways and the best at valuing horses, bartered a mount for Xantila, to speed them on their journey southeast. Temac made sure to secure an amenable mount, which would follow the others as this would be Xantila's first time riding and she would have much to learn. Each of the company were careful not to reveal too much about themselves as they still meant to keep their movements as secret as possible until they knew what was going on in Arinach.

Five days of uneventful travel after leaving the boughs of Azin Heart, two of them in the forest and three in the open lands, avoiding the local population where possible, the company arrived, without ceremony, at the coastal town of Tellac. The weather had turned increasingly blustery and one of the famous, autumnal, coastal storms was threatening to break. Despite being uneventful, their journey had still been productive; they had used the time to arrive at a cover story to explain who they were and why they were traveling through Tellac. They had purchased a wagon from a farmstead far outside Tellac and were posing as traders wanting to buy fish and carry the produce down to Baxen. With They pretended to have sold their previous wares just outside the town, so as not to appear empty-handed traders as they explored the Tellac marketplace. As they passed into the town, Koran slipped away to enquire from his local sources of any news from Arin. Teloran took the lead in purchasing their fish, which was heavily salted and sealed in barrels to preserve their freshness on the journey to Baxen.

They stayed overnight in a seafront inn called *The Leaping Cod*, which was used to housing traders and thus had room for their wagon, goods and horses. Late that evening Koran slipped back into the inn and joined the rest of the group to let them know what he had been able to discover.

"I think we need to be on the road again as soon as possible." Koran told them, "I haven't liked the snippets of information I've heard at all, although I admit it has all been a little vague."

"Vague," Commented Olin, "In what sense?" Voicing what the whole group were feeling, wishing that Koran would hurry and get to the point.

"There has been almost no information or, for that matter, traders coming out of Arin recently." Koran continued, "Only a single Royal Edict. No one is to talk to strangers and trade is to be limited as much as possible with outsiders, especially with visitors from the Sambarian lands."

"I wondered why I was having difficulty and getting odd looks whilst trading." Commented Teloran, realization dawning in his voice, "Lucky for us that coin is so universally required!"

"I think we should get a good night's sleep and hit the road as early as possible tomorrow. I'm eager to get to Baxen to see if we can get any clearer intelligence from there." With that Koran made his way to the rooms they had hired for the night. Outside the wind was picking up and gusting against the side of the inn, making the building creak.

"I think Olin and I will remain downstairs a little longer, we can check no one is taking too much interest in our activities, mercantile or otherwise." Replied Temac, as Olin got up to order them more beer.

"I think I'll also stay with you for a while," Said Teloran, "Another drink will dim the noise of the storm growing outside enough for me to sleep." That decision made, Koran, Teran and Xantila retired upstairs whilst the others remained for a further drink.

Olin, Temac and Teloran did not notice anyone watching them as the evening drew on and most of the inn's patrons left for their homes. The storm outside grew stronger and stronger.

"This storm is unseasonably strong." Said the innkeeper, looking at the creaking walls around him, "It's not very comfortable, but perhaps you'd like to go and wake your friends and suggest they sleep in the cellar. That's where my family will be sleeping tonight… an old habit to protect us form the worst storms." The innkeeper finished.

"Okay," Nodded Teloran, "I'll go and get the others."

A short while later they were all safely wrapped up in, what turned out to be, a large cellar beneath the inn with plenty of room for them all. The storm above continued to rage and they all slept fitfully until the morning came.

Morning broke and the sound of the storm had gone, though water pooled around their feet in the cellar, which had not drained yet. Eager to get somewhere they could dry their feet, the companions climbed the stairs to the ground floor, Olin in the lead. At the top of the stairs, the others heard him utter a startled curse, "By Grukan!". As they also reached the top of the stairs, they realized why. There was little left of the inn, just a few boards of wood from the once board and batten walls. The top floor had been swept clean away by the power of the storm and shreds of it were embedded in several other buildings around the seafront. Bizarrely the rest of the sea front was not affected any way near as badly… a few broken signs, doors and windows, but not much else. The innkeeper was muttering under his breath.

"Unnatural I say and unseasonable; the strongest storms come across the inner sea in the summer. Why have the gods decided to ruin me?"

"I'm sure you'll find help, both physical and financial to rebuild," Said Teran, trying to ease the innkeeper's distress. "Here, take some extra money from us. We would have been blown clear away if you hadn't invited us to your cellar last night." Teran finished, pressing a small purse into the innkeeper's hands.

"You can't afford to be too generous either," Exclaimed the innkeeper, "You lost your horses and your wares last night in that storm too." Teran cast his eyes around the inn properly for the first time and realized that the man was right. The stable yard had been completely destroyed too and their horses, wagons and goods were all gone, probably swept out to sea, though hopefully the horses had bolted somewhere to safety.

"Still, for our lives you deserve that gold." Answered Teran, continuing to look around. As he was casting his eyes around the debris, something caught his attention, which he had nearly missed.

"Xantila, Koran, look at this!" He called, bending down and picking up a simple clay disc, about the size of a token, from the floor. It was plain on one side, but the other bore a symbol. "Do you recognize it?" He asked.

"A dagger with a snake entwined." Answered Xantila, "It's the same mark we found on those mysterious bandits which assailed you in Azin Forest."

"Yes, definitely," Agreed Koran. "Do you recognize this?" He asked the innkeeper.

"Never seen it before in my life." He replied.

"This is a bad sign," Continued Teran, a small note of fear in his voice, "Something very strange is going on. Best we break the bad luck." With that he dropped the token to the floor and stamped his foot unto it, cleaving it in two. As he did so, he felt a rush of wind, as if some power had fled. He picked up the fragments of the token and wrapped them in a cloth to take with them.

"We might need it for future reference." He simply said, but in truth he was disturbed by the feeling he had upon breaking the clay token and wanted to examine it further. Olin broke his reverie,

"Best if we're on our way, wares or not, we still must not be late." He said significantly. So, the companions gathered themselves and went in search of some new mounts to speed their journey to Baxen, as well as tents for shelter and other provisions for the journey. Xantila decided that her Rangers' garb was too conspicuous for their onward journey and so sought out traders selling clothing which was closer to the local custom than her forest leathers.

As they were haggling with one particular trader, Olin caught Teran with a contemplative look upon his face.

"I know that look by now," Said Olin, "What have you got on your mind, Teran?" Teran took a big breath,

"I think we need to split up the group." He suggested tentatively. Temac, turned around sharply, interrupting his haggling with the horse trader,

"Split the group? We've barely been safe with the numbers we do have."

"That's exactly it," Continued Teran, "We're attracting strange attention anyway and an even smaller group would be able to slip in and out of Arin and Narsos more easily. Also, if our pursuers are expecting a group of this size, being half the size might throw them off our tracks…"

"It's not the *most* convincing plan you've come up with." Commented Koran.

"I just have this strange feeling, okay?" Retorted Teran, "Like everything is just heading from bad to worse and we need to break the cycle." Olin looked thoughtful,

"How would you suggest we split up?" He asked Teran.

"I think Xantila should be in the group to continue south. I don't think she'd except another option." Teran looked at Xantila and she nodded,

"Quite right!" She stated, "My skills will be of more use as we travel into the great forest of Narsos than the rest of you put together!" Teran cleared his throat,

"… anyway… I also think Koran should go because

he has the most contacts in Arin, whom we can draw information from. The final member of the group is open to discussion."

"We need to choose between Temac, Teloran, Teran and myself." Stated Olin.

"So, you think we should go through with this idea?" Queried Koran.

"Yes," Responded Olin, "I agree with Teran on this occasion. There was nothing natural about that storm last night and so I must conclude our pursuers have unnatural abilities. I think that Conclave needs to hear about this because although we can't connect this to what is happening in Arinach or Narsos yet, it is more than should be occurring in our lands."

"If this is a course of action we're agreed on, then I want to make a request." Koran chipped in, "I'd like Teran to be the third member of our group heading towards Arin. He and I know each other very well and are used to backing up each other in fight."

"He means anyone else in the group would have to suffer getting to know him better." Teran joked, winking at Koran who adopted a false scowl. Olin looked like he was of two minds,

"I feel that as the designated leader of the group, I should continue with you, but I also think your logic is good, Koran." Olin took a breath as he considered his next words, "We'll split the group as you suggest. Temac, Teloran and I will head towards Korrath to report and then onwards down to Cheros to report to Conclave whilst you, Xantila and Teran will continue the journey southwards to Baxen then eastwards to Arin and eventually southwards into Narsos itself."

Temac had concluded his haggling with the horse

Child of Rydos

trader and had a mount for each of them now as well as supplies.

"Well, we wanted to get an early start and we've already been severely delayed because of that storm." Temac stated bluntly, "It's best we're all on our ways. We know our duties and what's at stake." And with one quick motion he was mounted and secure in his saddle. The others mounted with considered skill, though not quite as gracefully as Temac, who being Hruntan was practically born on horseback.

"May the gods guide you on your journey." Olin said, raising his hand in salute to Koran, Xantila and Teran.

"You too my friend." Responded Koran and with that the company split and went their separate ways. Koran, Teran and Xantila continued south towards the town of Baxen and deeper into Arinach, whilst Olin, Temac and Teloran cut back towards the west to Korrath to report their findings so far.

Chapter VI – Little Thieves

Baxen was a large, dirty, fortified town. The landscape around it was arid and dusty. Three days after leaving Tellac, Koran, Xantila and Teran rode into the town through the north gate and asked directions for a reasonably priced, but comfortable inn. They were directed to *The Desert Prince* by a very enthusiastic beggar on the side of the street and so, after giving the beggar a few coins, they set off there at once. The inn was situated in the poorer part of town, near the south gate. The streets here were even dustier than those in the north of town, the buildings more poorly constructed, and the number of beggars on the streets drastically increased. The inn itself, though, looked well-constructed and as they drew into the stable yard it looked well swept and clean. They were greeted by a small boy who took charge of their horses and they ducked into the inn to ensure themselves rooms for later that evening. The interior of the inn was quiet, but it was only late afternoon. The inn keeper introduced himself,

"I'm Bardin, the owner of this fine establishment," He began, "You won't find an inn with finer food and drink for such a good price anywhere at all east of Korrath"

"You don't need to work so hard on the sales pitch, my friend." Replied Koran quickly, "We would like board and lodgings for the night and for our horses in the stables outside." The innkeeper looked slightly relieved and Teran guessed that business had taken a slight dive recently, perhaps because of the trade embargo in Arinach.

"I've got two fine rooms on the first floor that you're welcome to and the cook has been brewing up a hearty dumpling stew for dinner." Bardin replied.

"That would be most welcome, we've been on the road for a few days." Answered Koran as Bardin showed them to their rooms.

After having washed and tidied up the party returned to the common room and settled down for dinner at a corner table. Over dinner they spoke quietly with each other, constantly checking that no one was taking more interest in their conversation than they should as they discussed what they should do next. They agreed that they should split up and frequent as many of the streets and inns in the town as possible to pick up the local gossip. Koran would also seek out the Gerakan Intelligence contact in this town to see if any more had been heard about matters in Arin. After they had finished eating, they therefore split up and spread out across town. Koran heading towards the west, Xantila to the east and Teran back towards the north, taking his time as he passed through the poor quarter. Koran's route took him through the merchants' district of the town. It became extremely obvious that the town had seen better times as many of the shops showed signs of recently being boarded up as business dropped off too much to continue. Where the shopkeepers had moved out, the beggars had moved in. Eventually Koran found the shop he was looking for, which was run the Gerakan Intelligence contact here and he stepped inside.

Xantila's journey took her through the wealthier parts of the town and though the residents here were more resilient to the effects of the town's recession, the signs were still evident to someone with a keen enough eye. It was the paintwork which was in need of refreshing and the crumbling stonework or rotten woodwork which had not yet been repaired, which were the most obvious signs of the dwindling prosperity of the the town.

Later that evening, Teran was strolling back towards the inn with much on his mind. The chatter he had overheard confirmed that a trade embargo had been issued from Arin against the other nations of Sambar. There were also rumours that the recent changes had begun when King Arran had appointed a new advisor. Teran had not been able to glean any real details about this advisor, except that he appeared to be of foreign lineage. Teran thought it all too much of a coincidence. As Teran approached *The Desert Prince*, a group of children were playing in the dusty street, kicking a ball around. As they were kicking the ball, one of them missed their mark and the ball flew accidentally towards Teran, all the children yelling towards him to catch the ball. Teran did so and threw the ball back to the children so that they could continue playing. At that moment, Teran realised Xantila had come up behind him and she was dragging another small child with her, whom she held strongly by his wrist.

"Xan, Wha…" Teran began to ask, as Xantila interjected,

"Check your pockets, Teran, I think you'll find there is something missing." Teran reached down and patted himself, realising that, indeed, one of his money pouches had disappeared. He looked towards the young boy, who was holding it in the palm of his hand whilst trying to look as apologetic and innocent as possible. At the same time, all the children who had been playing scattered, leaving the street deserted.

"You didn't think it was an odd time of day for children to be playing in the street?" Xantila asked Teran.

"My thoughts were elsewhere, so I wasn't really thinking about it." Responded Teran defensively.

"My guess is that it was all a ruse to distract you, whilst this young man here could do his business." Xantila responded, glancing towards the boy for confirmation, who meekly nodded in response.

"I'm really tired of being targeted so much. Let's take him inside to question him." Said Teran, gesturing towards the inn with a sweep of his hand. Xantila nodded, dragging the resistant boy along with her, as they returned to the common room.

The common room of *The Desert Prince* was empty, apart from Koran, sitting at a table in the corner, and Bardin, propped on a stall behind the bar. Koran simply raised an eyebrow towards Xantila and Teran as they approached with the boy. Teran responded to Koran's simple query,

"Xan caught him trying to steal from me. We thought a few questions might be in order." With that, Teran sat down and indicated that the boy should do the same, whilst Xan stood behind the boy, with her hand on his shoulder, making sure he realised that he was not going anywhere until their questions were satisfactorily answered.

"What is your name?" Teran began.

"Banir, sir," The boy responded hesitantly.

"Banir," Teran repeated, not entirely convinced the boy had given his true name, but that was not really important. The main reason Teran wanted a name was to put the boy at greater ease whilst he questioned him. Teran continued with some preliminary questions, "Do you live in Baxen?" Banir nodded. "Who put you up to stealing from me? What were you meant to try and steal?" Banir looked confused and a little scared, shaking his head. "We need some answers, Banir…"

"I don't understand what you mean…" Banir responded hesitantly, "No one commissioned us, newcomers to town are fair game, especially since you hadn't been marked yet by anyone else."

"Who would want to mark us?" Teran asked sharply. Banir rolled his eyes,

"You might be dressed simply, but it's obvious from your boots that you're wealthy. Me and the kids were lucky to mark you first, anyone from the guild would have picked you out as a good target." Teran looked down at his feet with chagrin, they obviously had not been careful enough with their disguises.

"But who do you work for?" Teran responded. Banir looked dumbfounded.

"The thieves' guild of course! Who else goes around trying to pinch purses? I have to say your companion," He said nodding towards Xantila who stood behind him still, "Caught me off guard. No one has ever spotted me thieving before and caught up with me."

"So, you're not working with the others?" Teran asked.

"I don't know what you're talking about." Responded Banir, "Can I go now?"

Child of Rydos

"What shall we do with him?" Teran asked the others.

"I think we will have to let him go. We can't afford the attention of taking this matter to the local constabulary, nor can we lock him away or take him with us." Koran contributed at this point. Xantila nodded in agreement and removed her hand from Banir's shoulder. Banir immediately leapt up and made towards the door.

"Wait! Take this," Exclaimed Teran, throwing his pouch of gold towards Banir, "Consider it a payment for your continued silence about this meeting." Banir turned, caught the bag in mid-air, nodded towards Teran, and ran straight out the door without breaking his stride. Xantila ran to the door and looked up and down the street, but there was no sign of the little thief.

"He's good." Xantila commented as she returned to the table and sat with Teran and Koran. Xantila shared her own evening experience with the others, mirroring exactly what Teran had already discovered. Then Koran spoke about what he had discovered from his local contacts.

"My contacts confirm that King Arran and Queen Belna have a new advisor and that he does not appear to be of local stock, though they could not comment on where he might be from. The conservative policies flowing out of Arin definitely stem from the time that this new advisor appeared on the scene." Koran began. Teran and Xantila nodded, knowing more was coming, by the way in which Koran was revealing the facts, methodically building to a climax, "All the agents sent into Arin have not returned. There must be foul play at hand, but it is not clear whether the king and queen are complicit in this action, or whether something works within their kingdom without their knowledge."

"I think it is clear that we need to travel all the way into Arin itself to get to the bottom of this situation," Responded Teran, "Before we turn southwards into Narsos to explore what is occurring there."

"Agreed." Concurred Koran.

"Agreed," Added Xantila, "Let's get a good night's sleep and begin our journey eastwards tomorrow with first light." With that the companions retired to their rooms for the evening, leaving the innkeeper, Bardin, to finish clearing up the bar before he too retired for the night.

Chapter VII – Frozen Delight

Two days journeying west from Tellac had brought Olin, Temac and Teloran safely to the border between Arinach and Hrunta without incident. The sun was setting in the west bathing the Hruntan plains in glorious shades of orange and red, uninterrupted across the flat plains by any hills or mountains. The companions were using the last rays of light to travel as far as they could this day. As the final glimpses of colour faded from the horizon Olin raised a hand calling the group to a halt for the evening. They split instantly into well-rehearsed roles, Olin pitching their tents bought in Tellac, Temac collecting firewood and Teloran seeing to the needs of the horses. As Temac returned with scraps of wood for the fire, the horses, which Teloran was caring for, became agitated, whinnying and straining their stays to get away. Confused, Teloran tried to comfort the animals. The temperature began to rapidly drop so that they could see mist forming as they breathed.

"What is going on?" Temac asked, confused by the temperature change. Olin and Teloran had noticed it too and had leapt up, grabbing their weapons and looking towards the east.

"Temac, look to." Shouted Olin, gesturing towards the direction he and Teloran now looked. The air was continuing to rapidly cool and the wind was picking up. Snowflakes began to form spontaneously in the air, swirling around in the growing wind. Soon a tempestuous blizzard was swirling before them, blocking all from their sight. From the centre of the storm came a keening noise. Olin looked stunned, colour draining from his naturally pale face,

"Tha... That can't be!" Olin stammered.

"What is it?" Shouted Teloran over the howling of the wind. A pair of glowing red eyes appeared in the midst of the blizzard and a being of gigantic proportions stepped towards them, towering twice as high as Olin's six and a half feet. It was approximately humanoid in form, but with legs which bent backwards at the knee, like those of a horse, with arms which dragged along the ground and great hands which ended in long talon-like fingers. It had a head that lacked ears or hair and was elongated, the top of the cranium coming to a sharp point, a mouth that looked like the darkest pit as it howled towards them and two piercing eyes glowing the deepest crimson. Its body appeared to be made of ice suffused with a dark mist. Every time it howled the blizzard seemed to intensify.

"This isn't possible." Screamed Olin above the din, visibly shaken to his core, "It is a frostling from the northern wastes. A being of great power and very difficult to combat. Don't let it strike you directly." The beast was moving slowly, so Teloran shouted back over the storm,

"That shouldn't be too difficult, it is slower than an old, fat Hruntan horseman on foot and in full armour." Showing inappropriate humour for the occasion.

"Don't underestimate it." Olin shouted back. Just then, as if to mark Olin's comments the frostling raised its right arm and it grew into a long, icicle-like spear which it thrust out at high speed towards Teloran, who barely dove out of the way in time as the rapidly growing icicle spear shot past him into the trunk of a nearby tree. Frost began to spread outwards along the bark of the tree from the point of entry of the spear until the whole tree was rapidly sheaved in ice. The frostling drew back his arm and the tree shattered into tiny pieces. Teloran's and Temac's eyes widened at the attack. Olin simply grunted,

"I told you to be careful. The only thing they're scared of is daylight and fire and since morning is a long way off and I don't fancy trying to battle it all night, Temac I suggest you start trying to kindle that firewood. Teloran and I will try and distract it." Olin commanded, being the most experienced at fighting frostlings, amongst the plethora of other strange beasts which inhabited the northern ice land wastes above Ruorland.

Teloran and Olin began to circle around the frostling, Olin striking out at it with his axe, Teloran with his broadsword. The plan seemed to work because the frostling began focusing on Olin and Teloran, allowing Temac the time he needed to try and set a fire to the wood he had collected. The blows Olin and Teloran landed on the frostling did not really seem to damage the beast, their weapons seemed only to lightly scratch the ice, but it seemed enough to irritate the beast into focusing on their dance, rather than pay attention to Temac's business. Teloran and Olin were having to move extremely fast to avoid the deadly blows from the frostling and they were already beginning to tire from the exertion, imperceptibly slowing, little by little.

The frostling roared, a sound like a thrashing storm of hail, and stretched forth its arms. Its claw-like fingers froze together into points and its arms lengthened until both its upper limbs resembled spears of ice. Newly equipped the frostling was now striking rapidly towards both assailants. Olin swung his axe in a mighty blow, hoping to shatter the spear arm which had just narrowly missed him, but the frostling had played a ruse. Its spear arm dropped off and a new one instantly grew in its place. It struck towards Olin, missing Olin's body, but striking his axe driving the flat of the blade into Olin's right leg, crushing bone. He screamed in pain and dropped to the ground. The frostling raised its arm for a killing blow, but suddenly paused, looking towards Temac, and growled.

Temac had been trying to ignore the fight, keeping only as much attention on the fight as was necessary to ensure he was not about to get embroiled in it whilst he continued the work of lighting the fire. He had found his tinder in his pack and been trying to get a spark to light the kindling wood. It was as the first sparks caught in the kindling that the frostling had focused its attention on what Temac was trying to achieve. Temac saw that the frostling was suddenly focused on him, but he needed more time to get the fire established.

"Hold it back for as long as possible!" Shouted Temac to Olin and Teloran. Teloran knew that Olin was incapacitated so that it was up to him to slow the beast's advance. He leapt into the frostling's path stopping its immediate pursuit of Temac. The frostling was fast and now that Teloran was battling it alone he was not able to move quickly enough to keep up with the onslaught for long, especially as he was already tired from fighting the frostling. Teloran barely managed to raise his sword in time to block a sideways blow from the frostling which sent Teloran sprawling across the ground.

Child of Rydos

The frostling loomed above Temac, poised to strike at him as Temac lifted a lighted branch. The frostling veered backwards trying to get away from the flame, keening at a high pitch as it backed away. Temac tossed a flaming brand to each of Teloran and Olin.

"Try and surround him," Called Olin, "I can't move so you'll have to drive it towards me. The fire will destroy its body."

"This thing is huge. Will this small amount of fire be enough?" Asked Teloran, concernedly.

"Hopefully," Responded Olin, "They are beings forged of magic and melt incredibly quickly when they come into contact with fire." Temac and Teloran came at the frostling from opposite sides, driving it backward towards Olin, who was also holding his fiery branch aloft. It was cowering now as its icy form began to lose its integrity, water beginning to form in rivulets and flow down its body.

"It looks like its working, but… I don't think this fire is going to be enough, my branch is already dying out." Teloran was the first to notice, but he was right, their flames were not going to be enough, and it looked like the frostling was realizing that too because it was beginning to rise from its cowering position, a new gleam in its dark eyes.

Temac cast his eyes about him looking for inspiration and then he spotted their tent awning. Temac darted towards the awning, and set his dying flame to the tent fabric. The sheet started to burn and so it hoisted it up throwing it over the frostling before it could rise and either escape or attack again. Olin and Teloran both grabbed corners of the fabric, forcing the frostling to the ground. As the flames consumed both the tent fabric and the beast it began to scream in an unearthly manner. Then suddenly, it was gone. A black mist rose from the flames and dispersed into the air.

"Thank Marah!" Exclaimed Teloran, invoking the god most worshipped by the Laconians, "We managed to finally kill the beast."

"It is dead, but it is not destroyed." Said Olin weakly. His words brought Temac's and Teloran's attention back to their injured comrade. They moved quickly towards him now to see how badly he was injured. The head of Olin's axe had obviously crushed some of his bones in his right leg. There was not any bleeding, so Temac did what it could to splint Olin's leg in a straight position so it would be more comfortable and so it would have some opportunity of healing.

"You're not going to be walking, or riding, any time soon. But I don't think you're going to die either." Temac told Olin, then asked, "What did you mean when you said that thing wasn't dead?"

"It takes more than fire to kill a frostling. It is a dark spirit from the northern wastes. Melting away the ice is the only way a normal warrior can hope to battle them. Melting the ice deprived it of its body, its form. Its spirit will have flown back to the northern ice caps. It will be able to regrow its body, but it will take years, maybe centuries, for the ice to build up around it again so that it can claim a physical body again."

"You mean they are indestructible?" Asked Teloran, incredulously.

"No, not indestructible either. But it would take the power of a cleric or a mystic to damage its non-corporeal form and unless either of you is keeping some secret life-choices from me, I don't think that any of us could do much more than we already have." Olin said, allowing his sense of humour to show through, despite the pain he was in.

"It is good to see your odd sense of humour hasn't failed you, Olin." Temac commented.

"What concerns me more," Olin began, "Is how the frostling got here at all."

"What do you mean?" asked Temac.

"It should not have been able to travel this far south. Direct sunlight would have destroyed it. It would have had to travel all the way down from the northern wastes, finding shelter each night. It just isn't possible. Why would it have wanted to come this far south anyway? Frostlings are not known for their intelligence, just for their rage." Concluded Olin.

"Another mystery to report to Conclave it would seem." Sighed Temac, "We may as well try and set up camp. We're not going anywhere this evening and it probably isn't a good idea to make Olin move until the morning anyway."

"No argument from me!" Olin commented gruffly, trying to hide the pain he was feeling. Noting this, Temac and Teloran set about making camp around Olin. They were one canvas down so they erected one canvas over Olin to give him shelter and they erected the other next to it, planning to share it between themselves. Temac went to check whether the horses had survived the attack or if they had managed to break their tethers and flee in fear when the frostling arrived. Temac found the horses agitated, but thankfully all present and uninjured. He saw to their needs before returning to Olin and Teloran.

Exhaustion began to finally get the better of all three

of them. Temac distributed a few of their cold rations between them to make sure they took some food before they fell asleep. Meanwhile Teloran found Olin's bedroll and helped him into it before he and Temac both fell into their own rolls and slept soundly until first light.

Once morning had broken and they had breakfasted and disbanded their camp, Temac and Teloran fashioned a makeshift sled by banding branches together in order to lay Olin upon it and drag him behind his horse. It was the only way they could work out to move him, at least until they found a farmstead and farmer who was willing to sell them a wagon. It had not taken them long to fashion the simple sled and so they were able to continue their journey westwards towards Korrath without too much delay. The major delay would of course be the speed of the sled itself. As they set off the sled churned the soft ground creating ruts in the soft soil under Olin's weight. The destruction obscured a large mark burned into the grass of the snake entwined around a sword. There was a rush of wind as the soil was churned up. The companions noticed the temporary rush of wind, but assumed it was a random gust of wind as they had had not noticed the mark in the darkness of the night and the business of the morning. The onward journey was slow and Olin was making his discomfort known by complaining loudly, though Temac and Teloran suspected it had more to do with the embarrassment of being dragged behind a horse and being unable to stand on his own two feet, rather than the pain he was in, as usually Olin was very stoic.

Chapter VIII – Children's Games

Teran, Xantila and Koran set off early in the morning from Baxen, the sun having barely risen over the horizon. They headed through the dusty streets towards the east gate of the town, towards the rising sun and towards Arin, the capital of Arinach and the boundary marker for the edge of the Arinach desert. As they were making their way through the town all three of the companions had the feeling they were being watched and followed, though none of them could make out a mark, so they did not mention it to each other. As they left the town behind them and got further into the open countryside, the niggling itch that they were being followed lessened. They did not race at breakneck speed across Arinach because such haste would have been unusual and noteworthy to those they encountered or passed by and would have also exhausted the horses.

They saw very few people on the road; trade was definitely being restricted rather extremely in this part of the country, as Koran's contacts had reported. As the day progressed, the sun arched gracefully through the sky from the east to the west. As the sun began to sink towards the west, Xantila, looking towards the setting sun, noticed a dark smug on the horizon, which appeared to be getting slowly larger.

"I think someone is following us. I thought someone marked us in Baxen as we left, but I couldn't spot anyone, then the feeling faded, but I'm fairly sure that smudge on the horizon is someone trying to catch up with us." Xantila confided with Teran and Koran.

"What do you want to do? We need to set up camp for the night soon. Shall we try to lose them in the dark first or shall we hope we can outnumber or outsmart them if it comes to a conflict?" Koran asked.

"You're assuming they are hostile." Commented Teran, "I suppose our luck so far would suggest that you're right. I think it'd be good to take precautions, but I don't see anywhere convenient where we could hide. The landscape is too open."

"Agreed," Added Koran, "So we stand?"

"We could move off the road a little way and refrain from a campfire. It is entirely possible that they will miss our position in the dark." Suggested Xantila. Teran and Koran agreed and they set the plan in action, hoping to avoid further conflict.

It was a cold night to camp outdoors without the benefit of a fire, even with the comfort of the tents they had procured in Tellac. Nearer the desert the nights got cold, even in mid-autumn. Xantila, Koran and Teran sat on the ground, their backs to each other. This gave them both extra warmth and allowed them to keep watch all around their position. The night wore on and they were not disturbed, nor could they see or hear anything out of the ordinary. They needed some rest so they switched their pattern and two of them slept whilst the other kept watch over the camp. It was Teran's turn to keep watch and he was peering out into the blackness of the night. There was a new moon this night, so it was only the starlight that broke the thick darkness of the night.

"You can't hide from me that easily." A voice cut

through the darkness from behind Teran, causing him to jump and spin around in surprise. It took him a moment to place the voice, but he knew he recognised it.

"Banir?" He queried to the darkness.

"Do you know anyone else who could find you in this darkness?" Banir responded, stepping closer to Teran so he was visible in the dim light. Teran hesitated in his replied,

"What are you doing here? Why did you follow us?" He was beginning to grow suspicious of the child's motives. These were not the actions of normal street urchin and Teran wondered if his actions were related to the incidents of the other mysterious assailants and experiences the companions had undergone.

"I've grown a little bored of life in Baxen. I don't find pickpocketing the locals interesting or challenging enough anymore. It looked like you were set for an adventure and I thought you might be able to use my skills. I'm very good at what I do." Banir added, "That is, sneaking around unnoticed."

"What do you know of our adventures?" Asked Teran.

"Nothing much, except that you are obviously worried about being followed and that you're headed towards Arin and the dessert or further." Answered Banir.

"I'm not certain about this. Since you were the one following us we might as well light a fire to warm up and get the others involved in this conversation. I'm not convinced of the wisdom of trusting a thief, you need to convince me that we can trust you despite the unhealthy interest you seem to be taking in our affairs." Teran continued. He was thinking about how useful the boy could be in sneaking around in Arin. He was feeling surprisingly well-disposed towards this boy and felt trust towards him, though he knew that he should not be so naïve. He also was concerned about sending the boy back to Baxen by himself, the road is not particularly safe for such a young traveller by himself.

Teran began building a fire, as he suggested, meanwhile he continued his questioning of Banir, changing tack slightly, "How did you catch up with us anyway?"

"My horse is tethered a little way outside your camp." Banir answered.

"You stole a horse?" Teran assumed, not very pleased with the attention that would throw in their direction from the townsfolk of Baxen.

"Um… No… much against my better judgement I spent some of the money you gave me on purchasing a horse. I got the impression you didn't want to make too obvious a trail of crumbs towards where you were headed, so I made sure to be as discreet as possible." Banir said somewhat abashedly. Teran was impressed by the boy's sensitivities,

"That was very astute of you." He responded. Xantila and Koran had been roused by Teran's and Banir's talking and by the fire building, so they also started paying attention to the conversation now. "Why don't you fill us in on some of your background. How did you get mixed up with the thieves' guild in Baxen?" So it was, that Banir began to weave his life's story for Teran, Xantila and Koran,

"I never met my father. I don't remember my mother ever mentioning him. We used to live in the poor quarter in Baxen, in one of the shacks that are built up against the town wall. We shared the small house with four other families. It was fun for me because there were other kids around. I don't think my mother appreciated it much, but we couldn't afford anything grander. She was a seamstress of sorts, my mother; at least that is how I like to think of her. It sounds worthier than a rag lady, but in truth that is what she was. She would salvage or buy clothing discarded by others and patch them back together to sell on to those who couldn't afford the expense of tailored clothes. There wasn't much business in it, but it kept us fed. Most of the time." Banir paused in silent recollection. "We were not treated well by others who were more fortunate than ourselves. I remember, in particular, the children of the merchants and other wealthier families would use mother as sport, throwing rotten food at her as she wound through the streets with her cart trying to collect any rags she could…"

"What happened to your mother?" Xantila injected in a soft, concerned voice. She sensed by the way in which Banir was telling his tale that there was more to come and that he needed help to tell it.

"She… it was during one of those very cold, wet winters that we occasionally get near Baxen due to the winds blowing from the north-east from across the inner sea." He began, "She caught lung waste, there was nothing we could do, we didn't have the money for a healer. For fear of catching her disease the other ignorant families sharing our hovel of a home threw us out." Banir paused, tears welling up in his eyes, "She died in a street gutter, no roof over her head, no warmth, only me besides her. A town constable collected her body the next morning and disposed of it in a common grave. I followed to see where. No one gave any attention to a lonely boy on the streets."

"Were you able to return to you home then?" Asked Koran, concern afresh on his face. Though Banir spoke of events long passed, his skill in weaving the story and the sorrow of it caught the emotions of those who were listening.

"No, the fools still feared that I might have contracted the lung waste too. They slammed the door in my face. I was so angry with them then. I blamed them for it all, though in truth, I don't think my mother would have survived whether she was under a roof or outside and exposed to the elements. The sickness had taken a strong hold of her. But it was such an undignified way to die and I loved her so much." Responded Banir, some residual anger in his voice, but tempered by the years and the needless waste of it all, "I sat there in the street, unable to bring myself to any action after that. I wasn't aware of what was happening around me, my thoughts were turned entirely inward. I don't know how old I was then, but I can't have been more than four years old." Xantila let out an impromptu gasp at realising the extent of Banir's terrible history. It was amazing the boy had survived at all. Banir continued, "I don't know how much time passed, it could have been merely hours, or it could have been days. Eventually, practicality won out over introspection. My stomach called to me and I realised I was ravenous. I looked down and realised that someone must have thought I was a sorry case and had thrown a few coppers at my feet where I sat. It was enough to buy a loaf of bread to assuage my hunger." Banir paused to give himself breath and collect his thoughts for the continuation of his story, "I realised then that I might be able to survive by continuing to beg... it sort of worked for a while, but whilst people are somewhat generous to a young ragged mouth to feed, they are not overly free with their money. I sometimes went days without enough food and would be on the verge of fainting. Then one day, I saw a young street urchin pickpocketing a well-dressed passer-by and I realised to myself that perhaps I could try and do the same. After all it had to be better than starving and if I was caught the worst that would happen would be that I'd end up dead and I was already more than half-way there anyway. I already had quite a head start because no one really wanted to look at me anyway or acknowledge my existence so it wasn't hard to sneak up on people. I quickly found that I was quite good, actually. I rarely had trouble picking pockets and I was never caught... at least... not until the thieves' guild found me. I was doing pretty well for myself really. I wasn't going hungry anymore and though I wasn't able to afford a proper roof over my head, I could at least afford clothing for my back. One evening, just after I'd lifted a good, hefty purse, I was intercepted by a cloaked figure who forced me into a side alley and clocked me on the head. When I came around I found myself in a room, bound to a chair, with bright lights burning in my eyes. Behind the lights, I could see the outline of a number of figures. Out of the shadows a voice began to question me. They were the guild of thieves. They didn't let just anyone steal on the streets of Baxen, after all it might bring thievery a bad name..." Banir grinned and continued, "I told them my story, as I'm telling you.

They were impressed at the number of lifts I said I'd managed to do without them noticing me. They took me into their fold and I've worked for them ever since. In return for a share of my takings they gave me a roof over my head and taught me how to develop my skills." Banir paused, "Until yesterday when Xantila caught me trying to lift your purse, Teran, they were the only people who'd ever caught me stealing. I'm real good." Banir finished, without any hint of modesty in his voice.

"If life was so good as a thief in Baxen, why have you hot-footed it out of the town to follow us well into the dead of night?" Asked Koran

"Like I said, I fancied the adventure." Banir responded, though he looked a little confused. "It is odd really," He continued, "I was completely content with my life, doing well even, until you showed up. I can't explain, but as soon as I saw you Teran I knew something special was occurring and that I needed to be involved. I honestly think my skills can be of use to you and I'm not exactly a huge drain on your supplies as I'm so small."

"Go and wait by your horse so we can discuss it amongst ourselves." Responded Teran. Banir nodded, understandingly, and took himself away from the centre of the camp to collect his tethered horse whilst the companions conferred.

"I think his story is genuine and that he believes in his desire to join us." Began Teran, "However, I am still concerned as I feel very strongly predisposed to like the boy and to trust him and I can't pinpoint why I feel that way."

"I know exactly what you mean." Agreed Koran, "I feel similarly but also feel suspicious because of all the strange things that have already happened on the journey. And he is, after all, a thief."

"If we send him packing though, he could alert others to our journey." Xantila pitched in, "We can probably keep a closer watch on him if we keep him with us. At least for now." They nodded towards each other as Banir was returning to the centre of the camp with his horse in tow. He looked up at Teran with a questioning look on his face.

"You can accompany us…" Teran began, interrupted by Banir's whoop of joy, "… for now. But, you must do exactly what we tell you and no sneaking off without explicit permission from one of us."

"Yes Sir!" Banir responded enthusiastically, just relieved to have been taken in by the group. He was not sure why he felt so strongly that he needed to join them, but for the first time he could remember he felt like his life was beginning to have some purpose to it.

Morning was beginning to rear its head over the eastern horizon as the sun's glow was beginning to win out over the darkness of the night. They were already all awake so the newly enlarged group breakfasted together and began the next day of their journeying towards Arin. They knew that Banir did not believe their cover story about being merchants, but they were not willing to reveal their true identities and mission to him just yet. Thus, they pretended to be ordinary messengers from the northern kingdoms of Sambar sent to entreat with King Arran of Arinach.

Chapter IX – Jewel of the Desert

Arin sat on the cusp between scrubland and desert. No river flowed past its gates, but the city itself sat upon an old spring, which serviced the city and allowed it not only to survive, but to thrive in a place which otherwise seemed inhospitable. The city was renowned for its flowing waterways, fed by the plentiful spring, which seemed miraculous and exotic in this dry landscape. Arin had once been a jewel among the cities of Sambar, boasting the height of sophistication when it came to art and architecture, since it had been a major trade junction between east and west. Much of the city's glory was now faded, surpassed by the wealth of Rydos. The approach from the west towards Arin was not too difficult for travellers. The desert began east of the city; the lands to the west were merely arid and its pathways and roads well-trodden as trade routes to the rest of the country and the other nations of Sambar.

As Teran, Koran, Xantila and Banir rode towards the city they could see that there were lines of tradesmen and normal folk queuing at the gates of the city, being interviewed by the gatehouse guards before they were permitted to enter within the city's walls. It also seemed that a shantytown had developed outside the city walls, which was news to all of them, as they had not gleaned information about this in advance. When they eventually got to the gates they realised why. The city was under martial law.

"Papers!" The nearest city guard, a man with a little,

Child of Rydos

round, red face to match his attitude, shouted at them; more of an assault on the ears than a request.

"We've just arrived, we don't have any." Koran volunteered calmly.

"No papers. No entry." The guard spat and turned away from them to talk to the next group in the queue.

"Wait! How do we get papers?" Asked Teran, at which point the guard swung his body back around towards them, smacking Teran across the face with the back of his armoured glove, sending him reeling.

"Don't waste my time." The guard shouted, "Push off or I'll throw you all in jail." Puffing up his chest as he delivered his threat. Koran went to dart forward at the attack of his friend, but Xantila reached out to grab him in time before things unravelled further. Banir helped Teran back to his feet and the companions melted away from the queue into the depths of the shantytown looking for somewhere to recuperate and work out what to do next.

They found an inn which looked like it had been built from the debris of other buildings called *The King's Head*, though the crudely painted sign which hung above the door looked rather more like it represented the king's posterior. Koran suspected the artistry was purposefully obscure. Koran entered the establishment with Xantila whilst Teran and Banir kept watch over the horses; they had seen hungry eyes look towards them as they passed through the streets. Koran approached the innkeeper to inquire about rooms.

"No space, mate." The innkeeper replied, and then continued, "No space anywhere in the whole shanty. We're crammed in here tighter than a barrelful of salted fish!" He finished, evidentially disgruntled by the turn his life had taken.

"Is there absolutely nowhere you can give us to sleep? We've been on the road for four days and really need somewhere to rest." Koran queried again. The innkeeper could see they were desperate too and, not wanting to turn down money unnecessarily, he paused in contemplation.

"If you're willing to share a couple of pallets outside in the yard with the horses you're welcome to the space. I know it is a little cold at this time of year during the nights. I'm sorry about that. But it rarely rains and it shouldn't be too bad if you stay close to each other and as long as you're sheltered from the wind." The innkeeper responded at last.

"I don't see that we have much choice. Can you at least feed us something hot to soften the deal?" Koran negotiated. Moved to embarrassment that he was going to charge them for sleeping in his yard, the innkeeper nodded in agreement.

That evening found the four of them crowded in the common room of the inn, eating their supper and listening to the idle gossip floating around the room, which was rife, especially after the clientele were a few pints of ale into the evening. The population of Arin were deeply unhappy, which meant they were keen to nurse their woes over a drink or two. Thus, it was that it did not take long for Teran and the others to piece together what was happening, even if they did not understand the reasons why. Most of the people living in the shantytown had previously lived in the poorer quarter of the city, within its protective walls. About two months ago the king had instituted martial law and had thrown all those who could not afford papers of transit and residency out of the city, which had meant most of those in lower paid occupations. There was only one office set up outside the city walls for the processing of papers and this was not only understaffed and overworked, but also incredibly costly. It could take months to procure the papers to be allowed inside the city and it was not guaranteed that every applicant would be allowed entry.

"We need to get inside the city. And soon. We can't wait a month or more to get the paperwork." Said Teran to the others as they sat discussing things at their table.

"Leave it to me." Responded Banir, getting up from his seat, "I might be gone a while."

"Wha..?" Began Koran. Teran snorted,

"It's not worth trying to stop him. He'll be back. I have a feeling."

"I thought we'd told him he was here on our terms." Retorted Koran, "That lasted a long time."

"Indeed." Xantila chipped in.

"Let's see what the evening brings. Banir can take care of himself and, somehow, I don't think he is in the process of turning us in. Besides, who, in a city run on martial law, would trust a thief?" Nothing else to be done, they leaned back and enjoyed their first evening of moderate rest for some time since they began their life on the road.

It was three hours later. The hustle and bustle of the common room was beginning to quieten down as people had drunk all that their money would allow and were now drifting to their beds in order to be ready for another day of hard slog tomorrow. Banir snuck back into the common room and slid into his place at the table that he had those hours earlier.

"So," Said Koran, focussing his attention on Banir, "What was all that about?" Banir reached into the inside of his vest-top and pulled out some documents, spreading them on the table in front of them.

"Papers which identify the four of us as merchants and allow us access to that part of the city and its facilities." Banir said smugly.

"Where did you get those?" Teran asked.

"I relieved some heavily laden merchants of them, easing the burden on their backs." Banir responded, giving the fully innocent impression that he really had just been helping those merchants out. Koran suppressed a laugh,

"They are not going to be very happy come the morning." He observed.

"We'll be long inside the city walls by then and there is no way to trace the theft to us. The paperwork, whilst official, is sloppy and vague. Not the way to run a true state under martial law." Banir responded, as if he'd had years of training in statecraft, rather than the few years on the streets of Baxen, which were, in fact, his heritage.

"Let's turn in for the night. It is already late and I doubt we'll get much sleep any way so we'll be up early, in time to try and beat the crowds and the queues into the city." Teran suggested. The others agreed and they settled their account with the innkeeper and headed out to the yard and to their pallets for the night.

The next morning broke far too early from Banir's point of view. He still had not fully recovered from the missed sleep from the day and night he spent pursuing

Child of Rydos

Teran, Koran and Xantila from Baxen to catch up with them. As he rubbed his eyes and sat up, he could see the others stirring. They returned to the common room where they were given a sweet rice dish for breakfast before they left to make their way to the city gate. There was already a long queue making its way towards the gate. They must have gathered literally as dawn broke to have beaten them there. It took about an hour for them to finally reach the guards at the gate again. This time the guard that they dealt with looked decidedly friendlier than the one from the day before. He was still officious and abrupt, but he did not resort to violence to deal with those waiting for entry into the city, unlike some of his colleagues.

"Papers?" The guard queried.

"Here you are." Teran volunteered, passing the stolen papers to the guard.

"What is your business in the city?" The guard asked in a bored voice, glancing down at the paperwork. They had made sure to examine the paperwork thoroughly before passing it over, so they knew the role they had to play to gain entry to the city.

"We're merchants hoping to buy silks in the city to export to Baxen and Tellac." Teran continued. The guard nodded, passed back the papers to Teran, and waved them onward into the city.

"Keep to the merchants' quarter, otherwise you'll be arrested. Also make sure you obey the hours of curfew. Finally, don't lose your papers, otherwise you could find yourself in serious trouble." The guard advised, turning his back to them as they passed beyond him and through the gate into the city.

This gate led directly in to what had been the poor

quarter of the city before the citizens deemed as unworthy by the state had all been evicted to outside the city walls. Most of the buildings inside had been levelled. The only buildings which remained standing were those that appeared to be of slightly better quality. There was evidence of new roads being laid and new buildings under construction. The old main road still existed and led towards the merchants' quarter, where their papers were valid, so they took the horses at a steady trot towards that part of the city. Their first order of business was to establish a base of operations and so they were looking for an inn which included stabling, hoping that it would be better than the previous night's accommodation. They asked for a recommendation from a passer-by once they finally left the derelict poor quarter and they were given directions to *The Jewel*, which apparently would match their requirements. When they arrived at *The Jewel* they were not disappointed. The stables attached to the inn were clean and spacious and the inn itself had large airy rooms which were built around a luxurious garden courtyard. The proprietor wanted an exorbitant amount of money for their stay, but that was not surprising given the pressures on business in the city and since, in reality, money was not an issue for them either. They agreed a price and settled into the inn.

The innkeeper, happy to have such well-paying guests, was very forthcoming with information about the city. He waxed lyrical about the wonderful plans the king had for the city. Arin was to become known as the 'Jewel of the Desert', a jewel to rival to pearl of the ocean, Rydos. There were temporary sacrifices to be made in terms of civil liberties to make sure the work could progress as quickly as possible, but it would all be worth it when Arin became the greatest city amongst the nations of Sambar and then the world. Teran listened to all this with great interest, but could not shake the feeling that most of what the innkeeper said was forced, that he felt he had to agree with it or face being classified as unnecessary and find himself outside the walls of the city like those from the poor quarter. Or worse, branded as a troublemaker or traitor and thrown in jail. Koran agreed with Teran's assessment, which he shared with the others once the innkeeper was out of earshot. They decided that they needed to spend some time gathering further information about King Arran's plans and why he was so focussed on them, before they progressed any further.

Chapter X – Cartwheels and Cabbages

Temac, Teloran and Olin had been travelling for about half a day before they came across the first farmstead since their encounter with the frostling.

"I see some buildings in the distance." Relayed Teloran, "Let us hope it is a farm or, at least, that they have a wagon or cart we can put you in Olin."

"It will be a farm." Commented Temac, "Most people in Hrunta are fairly nomadic, like the Ruors, travelling with their horse herds to the best grazing land. I can't imagine that there would be another type of building out here. Let's hope they're willing to spare us a cart, or at least let us buy one."

"It's about time." Olin grumbling, "Being dragged, practically along the floor, by my horse is humiliating." Temac suspected the real problem was the pain of all the bumps in the landscape, rather than the embarrassment of the mode of transport itself causing Olin's grief, but he elected not to mention this.

As the companions drew nearer to the buildings they could see that the land around was cultivated and that this was indeed a farm. They spotted a team working with horse and plough in one of the fields near the road and waved to them, hoping to establish the likelihood of being able to purchase a cart from them. The men who had been working on gathering in the harvest and preparing the ground for the winter months paused in their work and came over to the travellers on the road.

"We don't see many travellers on this road of late."

Child of Rydos

One of the farmers offered as commentary in a thick Hruntan accent as he simultaneously cast his gaze over, the now somewhat motely, trio that Temac, Teloran and Olin made since their frolic with the frostling.

"Why? Has there be trouble on the road recently?" Asked Temac, fearing that their journey was going to become even more complex than it already was.

"No." The farmer responded, "Just that no trade seems to be coming from over the border with Arinach at the moment. Bad for us, 'cos we often put up travellers for the night as there are no inns around here."

"We don't need a place to stay, but we wouldn't mind a hot meal and, if possible, a cart or a wagon to carry our injured colleague in greater comfort and with greater speed." Queried Temac, who had placed himself in the position of negotiator on the basis that they were now in his homeland. The farmer looked over towards Olin again, his face a mixture of disappointment from the lost overnight revenue and hopeful calculation as he considered how much they could charge for a cart or whether it would damage too much their ability to gather next year's harvest.

"Come with me to the barns up at the main house, we might be able to find something there to help you." Responded the farmer, then turning to the other labourers he said, "Carry on without me here until you break for lunch." They nodded towards him and the farmer then led them towards his home. As he led them there he started to converse with them, obviously desperate for news from the surrounding area. "My name in Gregac. This farmstead has been in my family for over ten generations." Pride evident in his voice.

"Very good to meet you, Gregac. I am Korac, and

this is Tellor and Olaf." Responded Temac as he indicated Teloran and Olin, hoping that Gregac did not recognise him as King Teslas' brother, as they had agreed to keep their cover as long as possible in case of spies from Narsos or Arinach working in the kingdoms. "We are traders returning from Tellac, having sold our wares, but we were ambushed by bandits who hoped to relieve us of our money. They were not successful, but Olaf's leg got broken during the fight and we have had to drag him behind us all the way since."

"Bandits?" Gregac asked, looking concerned, "How far away were they? That's not good news if they take it into their heads to start raiding farmsteads too, we're fairly isolated out here."

"Our attack came on the border between Hrunta and Arinach." Temac told him truthfully, "I don't think you have too much to worry about here though, as it seemed to me they were operating deeper out of Arinach and had strayed unusually close to the border in pursuit of us." Temac added trying to alleviate the farmer's fears as he did not believe the farm was about to be overtaken by frostlings. Gregac looked a little comforted, but not entirely convinced by Temac's assessment, as they continued towards the barns.

"Wait here. I'll just run into the house and let Marin know we've got extra mouths to feed for lunch. She's used to serving a big spread, so it won't be any trouble." Gregac told them as he darted forward towards his home. Marin, they presumed, was his wife. A little while later, Gregac reappeared from inside the farmhouse and re-joined them. "That's all sorted. Let's go and look at my carts to see if there is something we can spare which would suit your needs." Gregac suggested, obviously beginning to get ready to barter, not quite the country bumpkin one might naively assume a remote farmer to be. He led them to the nearest barn and Temac and Teloran followed him inside whilst Olin waited outside, trying to stand from the reclined position he had been occupying on the litter. The barn was actually fitted out as stable for the horses on one side and a dry store for various farm machinery, obviously intended to help with ploughing and harvesting, on the other. Near the back of the barn was an old open-topped cart, its right wheel cracked, which presumably had once been used to transport goods from the farm to the nearest market. The layers of dust upon it suggested it had not been used for some time.

"We might be able to scrape by without this one." Gregac suggested, indicating said cart. Teloran snorted and Temac stepped in and spoke before Teloran could say something which might damage their ability to barter with the farmer.

"It doesn't even have two wheels!" Temac began.

"Easily fixed," Gregac retorted, "I'll get a couple of the lads to swap it with the wheel from another cart to speed you on your way, and get that one repaired myself." He continued trying to sound generous. Temac could see the way this negotiation was likely to go.

"How generous." Temac responded without enthusiasm, "What price do need for it?"

"Ten marks." Suggested Gregac, his face a mask of neutrality. They could afford it, but it was a ridiculously price. The farmer was obviously trying his luck so Temac was not afraid to give a counter-offer.

"The cart cannot have been worth more than four marks when new." Came Temac's reply.

"I have to take into account the labour for fixing the wheel, the time it'll take me to replace that wheel and the extra hands I'll have to hire to make up for the slowed pace of harvesting without this cart to carry goods." Gregac stated, trying to make it seem like the world lay heavy upon his shoulders. He paused as if making all these calculations in his head, then suggested, "Eight marks."

"I can't believe your loss of revenue would be so much. The cart was thick with dust and obviously not being used with that busted wheel." Countered Temac, "Five marks at the most."

"Seven." Quickly reposted Gregac, obviously enjoying the haggling, "You'll not find another farmer or cart for a league in any direction."

"Five marks and six shillings." Returned Temac, sticking closely to his lower estimate, "And you'll include lunch for us too. It's a good price." Gregac grinned,

"You drive a hard bargain. It is a deal." And they shook on the agreed price and Temac drew the money out of his purse to give to Gregac. Temac would have happily paid the original ten marks as they desperately needed the cart to speed their journey and money was not a large concern at this point in their travels, but he wanted to stay in character to not raise suspicions about who they might really be. "I'll make sure the cart wheel is fixed whilst we're eating lunch so you don't delay your journey too much longer." Gregac told them as they made their way out of the barn. Outside Olin was no longer lying on the makeshift litter. He had obviously managed to lift himself up, either under his own strength or with a little help and was now sitting on a bench by an outdoor table at the front of the farm house, talking with a couple of the farm hands.

"Did you find me something a little more comfortable than that litter?" Olin called to Temac and Teloran when he saw them approaching.

"Gregac had an old cart, which Temac bartered for." Called Teloran in response. The farm hands both raised their eyebrows at this, obviously guessing which cart Gregac had sold to them. Gregac waved his arm at them,

"Go and swap that wheel with one of a similar size which isn't busted." He told them, "You can come back and have your lunch after that." The two lads, grumbling good-humouredly, sloped off to the barn to get to work. At that moment, a short lady of middle years, with flat brown hair, streaked with grey and scrapped back severely into a tight bun knot, came out of the house, carrying a large pot, which was steaming. Several small children were dancing in and out around her, chattering away. Gregac smiled at her as she approached. "This is my wife, Marin." He said proudly.

"Korac, Tellor. And have you already met Olaf?" Temac offered, indicating himself, Teloran and Olin in turn, making sure to be consistent in his use of false names.

"Good to make your acquaintance." Marin said, giving a slight bob towards them. "Gregac, go inside and wash your hands and bring out the bread and the bowls." She continued speaking almost continuously, just shifting her focus slightly from the guests to her husband. Gregac did what he was told immediately and without fuss or comment. Obviously used to obeying his wife's orders. He returned a short while later carrying a large loaf of freshly baked bread and a knife to slice it with. A couple of older children followed behind carrying bowls for the soup.

"Are all these children yours?" Olin asked of Gregac and Marin as Gregac got to the table and sat down with them. Gregac laughed.

"No, we've got quite an extended family here, they are my brothers' children for the most part. Though Gema, Greg and Marianna are ours." Gregac told them, indicating one of the boys who had carried the bowls, another boy a couple of years younger and a little girl who was currently clinging to Marin's skirts, one eye fixed on the strange visitors.

"We don't have much time for standing on ceremony here." Said Marin as she began serving out the soup from the large pot, whilst Gregac sliced the bread. "Please, dig in." She concluded as she passed the bowls to the guests before serving the family.

"Smells like cabbage." Commented Teloran, wafting the vapours from his bowl towards his nose.

"Aye. Cabbage it is." Marin responded.

"It's been a very good growing year for cabbages." Added Gregac, "Too many for us to sell them all at a price worth our bother, which has meant a lot of cabbages for us." He finished dolefully as he dipped his spoon into his bowl unenthusiastically. They must have been eating a lot of cabbages. Temac, Teloran and Olin fell to their bowls without fuss, just pleased for a warm meal after their battle with the frostling and the morning's travel.

"You're continuing west?" Gregac asked them as they ate. Temac nodded,

"Yes, we plan to head to Korrath. We have business associates there." He told Gregac.

"I hear there has been a steady increase in food purchasing recently. Not from single buyers, but generally good news for us farmers. I don't know why everyone is suddenly so hungry, but you won't hear complaints from us." Gregac continued.

"You've had lots of buyers here?" Temac asked.

"No, they haven't made it this far east yet. They seem to be buying from farmers nearer the capital first and making their way slowly eastwards, so I'm hopeful the trend will continue and we'll benefit from it too." Gregac told them. Then his face brightened as if he'd had an idea,

"You're merchants, you said. Why don't you buy some of our crop and take it with you, you could end up with quite a profit by the time you reach Korrath." He suggested. Temac shook his head,

"We're not agriculturalists. Our expertise and connections are not in buying food. With our bad luck on the road recently, I'd rather not take the risk." Temac told Gregac, creating a temporary lull in the conversation. Gregac looked a little crestfallen, as if he had suddenly seen before him the offer of a good year's profits suddenly dashed. Olin, Temac and Teloran had guessed why there was an increase in food purchasing. They were obviously trying to gather provisions for the army should it be needed, but not wanting to purchase all the food through one buyer, as that would lead back to the government too easily. Temac was fairly confident that the buyers would make it all the way to Gregac's farm, so he had little concern the the farmer would miss out and he did not fancy being slowed down by carrying all that extra load towards Korrath, even if it would have been convenient for the army.

As they were finishing their lunch the two lads came out from the barn, pulling the cart behind them. It seemed to be running smoothly. They laid the cart down and came eagerly towards the table hoping they could now have their lunch.

"There is plenty more in the kitchen." Marin said to them both and the lads grinned and dashed inside. Temac, Teloran and Olin thanked Marin and Gregac for their help and hospitality. Temac and Teloran hitched two of their horses to the cart and laid their belongings in the back. They helped Olin onto the back of the cart and Teloran sat near the front to drive the horses. Temac rode his own horse alongside. They waved a final thanks to the farmers and set off to rejoin the road towards Korrath.

"If they are simple merchants then I'm a Narsian snake dancer." Commented Marin to her husband. Gregac nodded in agreement,

"Soldiers of some sort I'd guess by the way in which they carried themselves. And only the one calling himself Korac is from around here. But their business is their own. They will not get any trouble due to us if others come asking for them." Gregac knew better than to get too involved in others' business, it only ever led to trouble. But he was no country bumpkin and had seen plenty of merchants and soldiers pass this way over time. He knew the difference in how they travelled and how they carried themselves. Marin just nodded in agreement. Then as the visitors disappeared over the gentle hills they turned back to their own business of running a farm.

Chapter XI – Horsemeet

It took Temac, Teloran and Olin another three days of travel to reach the river that swept around Korrath and which they had to cross to gain access to the city. Their progress had been good at first, with the addition of Gregac's cart to speed their journey, but on the second day the rain had set in. It fell lightly at first, but gradually the rain increased until it was sheeting down, driving hard into the ground and into their clothes. The road they were taking became churned up with mud and the cart's wheels only added to the problem. They had little choice but to persevere, however, so that is what they did. Trying not to let the weather dampen their spirits unnecessarily.

Olin had let Temac lead without complaint since his incident with the frostling and their crossing over the border into Temac's homeland of Hrunta. Korrath itself was situated upon a small rise above the plains that the river meandered around. From the east, the city was accessed by virtue of a wide stone bridge that could, should occasion warrant it, support a company of mounted cavalry, which the Hruntans were famed for. If they had approached from the west they would have seen scores of temporary caravanserai as horse traders made their way to the city in order to sell and buy stock. The majority of Hruntans were nomadic. They lived with their horse herds, pitching their tents wherever the horses needed to graze and moving on to new pastures when required. When they wished to trade they would make their way, sometimes with their herds, to one of the major towns or cities, such as Korrath, and pitch their tents amongst the caravanserai, granting them easy access to all the facilities major towns could offer for as long as they required. They never stayed too long in one place, as the nomadic life was in their very blood and they soon longed to return to the open fields with their herds.

Temac, Teloran and Olin made their way over the bridge and reached the city gate without anyone challenging them, though Olin received plenty of stares from passers-by wondering about how he was wounded. At the city gate, Temac caught the attention of one of the guards and identified himself. It was not necessary, as Temac was well known in the city, being the king's brother, and whilst the guards did not know what mission Temac had been on, they knew he had been away and that the king would want to see him. In less than an hour Temac, Teloran and Olin found themselves within the palace walls, in Teslas' private sitting rooms, waiting for the king to finish his afternoon audience, so they could report back on the outcome of their travels. One of the blue-clad guild healers was tending to Olin, who was reclined on one of the chaise longues, his leg stretched out so the healer could examine it properly. The break in Olin's leg was not too bad and they had treated it well, resting it properly and not overextending him on the journey to Korrath, so he was expected to make a full recovery. He would, however, still be out of fighting action for a few months and have to travel by cart or coach, much to his distain.

The king was eventually able to join them in the late afternoon and, as he arrived, he ordered a servant to

Child of Rydos

bring them afternoon tea, because he had not had the opportunity to eat since breakfast. Teslas waited for the food to arrive then dismissed all the attendants before he spoke to Temac, Teloran and Olin about the matter that really interested him.

"I wanted to minimize prying eyes and ears before we began to talk in earnest." Begun the king, "What has happened? You are back earlier than I would have expected and you are missing half of the company. Where are Teran and Koran?"

"We split the group in two at Tellac. It'll be easier to understand our motives if I start from the beginning of our journey." Temac responded to his brother. The king nodded in agreement and so Temac began to unfold their story. He began with their passage through Azin forest, being ambushed by mysterious bandits and rescued by the Rangers, then Xantila joining the company, then moved on to the mysterious weather patterns of Tellac and the decision to split the group there.

"You were right to report this as soon as possible. Though I believe these incidents are not wide spread; we haven't had any other reports of strange incidents." Teslas interrupted.

"If anyone was left alive to report them…" Muttered Teloran.

"True… but are you absolutely convinced magic is involved?" Teslas continued.

"Well there is the incident of how this happened." Olin interjected looking down at his leg and he told the story of their dalliance with the frostling. Teslas' face seemed to pale slightly as Olin recounted the fight.

"Magic must be involved, but it seems that you have

managed to come out on top each time. We have to hope that the same will be true if we end up fighting with Narsos, as I don't see what other choice we have." Teslas paused, thoughtfully, "Do you know what has happened to Teran, Koran and the Ranger, Xantila?"

"No," Continued Temac, "They must have nearly made it to Arin by now, but it'll still be a while before we can expect to hear anything. We just wanted to give this early report in case we decide we need to change our preparations for war." Teslas nodded at Temac's comment.

"It is interesting that the Rangers also want to investigate matters towards the south. I wonder if this means they will be willing to work alongside us, if it does come to war." Teslas ponderd out loud.

"I believe they might," Temac answered his brother, "I think the best way to discover this will be to talk to Xantila when the remainder of the company returns here."

"I will dispatch riders to Azin, Rydos, Ariss and Ruor, to update them on this news." Teslas responded.

"How is the marshaling of forces and the preparations for war progressing?" Asked Olin, not having liked being out of the loop for the duration of their travels, though it had been necessary.

"Each nation is gathering its armies as surreptitiously as possible as we discussed at Conclave." Teslas begun, "The Laconians are gathering at Azin, the Ruors are making their way through Gerak and gathering with the Gerakans along their border. The Rydosian fleet is fully supplied and ready to sail. Some of the fleet is up by the border with Gerak so that it can be used to speed the passage south of their troops. Here in Hrunta I've

Child of Rydos

secretly called Horsemeet and the tribes are all gathering outside this city, using the caravanserai to mask their presence, but Temac you would notice if you took a journey through the camps that it is a lot larger than it usually is at this time of year. We have more than our regular traders here." Temac, Teloran and Olin nodded at Teslas' news.

"What of the supply trains for the armies?" Teloran asked, "We heard from a farmer on your eastern border that food produce is being bought up."

"Yes." Responded Teslas, "In each of the nations we've been purchasing food supplies to lay aside for the army and create caches along the southern border of Hrunta. We've been making sure to use lots of different agents, disguised as independent traders in order to purchase the supplies with less suspicion. We've also started improving all the road networks between north and south, widening them and leveling them so that it will speed feet and supplies when need arises. All in all, I think we're about as prepared as we can be without blowing trumpets that we're planning to go to war and marching all the troops down to the border with Narsos, banners unfurled and flapping in the wind."

"Let's hope that Teran's and Koran's mission into Arinach is successful and that they can convince them to join us in our efforts so that we don't have to worry about the possibility of fighting a war on two borders." Olin contributed. Everyone was assuming that the planned foray into Narsos by Teran, Koran and Xantila would prove that the Narsians were preparing for war too and that battle was inevitable. Though there had been peace of sorts for over five hundred years, there was no love lost between the nations of Sambar and

Narsos and little trust.

"If you're willing, I could use each of your help in the preparations. There are lots of maps of northern Narsos to pour over and devise various battle strategies depending on what we find down there." Teslas requested of the companions. It was the implicit assumption that if Narsos was preparing for war then Sambar would take the fight to them in order to avoid the inevitable desolation of war spoiling their own lands as much as possible. "Temac, I could also do with your expert eye for some tours of the caravanserai to inspect the troops there and make sure that they're not getting slack due to having to keep cover rather than overtly train." The king continued. Temac nodded.

"Well, I don't know about you Teloran, but I think we may as well stick around and help." Olin said gruffly, "I'm not going anywhere fast with this leg anyway and all the fun will be happening here or southwards, so not much point in travelling northwards towards home!"

Chapter XII – Desert Deserters

It took a couple of days of intelligence work inside the city for Teran, Xantila, Koran and Banir to get to the bottom of all that had been happening in Arinach. They wanted to be fully informed before they confronted the king directly. They had been slowed down in their research by the fact that they had to keep up the charade of being silk merchants. Furthermore, all of Koran's intelligence contacts had either gone missing or hidden so far underground that they were not surfacing for air. They knew the king had plans for gentrification of the city of Arin, but it was not obvious where the resources for this were going to come from given all trade with the other nations of Sambar had been restricted. The two ideas seemed mutually exclusive so the companions thought it essential to understand as much as possible before planning their meeting with King Arran.

All of the information they had managed to gather had been either through idle gossip of merchants they were consulting and trading with for silks and gossip overheard in taverns, or through carefully directed tangential questioning of those whom they met so as to discover some of the finer details, without appearing too interested. It seemed that about two years ago a new advisor had arrived in King Arran's court. An exotic man of unknown descent, but certainly not from the kingdoms of Sambar. The king valued his advice and he quickly rose through the ranks of the king's court until Arran appointed him his chief advisor. That man's name was Agachen.

It also seemed to be around the time when Agachen arrived in Arin that the king began to grow in distrust of the other nations of Sambar and regard their success with jealousy. The change had not been sudden, but slow and subtle and it was only with the benefit of hindsight that it was obvious what direction the king's thoughts were taking. It was this growth of distrust and jealousy which had led to the king's edict against trade and his plans to make Arin rival the richest cities of the nations of Sambar. Furthermore, whilst trade with the other nations of Sambar had been restricted to almost nothing there were still many traders in the city. Some were from across the desert and those mysterious lands to the east, but most of them hailed from Narsos. Whilst trade with Narsos was not banned in the slightest, it was very peculiar that King Arran should single them out with favour above the other Sambarian nations given the historic lack of trust between Sambarians and Narsians. This nugget of information certainly explained how Arin could expect to have the opportunity for growth and gentrification despite having cut itself off from the rest of Sambar.

Once they had realised the number of Narsian traders in the city, Teran and Seban had focussed on getting information from them, whilst Xantila and Banir had continued focussing on their original sources of information. Teran and Seban were keen to see if they could draw any information out about preparations for war in Narsos. If the merchants in Arin did know anything about this topic they were keeping unusually tight-lipped about it. It was not clear that King Arran was consciously plotting with Narsos against the rest of

Sambar. These changes in trading patterns proved nothing except a suspicious mind. Koran had continued to try and catch up with his contacts in the city, but all his attempts to do so proved unfruitful.

Banir, Xantila, Koran and Teran had gathered in the corner of *The Jewel*'s common room after a long day of intelligence gathering to compare notes. They had decided that it was probably time to take the risk of presenting themselves before the king as a delegation from the other nations. They judged it prudent to pretend they had just arrived and for only two of them to do so, in case the others had to make a quick escape. They were deeply concerned about how suspicious the king appeared to be. The restricted trading and the martial law the city was being held under were as nothing compared to the stories they had heard of sudden disappearances of people who spoke out against the king's recent decisions.

They had just come to this conclusion when suddenly the door to the common room burst inwards, shards of wood flying everywhere, and men in the armour of the royal guard poured into the room surrounding their table and backing them against the wall. Swords were levelled at them all around.

"I wish we'd sat at a table near a window, the back door or stairs now." Muttered Banir under his breath, his years of training as a thief kicking in, obviously uncomfortable at being cornered without a route of escape.

"You are to come with us." A guard who was looked to be the sergeant in charge told them in a flat, matter of fact voice.

"Where are you taking us?" Banir queried, receiving a

blow with the handle of a sword from the nearest guard for his trouble. Banir's eyes rolled, whites showing, and he collapsed, Teran and Koran catching him just before he hit the floor. No one spoke any further to them, but it was clear they were being marched out of the inn. Teran and Koran had to support Banir's dead weight between them as the guards directed them out of the building.

"I didn't know them." The innkeeper was hurriedly trying to tell the nearest guard who would listen to him, "Their money seemed good and they kept to themselves. I wouldn't have had anything to do with them if I'd known they were traitors." Obviously anxious not to have his business ruined by associating with people in such ill repute with the crown.

"Don't worry yourself." The guard responded, "There will be a full investigation. If you're as innocent as you claim, then you'll be fine." The innkeeper was not too convinced of the truth of that and continued to look very anxious as the guard left to join the prisoner escort, which had begun to make its way through the city in the direction of the palace.

Banir had regained consciousness just as they reached their final destination. The four of them had been placed in the same cell in the palace dungeons. Conditions were cramped, but a least it was not damp, thanks to the local climate. There were no windows in the cell, but Teran guessed that at least a day must have passed since they were imprisoned there. This was only a vague estimate based on how quickly the candles burned as, though they had been fed since they arrived it had only been once, and his stomach told him that he was well overdue another meal; the uncertainty of the situation doing nothing to suppress his appetite. Banir had developed a large and nasty bruise on the side of his head where he had been clouted by the guard who took exception to his speaking. There was not much that any of them could do for him though, none of them being specialised in healing and, in any case, having no access to medicines. Questioning him, he seemed to have retained all his faculties, so Teran did not believe the blow could be too serious, as he had sometimes heard head trauma could be.

An indeterminate time later, still no food forthcoming, a contingent of guards appeared outside their cell.

"It's your lucky day." One of the guards said, no humour in his voice, "The king wishes to see you in person."

"Well we had wanted an audience…" Koran said under his breath to his fellow cellmates, his dry humour coming through despite the circumstances. The guard who had spoken obviously overheard him.

"These days the king sentences people without hearing from them as often as not. You're lucky, as you might be able to plead for mercy."

"But we haven't broken any kingdom laws!" Protested Banir.

"I heard you had stolen papers on your persons when you were brought in, or are you still claiming to be silk merchants?" The guard asked and Banir fell silent. He had forgotten about stealing the papers, an occupational hazard for one who made a living through thievery. "I don't know what the king wants with you and I don't care. I just want to make a living and keep on living as part of the bargain." The guard continued. "Follow me." He concluded, unlocking their cell and leading them past other cells, all occupied, and up stairs which led back into the main part of the palace. The other guards fell in around them to keep them from attempts of escape.

They were led into the king's main audience chamber. It was a large square room, with plastered walls painted with geometric designs in gaudy colours. The floor was layered with silk rugs of the highest quality for which Arin was renowned, patterned similarly to the walls. The roof of the audience chamber was domed, pendentives eased the transition from the rectangular to the spherical, revealing the sophistication of the architecture. The chamber itself had been cleared of the general throng of people who usually gathered to petition the king and only the king's guard and his closest advisors remained. King Arran himself sat on a large ornate throne, elevated on a dais at the far end of the audience chamber. Next to the king, his wife, Queen Belna, sat on a throne which was smaller and slightly less ornate, but still intended to inspire awe and confidence in the one sat there. To their surprise a third throne-like chair had been positioned on the dais, only slightly lower than the king's throne in which a third figure sat, presumably the infamous Agachen. It was usual for everyone, including advisors, to stand in the presence of the king and the honouring of Agachen by granting him a throne alongside the king was unprecedented.

Teran took a good look at Agachen, of whom they had gleaned a little from the general gossip, but not much. It was difficult to judge his height from his seated positon, but Teran guessed it to be average. He

Child of Rydos

sat wearing robes which were foreign in design, sleeveless revealing surprisingly well muscled arms for a court advisor. His skin was a deep olive colour and his eyes a dark brown, his face was round and he was bald. Where one might have expected a head of hair, Agachen sported an intricate pattern of tattoos in geometric shapes in red and black ink, the meaning of which was unclear, but it gave him a harsh look. His eyes were fixed on the four companions, hatred and distain obvious in his face.

They were brought to stand before the edge of the dais and then forced by the guards to prostrate themselves before the king.

"Why are you plotting against me?" The king asked coldly.

"There is no plotting in our hearts, Your Majesty." Teran began.

"Don't lie to me, Teran, son of Lysan." The king rejoindered, "I recognise you and Koran, son of Gethas. You have been in the city many days, trying to spy on us. Did you think your activity would go unnoticed? I have eyes and ears everywhere in my realm. I always see treachery and deal with it accordingly." Teran swore inwardly. They had hoped by scouting out the trouble before approaching the king that they would be better prepared to parlay, but now that very action had thrown them into deepest trouble.

"My Lord," Koran put in, "We were concerned for you. Arinach has always been a strong part of the kingdoms of Sambar, but recently you have grown distant. We came to try and find out the reasons why. We feared you were being forced to act against your will."

"No one forces the royal hand to do anything!" King Arran screamed suddenly at them. Queen Belna flinched visibly and her face paled at the king's outburst and Agachen leaned over towards the king and whispered something in his ear, which seemed to calm the king down. "You are the treacherous ones. The kingdoms of Sambar have grown jealous of the Jewel of the Desert. You were sent here by your fathers, mere pawns in their game, to see if our success and growth in wealth is true and you have come here to try and undo us." The king continued.

"Majesty," Teran began, "It is not true. Yes, we were sent here by Conclave…"

"A secret Conclave which Arinach was excluded from! I know it all!" The king interjected, his voice high pitched in fervour. Queen Belna again looked nervous, but this time Agachen did not immediately move to sooth the king.

"… No, Majesty, you were invited. I do not know why the message would not have reached you. We have tried many times in recent months to contact our brothers and sisters in Arinach to ask after your wellbeing." Teran continued. The king looked slightly confused by this, and the queen leant over to speak to the king, but Agachen interfered before she could speak, leaning over and whispering in the king's ear again and this time the king's face hardened.

Teran took a deep breath, then decided to take an even bigger risk. He did not think he had much to lose as this meeting was not going at all well so far. Teran turned and fixed his gaze on Agachen. Koran, guessing what Teran was about to try, shook his head slightly in the negative, but Teran ignored him.

"Arran, this man is the spy and the imposter!" Teran claimed, pointing a finger at Agachen, who looked slightly surprised by the outburst. "This foreigner, Agachen, has poisoned your mind with mealy words, turning you against your true friends. The nations of Sambar have been as one since the days of our forefather Am Bære, always have we come together in peace, and always have we come to Conclave when called. Always we have helped each other in our need and supported each other's growth. This worm, this Agachen, has made deserters of this desert people. He has forced you to relinquish your sacred oath towards the other nations of Sambar which you made when you were crowned king of Arinach." The king looked stunned, but Agachen looked furious. He rose from his seat and pointed his own finger back towards Teran and his companions.

"How dare you?!" Agachen shouted, losing his temper. "How dare you slip like snakes into the king's city with mischief in your hearts and come here accusing the king of relinquishing his sacred duty and besmirching his judgement before his most trusted advisors?" His face purple with rage.

"You are the slippery serpent in this room, not us." Teran continued, completely in control of his emotions, unlike Agachen. "I don't know who you work for, but it is not King Arran's interests that you are serving, but your own and those of Narsos."

"Do not speak of what you do not understand." Spat Agachen.

"Your Majesty, what Teran says is true!" Joined in Koran at this point, fearing that Agachen might be about to gain the upper hand with the king again. "Look at how he has you treating your own people whom you love. The city is under martial law, people have been thrown out of their homes and out of the city. People are living in fear of their lives. This is not the King Arran whose generosity and kindness is renown throughout the kingdoms." Queen Belna and the king's other advisers sat rigid with fear etched upon their faces, but also grateful for the stand Teran and Koran were making. Agachen looked more and more enraged, but as Teran looked now at the king, it seemed like a weight had been lifted from the king's shoulders.

"Wha..." King Arran began groggily, "What have I done?" Then he turned to look at Agachen, "You!" He said with venom in his voice, "Guards seize this man, Agachen, he is a traitor to the crown." The guards started forward and Agachen looked around, realising that he was far outnumbered.

"You have cost me dearly today, boy!" Agachen sneered at Teran, "But this is only a minor set back, do not think that you have won anything by your actions today." Agachen clapped his hands together, there was a blinding flash and he was gone.

"What?!" Exclaimed King Arran, Teran and Koran all together. A stunned silence fell across the room.

"I feel like I've been living inside a dream..." The king continued at last.

"If Agachen was a magician, as he appears to be, then he could well have had you under some spell." Teran offered.

"It is of little comfort," The king continued, "When I think of all that I have done under his influence." Then he turned to Teran and his companions and said, "I have not treated you hospitably so far. Is there anything I can do for you?"

"You could feed us?" Suggested Banir, "Your jailors don't exactly go in for haute cuisine." The king laughed at the boy's spirits. Queen Belna and the king's advisors, looked increasingly releaved at the lightening of the king's mood.

"Done!" The king proclaimed.

That night saw Teran, Koran, Xantila and Banir as guests of honour at a grand feast. No expense had been spared and every well-to-do family had been invited to the celebrations. Musicians and entertainers weaved their way through the crowded tables to create a jovial atmosphere and to offer release from tedious conversation for those who found themselves seated next to a bore. The king had announced a day of celebration and had released food and capital to the general city, abolishing the martial law and allowing those living in the shantytown to reclaim their old lives if they wished. King Arran could tell that he was going to have to re-examine any petitions related to the past couple of years and smooth a lot of relations with his people, but tonight was about celebrating the nation's release from the hands of Agachen and to discuss with Teran and his companions about the recent events in Arinach and the news from the rest of the kingdoms of Sambar. The palace kitchens had panicked themselves at the short notice for the feast and had roasted every type of animal they could lay their hands on in order to make the feast seem exotic, but these had also been artfully blended with various spices used in Arinachian cooking to create truly mouth-watering dishes for them all to try.

"I wouldn't have believed magic like that existed if we had witnessed it with our own eyes." Arran was telling them as they sat eating.

"It is certainly worrying in the extreme." Koran responded to the king, "Was Agachen from Narsos?"

"I don't know where he was from, he never said, now that I come to think about it. But he was certainly persuasive in strengthening our ties with the Narsians and cutting off our links with the rest of Sambar." The king answered Koran's question, concluding, "Near the end, he spoke of how money would flow into Arin if we assisted the Narsians in their conquest."

"War is a certainty then, it seems." Xantila commented, who had become increasingly contemplative since the incident earlier in the day with Agachen.

"Yes, it is even more important now that the next stage of our journey takes us into Narsos so we can do some reconnaissance." Teran suggested to the group, "But we also need to get word to Conclave about what has passed here. Who knows what sort of magic the Narsians could wield against us if Agachen's magical prowess is anything to go by?"

"I will send birds and runners to the other rulers, so that you can focus on your continued mission to the south." Arran said.

"And of course, we'll supply you with anything you need for your onward journey." Queen Belna added, "It is the least we can do after you have returned to us my husband and our king."

"Something about Agachen made my skin crawl." Xantila interjected suddenly. The others nodded

Child of Rydos

vigorously in agreement. "I know it's not comfortable to contemplate, but could you tell us anything more about your experience of him, King Arran? It might help us in our journey southwards." The king seemed to pale slightly, but at last he nodded and began to speak.

"Yes... yes... I think you're right, I must speak, though it makes me nauseous to think of it now..." Arran began, "It all seems so clear retrospectively, but at the time nothing seemed out of place. I'm guessing, now, that Agachen must have been subtly weaving his magic from the very first moment he stood before me. It was about two years ago. I was holding one of my usual open court sessions in the morning when Agachen, who must have queued like every other petitioner, stood before me. He offered me some advice about a land dispute that two of my farmers had been having and it solved the problem. I felt a strong instinct to trust him and offered him a place amongst my advisors... I wonder at that immediate trust now... At first, Agachen's advice was much along the same lines as that initial incident, but over time his advice turned to suggestions and the suggestions grew more bold and decisive. Through it all I had a strong sense that I should trust his words and that he was leading me to greatness." The king paused for some time, looking downwards, "I feel so foolish now." He finished.

"I do not think you are a fool, Your Majesty," Xantila responded gently, "Suffering from the influence of a powerful magician, yes, but no fool." She finished with conviction and a slow, sad smile broke across the king's face.

"Yes... perhaps you are right..." He responded.

Teran then took up the narrative and filled in King

Desert Deserters

Arran about their journey from Ariss to Arin and all that had beset them on the way. Filling in the story about where Koran and he had collected their companions who now dined with them, Xantila and Banir. The news of their misadventures on the road did little to comfort King Arran. Teran also told the king what he knew of Conclave's plans for preparations for war with Narsos, knowing that the king would now be more than keen to help, if only to purge himself and his kingdom of the bitter taste of betrayal left by Agachen's influence.

They then began to discuss, in earnest, the next stage of the journey for the companions. They agreed that the most sensible route into Narsos would be via T'emar, which was on the border of Arinach with Narsos and sat in the shadow of Narsos forest. They could follow the river there to its source in the forest and continue heading more or less in the same direction and would arrive at the city of I'sos in Narsos. It was the route that the traders from Narsos in Arin had been using, so it would not be difficult to travel and they could continue to masquerade as merchants as it was a well rehearsed ruse by now.

By the time they had finished all these discussions the meal was nearly over and the servants were bringing around platters of sugared almonds and pots of coffee for the diners to enjoy. Banir, who had been very quiet the whole evening, slowly but surely making his way through mountains of food, spoke suddenly now, addressing himself to Teran and Koran,

"So... you're princes of the realm?" Banir asked. Teran had forgotten that they had not told Banir who they really were and had only supplied him with limited information about their plans and reasons for journeying to Arin to see King Arran.

"Um... yes we are." Teran responded to Banir, somewhat embarrassed.

"I knew there was something special about you guys. If I had to leave Baxen I certainly chose the right crowd to do it with." Banir said, a grin breaking across his face.

"Will you take the boy south with you?" King Arran asked Teran and Koran. Koran looked towards Teran. Teran felt a strong urge to keep Banir close by, which he could not explain. Given recent experiences with Agachen this feeling concerned Teran, but he fought it to the back of his mind.

"Yes," Teran answered the king, "He seems fairly adept at keeping out of trouble, unless we're getting him in to it, and his skills have already proved useful. They might do so again before our journey is out." Teran seemed surprised by his own answer, as did Koran and Xantila, but they did not raise an objection. Banir looked surprised too, but more by the idea that he might not automatically be part of their party now.

"Well, the evening wears on and I suspect you'll want to start early on the road tomorrow. You'll have fresh mounts and supplies ready for you whenever you need them in the morning." Arran stated as he rose from his seat, causing all the din of the dining hall to subside. "Now, I'll bid you good night." He said, nodding towards them, then in a louder voice to the rest of the hall, "Good night to you all." With this he took Queen Belna's hand and she rose to join him and they exited the hall. As soon as they had gone the noise levels rocketed and the heavy drinking and carousing began in earnest. Teran and his companions finished their drinks and also retired to the chambers that the king had provided for them to enjoy a good night's sleep in proper accommodation before they found themselves on the road again the following day.

Chapter XIII – Wizard's Wrath

Teran, Koran, Xantila and Banir had made good speed since leaving Arin two days ago. The terrain had been easy and the weather had been kind. There was some light drizzle today, but nothing which really hampered their progress and the rain itself was too light to turn their moods sour, especially since they were all focussed on what they might find once they crossed the border into Narsos. It was approaching evening now and they were hoping to find a small village to spend the night, rather than having to camp rough. As evening grew on and the darkness drew in though, this became less likely as none of them knew the road well. It was not worth the risk of losing their way in the dark. There was still about a day's journey left for them to reach T'emar, where they would certainly find indoor, if not comfortable, accommodation and this kept their spirits up. They moved off the track, which passed for a road, a little way in order to set up camp. Darkness had fallen near completely now for though the moon was growing towards full, thick cloud obscured it tonight, thus the only light was that of their campfire which illuminated their tents. Their thoughts had just turned to dinner when they heard the crack of a stick breaking underfoot and they all spun round to face the direction the sound came from.

"Who's there?" Teran called into the darkness. A figure wrapped in a black cloak emerged from the darkness, keeping a good distance from them, so as to remain partially in the shadows. Instinctively, each of the companions went to reach for their weapons, but they found they could not twitch a muscle.

"You cost me my place at court, boy!" The figure spat, focussed on Teran. The figure took a step closer and pushed back the hood of its cloak to reveal Agachen's face, his eyes full of hatred. "How did you manage to resist my enchantment? Who are you?" Teran didn't know how to answer the magician as he had not been aware of the enchantment until it broke and it had not occurred to him that it had been focussed on anyone other than King Arran. "Who are you?" Agachen asked again, raising his voice in anger.

"I am a child of Rydos." Teran answered, still not really understanding the magician's question, so giving the only valid answer that he could think of, but he did not really think Agachen was concerned with geography. "I am a son of the late King Lysan and of Queen Liliana of Rydos." Teran finished. Agachen looked peeved at the sort of answer that Teran had given, but a thoughtful look spread across his face.

"Surely he would know and would act to save himself." Agachen muttered to himself. "It matters not," Agachen said in a louder voice now, directed once again towards Teran, "You shall die here and now and that will bring an end to your interference." Agachen raised a hand and began to speak an enchantment. Flames of increasing intensity began to grow around his hand. Agachen raised his hand higher as if to throw the flames towards Teran when an arrow pierced that hand and he screamed in shock and drew his hand protectively towards his chest. His concentration lost, the flames disappeared. Agachen's eyes darted in

Child of Rydos

surprise towards the direction the arrow had flown from to find Xantila nocking another arrow to her bow and ready to fire.

"How...?" Agachen asked in a confused tone.

"You should pay more attention to who your captives are." Xantila responded, "I may not be a magician, but the Rangers of Azin have a sort of gentle magic of our own. We are not to be tamed by the likes of you!" She finished as she raised her bow. Agachen had no doubt that he could best Xantila in a fight, but he was concerned by this group of companions and their apparent ability to thwart him. He was shaken by their triumph in Arin and by events now and decided it was better to live to fight another day than risk all now in a petty fight. There were more important things for him to be focussing on at this moment in time. Agachen swirled his cloak and faded back into the darkness. Xantila loosed her second arrow but it sped into the darkness, not finding a mark. The others felt the magic holding them in place dissipate and they all rushed forward their weapons now drawn to chase after the magician before he could accomplish any more mischief, but he had vanished, no obvious trail to follow in the dark. Not wanting to explore the dark more than necessary, the companions regrouped by their fire. This time they kept a more concerted watch for figures approaching their camp in the night whilst they prepared dinner from the provisions King Arran had supplied them with.

"Xan, I didn't know the Rangers had magic." Teran said to Xantila as they sat eating.

"It isn't magic as you would normally understand the term." Xantila responded, "It isn't something we share with others usually either."

"No, the Rangers are certainly not known for talkative over-sharing." Commented Koran.

"I cannot describe it easily. It is more like an affinity with nature really." Xantila continued, being surprisingly open with the group. Teran guessed it was the recent events of the past days that made Xantila feel like she should share some of her nature with the group, in case it became important or her skills were needed. "It is the same affinity which keeps me in tune with my environment and guides my aim when I shoot. It is not strong magic like that of Agachen's. If he had not been so intent upon Teran, I think he would have noticed me working against his magical bonds and have easily been able to prevent me from breaking free." Xantila admitted, "I just think he underestimated us." Despite Xantila's modesty over her abilities, the others were looking at her with a newfound respect for, and surprise at, her abilities, reassessing what they knew of the Rangers of Azin forest.

"Agachen was incredibly focussed on you, Teran. Can you think why?" Koran asked at this juncture.

"No," Teran began, "I've no idea. I hadn't a notion that I did anything to resist him in Arin, at least not in magical terms, along the lines that Xan just described. I just spoke my mind about what I saw."

"Evidently, Agachen didn't think you should be able to do that. I didn't realise his magic was working on all of us either, until he admitted it just now, but now that I dwell upon it, in the throne room in Arin I wasn't able to put two and two together in his presence and declaim him. It wasn't until after you spoke out that my mind started to work clearly, which is unusual for me." Koran responded.

"I just felt itchy in his presence." Xantila added, "I didn't trust him, but I don't think I could have found the words you did either, Teran."

"Don't look at me." Banir chimed in at this point, "I'm just a thief, I'm not used to grand affairs of state… yet." Teran noticed the addition of the word 'yet' and thought that Banir certainly had some ambitions for himself now that he had fallen in with their group. "I think I heard Agachen mutter something to himself just before he tried to cast that spell on you, Teran. I didn't catch it, but did anyone else? I wonder if it was important…"

"Something about saving himself, I think." Teran responded.

"It was you he thought could save himself, Teran." Xantila corrected.

"Me? I just don't understand why he was so focussed on my actions." Teran said confusedly.

"As Xan said, we're just lucky he underestimated us as a group. I doubt he'll make the same mistake twice and somehow I'm guessing we'll see him again." Koran contributed.

"That's not a comforting thought on which to end the night." Teran said, his thoughts ranging far and wide to see if he could work out why he had such an effect on the magician. It might be of importance if they met again. He could not say why, but his thoughts were drawn back to his childhood growing up in Rydos.

Seban and Teran had been fighting. It was not unusual state of affairs between them. They were so similar in age that they were often compared to each other and were always competing for their parents' attention, which were often drawn away from them to dealing with matters of state. Recently it had become even more difficult to get the attention they each craved. Since their sister Loren had been born, their mother's attention was, quite rightly, focussed on the newest addition to their family. There was nothing sinister to their squabbles and they always made up eventually as, actually, they enjoyed each other's company and the opportunity to play together, for the most part.

On the occasion of this particular fight, their father Lysan's attention was diverted from them due to the session of Conclave being held in Rydos. Lysan was therefore especially focussed on matters of state and Liliana was focussed between that and caring for their new-born sister. Seban had started today's fight by claiming that their parents did not really love Teran as much as him because he was adopted.

"I am not!" Teran said agitatedly.

"Yes, you are. I overheard countesses Harana and Selani talking about it." Seban said antagonistically.

"Liar!" Teran shouted, taking the first swing at his brother. Things had quickly deteriorated from that point as the boys wrestled each other to the ground, pulling hair and tearing at clothing, even resorting to teeth, indeed, anything to gain the upper hand in the fight.

"What's going on here?" A voice shouted, bringing both boys to a sudden halt in their activities as they jumped up and away from each other to face Swordsmaster Beran. Beran had been promoted to the rank of swordsmaster, the head of King Lysan's guard, following the previous swordsmaster's retirement due to

Child of Rydos

the infirmity of old age.

"Nothing Sir!" Both boys chimed simultaneously.

"Nothing?" Beran quipped, "It doesn't look like 'nothing' to me. You boys know that you should not fight, it causes your parents to worry and they have enough to occupy their minds at the moment without the two of you piling on extra concern." The swordsmaster chided them, "Who started it this time?"

"Seban did!" Teran chimed in, before Seban could twist the turn of events into his own narrative, "He said that mother and father didn't really love me because I was adopted and I told him to stop lying." A shadow of concern passed across the swordsmaster's face.

"Where did you hear that?" Beran asked Seban.

"It's true! I overheard countesses Harana and Selani talking about it." Seban responded trying to justify himself. Beran noticed Teran clenching his fists, but he knew better than to let fly at his brother again in Beran's presence.

"Both of you, come with me." Beran responded, sweeping past them and heading through the palace in the general direction of the royal apartments. Both of the boys fell into step behind Beran.

"Now look what trouble you've got us into." Seban whispered to Teran.

"Me? You started it!" Teran retorted. The swordsmaster cleared his throat loudly and both boys fell silent for the rest of their journey.

Beran led the boys to their mother's chambers, nodded to the guard by the door and knocked. A young maid opened the door to find the swordsmaster standing there with the queen's two sons. Guessing what had taken place, she told the queen whom it was who wished to attend her and then invited the three of them into the queen's sitting rooms. The queen passed the baby, Loren, to the maid who retired to another chamber with the little girl.

"Which of you started *this* fight?" The queen asked her two sons as they stood before her. Swordsmaster Beran, who stood just behind them, answered before either of the boys could,

"It seems that countess Harana and countess Selani have been gossiping in the corridors about Teran." He told the queen. The queen looked up at him, an understanding in her eyes.

"Come and sit down, both of you." The queen said to her sons, indicating two chairs opposite the one where she had obviously been sitting before her disgraced sons arrived. The queen sat opposite them. "Thank you, Beran," The queen said kindly, "I think I can handle this from here. I know it is not what you are paid for, but could you do me a favour and ask the countesses to come and see me this afternoon?" The queen asked Beran, effectively dismissing him from her chambers before she returned her attention to her sons. Queen Liliana leaned forward and took one of each of her sons hands in hers.

"Teran and Seban, you must not fight each other. Especially over this. Lysan and I love you both equally." The queen began.

"I told you it wasn't true." Teran said, turning to his brother.

"You *are* adopted, Teran." His mother said gently.

"What?" Teran said with shock, too stunned to say anything else.

"I found you in the forest when you were a baby and

your father and I adopted you." The queen continued and then related the story to both the boys in full. It was important to her that both the boys understood what had happened and that it made no difference to either her or Lysan about how much they loved either of them.

Teran was not sure why that particular memory surfaced now so many years later and so far from home. He thought it was probably linked with the fact he'd referred to himself as a child of Rydos when Agachen had asked who he was. That was how he had thought of himself ever since he had found out about his adoption. He did not mean it as a slur upon his family, who he had no doubt loved him. Love was not measured through words or actions. Love simply was. It transcended fears and doubts. Teran supposed that this memory surfaced now because he missed the advice of his brother, his sister, his mother and, especially, of his late father. He lapsed into brooding and decided it was time for him to turn in for the night. The others were also tired from the day's travelling and from the encounter with Agachen and so thought nothing unusual about Teran's need for sleep. Koran elected to keep the first watch and the others joined Teran in attempted slumber.

Chapter XIV – Army Ambulation

It had been several days since Olin, Teloran and Temac had made it to Korrath to report their findings to Teslas and thereby the rest of Conclave. Olin still had a long way to go with his healing, but the local healers' guild here had given him a set of crutches which had allowed him some freedom of movement, albeit at a much slower pace than he was used to. Olin, used to the freedom and open skies of the northern ice lands, had been going stir-crazy until the crutches afforded him some much-desired freedom. The one constraint of their use was that he was not supposed to overextend himself too much, otherwise it might hamper his healing. Olin was using this newfound freedom to assist Temac with his inspections of the army amongst the caravanserai and had taken to daily ambulations to the west of the city.

Olin, who had a keen eye and good memory for such things, was growing increasingly familiar with the lay of the land, with the relative positions of different camps, familiar faces, of where the water supplies were located and increasing other detail with each passing day. He was limping along today when something bothered him. He was not sure what it was, but it caused him to pause momentarily. Olin looked back along the path he'd just travelled and he realized what it was that had filtered into his mind to cause him to catch himself. The gate to the well enclosure he'd just passed was open. It had always been shut every other time he had passed by and he knew that this was the norm, because the Hruntans were generally fastidious about isolating these water supplies from the animals which accompanied the caravanserai. Water could be drawn from them to give to the animals, but the areas around the wells were kept enclosed to help prevent supplies from being contaminated. Olin turned himself around on his crutches and went to try and shut the gate. He reached the enclosure and was about to shut the gate when he realized there was someone crouched by the well. He recognized the figure, robed in blue, as one of the healers who had checked on the progress of his healing leg.

"Oh, sorry." He said, "I didn't realize anyone was drawing from the well and I came to close the gate." The healer rose and turned towards him and Olin noticed that he didn't have a jar with which to collect the water from the well. It also occurred to Olin that this was a peculiar place for the healer to be drawing water. If there had been someone ill nearby to which he was tending then he would have sent an assistant to do this duty. "Hezek, isn't it?" Olin said, remembering the healer's name, "Can I help you at all?" Hezek looked directly at Olin, taking in his measure, his crutches and garb then looked around and, seeing the area was quiet, spat at Olin.

"Cripple!" He sneered and darted at Olin with alarming speed, drawing a knife from his robes as he advanced. Olin, always the warrior, responded with equal speed. Balanced on one leg he used his crutches as a shield to deflect the blow from Hezek. He did not have time to try and draw a weapon in the midst of the flurry of blows. Olin used his sheer strength to make up for his lack of agility. He parried a number of knife blows and eventually managed to get the crutches caught through Hezek's leading arm, twisting it round, forcing Hezek to drop the knife and bringing him to his knees.

"Yield!" Olin roared, bringing his full weight to bear on Hezek's more diminutive frame. Olin knew he had won the fight and now he would get some answers about what was going on. Hezek knew it too. Something was wrong. Hezek's body suddenly went weak under Olin's weight and he could feel Hezek shuddering. Olin dropped his body and turned Hezek over. His skin was becoming pallid and a blue tinge was appearing on Hezek's lips. Hezek let out a weak laugh.

"By Grukan!" Said Olin, invoking the god of the northern wilds, who was dear to the Ruors, but there was nothing he could do. The poison had already done its work and within moments Hezek was dead. Olin carefully prized open Hezek's now clenched teeth and saw that one of the teeth was crushed. The healer had obviously had a false tooth containing the poison, in case of capture. Olin couldn't believe it. There was only one real possibility. Hezek had been a Narsian sympathizer, spy and a traitor to the Hruntan crown. But what had he been doing at this well? He obviously had not wanted to be able to answer any questions about his actions.

The noise of Olin's struggle with Hezek had drawn the attention of those working and living nearby. It was all over before anyone arrived, but as the first curious onlookers arrived, Olin commanded them to fetch Temac, who was elsewhere in the caravanserai and to inform the king. Olin had no right of command over the people here, but they knew whom Olin was and

Child of Rydos

were not about to argue with the evidence of an obvious struggle and a dead body.

Whilst others got to the business of fetching the authorities, Olin picked up his crutches and limped towards the well to see if he could work out what Hezek had been doing. He could not see anything around the edges of the well to indicate why Hezek had been here. The bucket used to draw the water was not hoisted, but lay at the bottom of the well. Olin used the winch to raise the bucket. As the bucket surfaced he noticed that there was a small, unstoppered phial at the bottom of the bucket. He reached through the water to lift the phial out and sniffed it. There was no discernable scent, probably because the phial had been fully immersed in the water. Olin cursed. He had a very bad feeling.

At that moment Temac arrived with a couple of soldiers, breathing heavily, indicating that they had been running. Temac scanned the scene and looked towards Olin,

"What happened?" He asked.

"We've got trouble. It would be a good idea to fetch someone from the healers' guild who has knowledge of poisons." Olin responded, lifting the phial to show Temac. Temac cursed, reflecting Olin's earlier response, and sent one of the soldiers who had arrived with him to do as Olin suggested. "I was passing by and poked my head into the well enclosure here." Olin continued, "I saw Healer Hezek here crouched over the well. When he saw me he rushed at me, thinking he could best me because I was on crutches. He was wrong."

"You could have left him alive to question." Temac suggested wryly.

"Not my fault." Olin responded, "I was careful to do

just that, but look at his lips. He poisoned himself to avoid questioning." Temac inspected the body as Olin suggested and cursed again. "I came to inspect the well to see if I could work out what Hezek was doing and I found this phial. I suspect he has poisoned the water supply." Olin finished, bringing Temac up to speed. "Temac, we need to stop use of all the water supplies in the city and have them checked. We've no idea of whether he had any assistance, nor of how many wells he might have poisoned before this one." Olin added.

"Yes, you're right," Temac said in a resigned and tired manner, then turning to another soldier he said, "Issue the edict on my orders. All the water supplies are to be quarantined and checked for contamination." The solider saluted and speed off to follow his orders. At that moment Lanna, the Chief Healer in Korrath, arrived, escorted by the soldier who had been sent to the guild. It did not surprise Temac that Lanna had come herself; she was an expert in herbal remedies and poisons and also liked to lead through a hands-on approach.

"What has happened here?" She asked, seeing Hezek's body. Olin repeated his story again. Lanna looked completely shocked by Hezek's betrayal, but remained entirely focused on the business at hand. She went first to inspect the phial that Olin had found, knowing that this threat needed to be addressed immediately. She sniffed the phial as Olin had.

"If this did contain poison then it is either odourless when mixed with water or it has been so diluted as to leave no trace." Lanna stated, "If it has been diluted beyond effect then there is little to worry about. If, on the other hand it is an odourless, yet potent, poison then this could spell trouble." At this, Lanna laid down the medicine bag she had brought with her, unstrapped it, and rolled it out, revealing a collection of herbs and medicines. She took some of the liquids from the collection and approached the bucket of water that Olin had drawn. "This came from the well?" She asked and Olin nodded. She then proceeded to draw cups of water from the barrel and add various of the liquids to them, clearly in a specific and methodical way. She sniffed the contents of each and examined the colours created. After a while she sat back with a look of contemplation.

"Does this mean that Hezek wasn't poisoning the water supply?" Temac asked.

"No," Lanna responded, "It just means it isn't any of the more obvious poisons that could have been used."

"In Ariss, Kino, the messenger which brought us the first tidings of this brewing war was poisoned with Querien. Could it be that?" Temac suggested.

"Hmm…" Lanna began, "Not by itself, but if distilled with asp's venom…" Lanna returned to her medicines and mixed together a number of herbs with one of the remaining medicines and added this to a sample of the well water. It began to fizz violently and Lanna raised her eyebrows. "Extraordinary." She said, "I've no idea how it was distilled to be so difficult to detect, yet so potent. It *is* a modified form of Querien." She told Temac.

"Can you purify the well and test the other water supplies?" Temac asked.

"I can draw up the necessary potion to test the rest of the water supplies in the city, but it will take time. I cannot do anything to purify the supplies. The only solution is to draw as much water from the wells as possible and let them refill naturally. Then to keep testing the water until this reaction no longer occurs. It could take weeks, so let's hope that not all the water in the city has already been affected. Now let me examine Hezek." Lanna said returning again to the business at hand and moving towards the body to examine it more closely. She looked at his tongue and his teeth, examined his lips and his eyelids. She moved down his arms to examine his hands, fingers and nails. She paused when she reached his little finger on his left hand. "This is not Hezek," she said.

"What do you mean?" Olin said, "It's Hezek sure enough, he attacked just after I'd remembered his name. He was treating me for my leg earlier this week."

"I agree it looks remarkably like Hezek, with a similar height build, but it is not him." Lanna riposted.

"He doesn't just look similar, he looks identical! I've got a good memory for faces." Olin said in rejoinder.

"Yes." Lanna continued patiently, "Nonetheless it is not Hezek. Hezek lost the tip of his little finger to a spirited horse's bite when he was an adolescent." She continued, lifting up the offending hand. "This man's hand does not have the same injury. It would be easy to miss if you didn't know him really well. We both began studying at the guild in the same intake." Olin was taken aback.

"So, this man is an imposter? A doppelganger." Olin said, "How long ago do you think he infiltrated the healers? What happened to the real Hezek?"

"All very good questions." Lanna answered, "To which we have no answers for the time being."

"We need to take some action on this." Temac interrupted at this point, "Are there any other identifying features, anything else to give him away? We need to know how to identify other imposters. Assuming that it wasn't a fluke that these men look so alike."

"Look!" Exclaimed Olin, pointing to Hezek's body, drawing Temac out of his reverie. Before their eyes Hezek's face was changing, almost as if it was made of clay and being remolded by an invisible potter. When his features had finished altering a man of very different appearance remained. One who was obviously of Narsian descent. "Well that answers one of your questions, Temac." Olin said, "It seems that, once again, magic is involved and that it doesn't last too long."

"Assuming that it is a spell of short duration and not one that wears off with death…" Temac responded.

Later that day King Teslas, Temac, Olin, Teloran, Lanna and other of the king's advisors gathered in the king's private chambers to discuss earlier events and what had been discovered since. They had not rooted out any other imposters, but that did not give them confidence that there were none to be found. In all, three quarters of the city's wells had been contaminated with the poison. This was not an insurmountable problem given the River Hrun meandered around the edge of the city, but it was an inconvenience and if Olin had not discovered the poisoner then many more people would have died. As it was, a few hundred Hruntans had drunk from contaminated supplies and had died before it was realized what was going on. Their families were now arranging their funerals. Hezek had been found in one of the treatment rooms in the healers' guild in the city. He had been bound and tied up, but not killed. A metal medallion depicting two overlapping faces had been placed around his neck. An inspection of the poisoner's body had revealed he was wearing a complementary medallion. They had tried using the medallions again but nothing happened. They either needed an incantation to work, or their magic had been drained by their previous use.

The gathered council was discussing all these things when there was a knock at the chamber doors.

"Enter!" Called the king. The door attendant came into the room and spoke to the king.

"A message just arrived." The attendant said, "The bird was from Arinach stock." That caught the whole company's attention.

"Bring it here." Said the king and the attendant nodded to the boy from the bird tower who had retrieved and carried the sealed message here. The boy bowed and placed the message into the king's open palm. "Thank you." Said the king, "Let me see if it needs an immediate response." The boy waited whilst the king broke the seal and read the note. He knew a more expansive message would follow on foot, this was just a short message quickly delivered by air for speed. "You may go." The king said to the boy and the attendant and they both left the room.

"What does it say?" Temac asked once the door had closed.

"It is from King Arran. Teran, Koran and Xantila reached Arin. Arran was being enthralled by magic. The Narsians are definitely preparing for war. Teran and the others are now travelling into Narsos to do some preliminary reconnaissance." Tesles revealed.

"Magic!" Spat Olin, "Magic seems to be plaguing us every step of the way. What are we going to do?"

Child of Rydos

"We need the help of the mystics of Laconia." Teloran said.

"Yes," Agreed Teslas, "But I don't have the authority to make that command. Nor can it be discussed by runner, we need Conclave to authorize making such overtures. I don't hold out much hope that they'll help. We may well be on our own." The others nodded in agreement with Teslas.

"What is next?" Temac asked.

"We will move the army to Cheros, on the border with Narsos. The other nations will join us there too. Arran will leave the majority of his armies along his border with Narsos, but will come himself to Cheros so we can hold a full Conclave." Teslas responded.

"Moving the army will have the happy coincidence of lessening the demand on water supplies in the city, making life a bit easier for the local population after the water contamination." Olin commented.

"Teran and Koran will be aiming for Cheros too, once they have finished in Narsos, so that works well." Teloran added, then asked, "Will you come, Olin, with your leg?"

"Try and stop me." Grunted Olin, "I might not be much good in the heat of a major battle, but you can hardly suggest I'm of no use without two good legs!" This caused a small titter of laughter through the room.

"Things go according to plan, despite the unexpected." Commented Teslas, thinking of all that had transpired since the first meeting of Conclave. "It is late. It would be good for us all to rest, tomorrow will bring much activity." The king finished and dismissed the others for the night.

Chapter XV – Servitude is an Option

Teran and his companions had reached T'emar without incident the next day, though they had been hyper-alert to a near-exhaustive level on the journey there, fearing the constant reappearance of Agachen and this time a failure to fight him off. Their fears had been unfounded, however, and a good night's rest in T'emar had done much to calm their nerves. They were not intending to become complacent, but they had regained some perspective about the likelihood of attack around every corner. Morning had broken and they were making final preparations and sorting out supplies for the journey up river and into the forest. They had each set to their given tasks and arranged to gather by the southern gate of the town to set off.

Banir was the first to arrive, having been giving responsibility for the horses. Koran and Teran both arrived shortly after he did, but Xantila was late. Eventually she arrived coming, not from the town, but from the countryside.

"Sorry I'm late." She said before any of the others could speak, "You can't buy a single decent arrow in this town. I had to go looking further afield for some decent materials to fletch my own."

"Are you ready?" Said Teran, caught between amusement and peevishness. Xantila nodded and they mounted and set off up stream.

The first part of their journey was not difficult terrain. The ground was muddy near the river, but the path was relatively unimpeded. The countryside in this part of Arinach was gently hilly and in the warmth of the shining sun it was easy to forget the seriousness of their mission and recent events and just enjoy the journey for its own sake. The companions kept watch all that day, but crossed the official border with Narsos and reached the edge of the forest by nightfall. When they reached the forest's edge they found a small encampment of traders there of Narsian descent. They were travelling to T'emar laden with spices and clothes from Narsos which they had procured in I'sos. They said little else about the city, but seemed to be genuine merchants and also seemed to take the companions' story of also being traders at face value. Since there was no formal war between Narsos and any of the nations of Sambar yet the companions decided the best course of action was to act on friendly terms, but remain wary. They settled their camp neither too close or too far away from the merchants so as not to appear suspicious, set a watch for the night, and took turns to sleep.

Morning broke without any night-time incidents. Their morning preparations roused the other merchants who also breakfasted and got ready to travel, albeit in the opposite direction. Soon they were underway, delving into the forest, but able to follow a well-defined path, which was obviously the one the merchants used to move their wares. Light scattered down through the boughs creating a peaceful atmosphere that made Xantila, in particular, feel like she was at home in Azin forest. Eventually things became more complex as multiple paths branched off from the track. The travelling was harder as the forest obscured their view into the distance, but glancing upwards towards the sun whenever the trees thinned a little it was possible to tell that they were still heading in the approximate direction of I'sos and had not made any significant wrong turns.

The heat of the day was building up and humidity was rising as they travelled south. As they continued, they heard the noise of travellers up ahead. Wanting to avoid further unnecessary interaction with Narsian traders, or worse, they dove off into the underbrush, away from the path, hoping to hide their presence. Sure enough another troop of traders came trampling noisily down the path in the direction of T'emar. Teran and his companions melted back further into the forest growth and waited for the noise to subside to indicate their passing. Time seemed to drag on as they waited there, trying to keep their horses quiet and concealed amongst the trees. Eventually noise from the road dissipated and Teran sent Banir to sneak back to the roadside to see if it was clear. Banir returned a few moments later and Teran looked to see what the boy had to say. Instead, Banir was was just pointing past Teran a look of incredulity on his face. Teran and the others all turned around to see what Banir was pointing at, as their attention had been solely focussed towards the road, thus neglecting what else might be nearby. Behind them was a large creature with black fur and skin and long arms which looked something like a cross between a bear and a human. It grinned at them revealing large white teeth and made a growling sound flexing its arms.

"What is that?" Exclaimed Banir, finally finding his voice.

"I've no idea." Said Teran, "It looks like some hideous magical mutation between a human and a bear." His mind becoming overactive thanks to his experiences in Azin, Tellac and Arin.

"I don't know what it is." Responded Xantila, "But it is a natural creature. I can feel that this forest is its home." Teran had forgotten about Xantila's magical affinity, but was grateful for it.

"Any ideas what we should do?" Asked Koran, his eyes fixed on the beast, which appeared to be getting more aggressive.

"We've invaded its territory." Xantila said, now focusing on the creature, "Let me see if I can calm it, it would be better than having to fight and kill it." She raised a hand towards it and began to concentrate on her connection to everything around her. The creature was unfamiliar to her and so it took time to recognise its pattern and understand its relationship to its surroundings. Xantila used all her skill, honed from a lifetime of living in Azin forest, and slowly the beast seemed to calm and step backwards, disappearing deeper into the forest. Xantila turned back to the others. "We must go now." She simply said and begun to lead them back to the path.

"Thank you, Xan." Banir said in awe. The others echoed his thanks as they continued their journey through the forest, keeping to the well-trodden path.

"Not all dangers are of human origin." Said Xantila, sagely, "Much danger can come from not understanding nature properly."

The day was wearing on and the sky was beginning to dim, but the companions rode on, hoping to make as much distance as possible.

"Hang on." Said Banir, who had been scouting up ahead, "I think I hear travellers again. Do you want to try getting off the path again?" He asked Teran. Teran looked at Xantila. Xantila paused and closed her eyes in concentration.

"Sometime is wrong." She said, opening her eyes.

"Wrong?" Asked Teran.

"Good evening, travellers." A voice said, and a man in forest leathers and camouflage stepped out of the trees to stand in front of them. "What a coincidence meeting you in the forest." He continued.

"Why a coincidence?" Asked Banir, his senses on edge.

"I was looking for four more people to join me." The man answered.

"We're not available for hire." Said Koran.

"Who said anything about hiring?" Asked the man as lots of other men stepped out of the forest to surround them.

"I don't suppose there are any Rangers of Narsos to come to our aid?" Teran asked Xantila hopefully.

"Drop your weapons." The man continued. The companions did not have any choice but to follow the stranger's commands. At least they didn't seem to want them dead, unlike most of their chance meetings since their journey began. They relinquished the weapons they were carrying and the men surrounding them came forward to bind their hands behind their backs and tie them together in a line. "You will follow us." The one they assumed was a leader said. As night fell the group lit lamps and continued to walk. They were being led along the path deeper into Narsos and towards I'sos, as far as Teran could tell. If any of the group stumbled they were pulled to their feet by one of their captors. If they tried to talk they were struck in the face. All they could do was keep walking and contemplate what was happening. They walked all night without rest or respite. It was morning when they finally reached a clearing in the forest and found a whole camp there. There were many men there. The ones with weapons were all dressed similarly to their captors. The ones that were not armed were dressed in a variety of manners, what they all had in common was that their hands were tied or chained. There were horses picketed at the edge of the clearing and a number of cages on the backs of carts.

"Slavers." Stated Koran, getting struck in the mouth for the trouble. The others nodded, but did not speak yet. At least they knew what they faced now. They would have to work out a way to escape, but that would take time. If they were lucky the slavers would take them in the direction they wished to travel towards, the rumoured army encampments. It was quite likely. Slavery was outlawed in the Sambarian lands, but Teran knew that the Narsians had often used slaves to help support their army logistics corps as well as other aspects of society.

They were led to part of the camp where they were chained to a stake and left with a different guard. A few crusts of bread and some water were given to them to eat and then they were left alone.

"I know its completely backward compared to our body clocks since it is already morning, but we should try and get some rest. Who knows when we'll next be able to?" Teran whispered to the others when the guards were not paying attention. He assumed that they were in a staging camp for the slavers, designed so that they could collect their catches here before leading them in a train to other destinations. His assessment proved correct.

Teran had been unable to follow his own advice, his mind working overtime, thus he remained awake. During the course of the morning other captured slaves were brought to the camp. Just before midday their original captors returned.

"Get up, we're moving again." One of them said to Teran and his companions, coming forward, hoisting them to their feet, if they did not manage it quickly enough, and retying them together in a line, this time with manacles and a chain, which was joined to other slaves. In short order, they were underway continuing their journey southwest, if the sun was anything to go by. Teran was grudgingly impressed by the efficiency of these slavers. In fact, they had almost military precision and he wondered whether they were either official soldiers, or men who had dropped out of the army, using their training to gain profit elsewhere.

The day was monotonous. The scenery might have been pleasant, but that was hardly the focus of any of their minds as they walked in the heat of the sun, chains chaffing at their wrists reminding them of their predicament, as if they needed physical reminder. The slavers were annoyingly vigilant and it was, once again, impossible to say a word, let alone have a conversation, without receiving a blow because of it. As the day wore on, the toil of the night before began to catch up with the companions and they began to stumble frequently as tiredness overtook their concentration and muscles. Each time they stumbled they were struck for their trouble and then hauled to their feet by a slaver. After this pattern repeated a few times, a particularly nasty looking slaver with scars on his face and muscles bulging came up the line.

Child of Rydos

"Stop slowing the line!" He barked.

"We're exhaust…" Banir began as the slaver struck him across the face with such force that he fell to the floor. Teran and Koran, who were in front and behind, quickly lifted him to his feet.

"If you can't keep up, then you're dead weight." The slaver said, leaning emphasis on the word dead, making the meaning of his threat perfectly clear. Teran and Koran nodded and continued to hold up Banir until he was focussed enough to walk under his own steam again after the blow. The four of them kept especially close watch on each other from that point on, helping each other as needed so as not to slow the line.

The day continued in much the same manner and they reached their next camp just as evening was beginning to fall. This camp was set up similarly to the one they had been incarcerated at last night when they were first captured and obviously served as yet another staging area in a network of camps that the slavers were using. By Teran's reckoning, assuming they continued in the same vein tomorrow and if the maps they had viewed in Arin were correct, they should finally clear the forest tomorrow and reach the city of I'sos. They were chained again to a post and fed the same diet of bread and water. Again, whilst they were guarded they were given slightly more freedom, in that they could talk at a whisper to each other without being noticed.

"Today has been terrible." Said Banir, exhaustion clear in his face, "I've been in some difficult scrapes, but there is no let up to this. When can we make a move to leave this party?"

"We need to work out how to get out of these chains first." Koran said.

"That's the least of our problems." Said Banir and he glanced to see no guards were watching as he flicked open his manacles, gave them a spin in his hand and quickly reattached them. Koran, Xantila and Teran stared, their mouths open.

"You could do that any time you want?" Koran said, surprised.

"How many times do I have to tell you that I'm good? You think I'd let someone take all my lock picks away? I'm a professional." Banir said with mock hurt in his voice. Teran then returned to Banir's original question.

"I know today has been hard, Ban, but we need to stick at it just one more day, I think. If we run too early then they'll just catch us and incarcerate us more fully next time, or do something worse to us. Besides, we need to complete our mission and reach the army, or at least somewhere where we can gain intelligence about their forces. I'm hoping we'll find that at I'sos, as well as some fast horses. You'll get to practice your skills plenty before this trip is out." Teran told Banir.

"Even from I'sos it is a long way back to Cheros, mostly back through Narsos forest. Even with Xantila's skills it is likely we'd be caught. Our knowledge of the forest will not be better than the local Narsians, especially if it is those slavers chasing us. I suspect they operate extensively throughout the whole forest." Koran commented on Teran's plan.

"I wasn't suggesting that we made directly for Cheros through the forest. It is about the same distance to Ptanga as it is to I'sos and the route is across open land. Fewer places to hide, but easier to get across the distance."

"How does it help us to reach Ptanga? It is still a Narsian city." Xantila asked.

"The Gerakans are not the only ones with underground connections." Teran began mysteriously, then he elaborated, "My father set up a safe house in Ptanga at the docks there. If we can reach Ptanga we can chart a ship immediately and be safe away at sea. There are no better sailors nor ships in the Great Western Sea."

"It is a long shot of a plan…" Koran said.

"… but we don't have much choice." Xantila finished.

"Running free sounds better than not even trying." Banir added.

"So, it's settled, we continue with the slavers to I'sos then try and make a break and risk the run." Finished Teran. Conversation dwindled after that, as each of them tried to get as much rest as possible for the journey tomorrow. They were going to need all of their strength and endurance, and more, before this adventure was out.

Chapter XVI – Rope Tricks

Evening had fallen and Teran was looking up at the walls of I'sos from an enclosure in the slave market. It had taken them a further two days travel under forced march from the slavers, but they were now incarcerated in the Narsian city. He was being held in a roofed cage with about another thirty future slaves and had been split up from his companions. He and Xantila were in this cage, but Banir was in an adjacent cage and he was not sure where Koran was. In all there were a few hundred people caged here, some of Sambarian descent, particularly Arinachian and Hruntan, some of Narsian descent and others still of lineage unknown to Teran. He assumed that these latter people were from lands south of Narsos, which were unknown to the Sambarians. None of this had he factored in to his escape plans and he was trying not to panic when he considered how they could possibly escape.

He had started to realize that escaping might be even harder than he thought as they neared I'sos that day from the northeast. He had noticed other groups travelling towards the city, which was much larger than he thought, and it was obvious that these too were companies of slaves being collected in one place. When they had finally reached the city, been marched to the extensive slave market and been caged there, he fell into an introspective and depressive mood.

Child of Rydos

Xantila had noticed Teran's mood and understood the reason for it, but also knew that he needed to snap out of it if they were going to work together to make any good come of this situation. If they were going to break out they needed to try and do it tonight. If they left it any longer they could be sold off to different owners and be permanently separated, unable to find each other and unable to use each other's skills to aid the escape home.

"So," She whispered to Teran when she'd managed to get him in a corner by himself furthest from the patrolling guards, "How are we going to get out of this one?"

"I don't know." He responded despondently, "The problem is not breaking out of these cages. I'm sure Banir could assist us in that. The problem is that there are so many guards and unfriendly eyes between here and freedom that there is no way we will avoid being seen."

"Why not use that to our advantage, then, and hide in plain sight?" Xantila suggested.

"What do you mean?" He asked, brightening slightly as it was obvious that Xantila had thought of something that might get them out of their predicament.

"Let's orchestrate a mass escape. Let's free every slave here so that they can help us overpower the guards and so there will be so many loose ends to catch and tie up that we might slip through the net." She said.

"That is a brilliant idea. And it's one we can execute tonight without too much preparation, which is ideal." Teran complimented her, brightening considerably. "Let me go and have a word with Banir." He told her, then strode to the other side of the cage nearest to Banir's enclosure and tried to surreptitiously get his attention. He wished that he knew the thieves' sign language which Banir had talked to him about as they had been travelling across Sambar together. He made a mental note to ask Banir to teach him some of it as he continued trying to get his attention. Banir had been waiting for a signal from Teran, so did not take too long to notice that he desired his attention. It was difficult for them to converse across the gap between them without notice, but it was possible at intervals.

"Have you seen Koran?" Teran began. Banir shook his head in the negative. Teran continued, "Are you still able to employ your skills?" He did not want to shout out to the guards that Banir was a good escape artist. Banir shook his head in the positive this time. "Tonight. Everyone. We want a party. Spread the word." Banir nodded enthusiastically, showing that he had understood Teran's meaning. Teran returned to Xantila. "Well that is organized. All we can do now is tell our plan to the others here and wait for night to fall." Teran confided in her.

Night had fallen. Unfortunately, though the moon was waning in the sky it was only just past full and it still cast significant light on their imminent escape attempt. Banir waited until the patrolling guard had passed, then started work on the lock of his cage. Within short order he was out and ran over to Teran and Xantila's cage to unlock that one.

"We need to find Koran, but we need to open all these other cages, anyway, as we go." Teran said to Banir, who was already making his way to the next cage. Banir had been watching the guards since he had found himself incarcerated in the slave market, trying to calculate and memorize their patrol routes, for precisely the sort of activity that they were now undertaking. He knew, however, that it would not take the guards long to notice something was wrong as the freed slaves created greater and greater a ruckus as they fled their captors. Banir just hoped they found Koran before the guards managed to contain the trouble they were raising through their escape.

Nearly all the cages had been opened now and still they had not found Koran. The guards had not yet been able to stop them. Banir had not taken into account the fact that the recently freed prisoners would want their revenge on their captors. They had swarmed the guards, not caring that they were going up against armed foes. The sheer number of freed slaves meant that they had easily gained control of the compound. Some of the prisoners had taken the keys from the guards and were now going about helping unlock the cages. Finally, they came to the last cage, furthest from where they had started, and were relieved to find Koran waiting there.

"This is your commotion I assume." He said, a smile on his face as he gestured expansively at the prisoners running about the complex, overpowering guards and streaming out into the city. Reunited at last and their work in the slave markets done they quickly made towards the nearest exit hoping they could escape into the anonymity of the city and from there into the countryside. They joined the flow of escapees and soon found themselves on the streets of the city.

"Does anyone know which way north and west is?" Asked Banir, disorientated by his run through the slave markets and the lack of daylight to judge by.

"Didn't you ever learn to navigate by the stars?" Asked Koran.

"Never needed to. I knew Baxen like the back of my hand, day or night." Banir said defensively.

"We need to go this way." Xantila said pointing towards a narrow street opposite them. The crowds of escapees were rapidly dissipating now as groups slit up and tried their own luck in different directions throughout the city. "We need to melt into the darkness quickly and try and stay away from other groups, lest we be caught." Xantila continued anxiously.

"Just follow my example." Said Banir, taking point and heading in the direction Xantila had indicated. They could hear the alarm spreading throughout the city now as bells were rung to signal the mass escape and knew it was even more urgent for them to get away from the market and out of the city.

They had made their way through the city, several times coming close to other escapees or to search parties looking for them, but they managed to stick to the shadows and avoid capture. They were making their way down a street filled with boarded-up shop fronts when Banir paused.

"What is it?" Teran hissed towards him. Banir turned back and pointed to one of the shops.

"That may come in useful." He said, pointing towards some old rope, which was holding in the boards against one particular shop front.

"It doesn't look like it is fit for the job it is performing, let alone anything else." Koran snorted. Banir was already halfway through untying the ropes.

"Help me, so we can get out of here as quick as possible." Banir chided them. Help suddenly aplenty, they were away in short order with knackered rope in hand.

They reached the east gate of the city to find their way barred. The gates themselves were firmly shut and there was a strong guard standing at the gate. This was obviously a routine response to the ringing of the city alarm. Teran's mood, lifted by the plan and escape thus far, was suddenly darkened again as he despaired of any of them escaping beyond the confines of the city walls. Banir seemed to take the news of the obstruction in his stride and led them northwards, away from the gate but along the edge of the city wall. Eventually they got to a point along the wall where there were few lights from the streets and where the walls of the houses came close to the walls.

"Here is where we will make our escape." Banir stated.

"You expect us to walk through the wall?" Teran asked skeptically, looking around.

"No. Watch." Banir said simply as he launched himself into the air, bouncing between the city wall and the wall of the house opposite, finding purchase where Teran could swear there was nothing to cling to. Reaching the top of the wall, Banir checked there was no guard patrolling the walkway at the top. Seeing the coast was clear he lowered the rope they had pilfered earlier, tying one end securely around the crenulations along the top of the city wall.

One by one, Koran, Xantila and Teran made their way to the top of the way with the aid of the rope. Once they had all gained the top Banir threw the rope over the other side for each of them to lower themselves. They spotted lights in the distance on the wall, bobbing towards them, no doubt the normal patrol coming around, so they had to make haste with their descent. Xantila and Teran had made the wall and Koran was halfway down when the rope broke mid-descent, sending Koran to the ground. He landed sprawled on his back.

"Are you okay?" Xantila and Teran echoed simultaneously as they rushed towards him.

"Ugh…" was Koran's only response. Meanwhile the patrol was closing in on Banir, it would not be long before they sighted him. Nor could the others flee from the wall to the safety of cover in time. Against the wall they might avoid being sighted, but only if the patrol did not look directly down, but across the field they would be sure to be sighted fleeing the city suspiciously in the middle of the night.

Banir untied the, now useless, rope and threw the end down to the others. He then tossed his boots and socks over the edge too, causing confusion amongst the party. He then clambered over the wall, making his way slowly down the wall using every crevice and crack that he could squeeze his fingers and toes into. He was about a quarter of the way down the wall when he heard the voices of the approaching guards. Banir froze in his position, whilst the others looked up in horror. It seemed like time had slowed to a standstill. Banir's fingers and toes were screaming under the pressure of clinging securely to the wall without moving or losing his purchase. The guards paused directly above Banir, shining a light outward into the night and inspecting the approach to the city. Banir held his breath, but every noise around him seemed like a sounding gong, directing the attention of the guards towards him. Banir was sure that he would be discovered; yet as time drew on the guards, though they remained, had not called the alarm. Eventually they turned away and continued along the wall on their patrol, leaving the escapees undiscovered. Banir let out a huge sign of relief, nearly unbalancing himself in the process, and continued slowly down the wall.

"I can't believe we were not discovered!" Teran exclaimed, under his breath, once Banir had secure footing on the ground.

"Th'an must be watching over us." Banir said, smiling and invoking the blessing of the god of good fortune, celebrated amongst thieves.

"It is not over yet." Added Koran, "We need to steal away from here as fast as possible. It cannot be doubted that most, if not all, of the freed slaves will be recaptured. The slave trade brings in a lot of money and money pays for muscle."

"Let us away." Xantila said, glancing up at the wall before beginning to make her way westwards, away from the city and towards freedom. Banir grabbed the remains of the rope to leave no trace of their passing and joined the others as they struck out across land.

Chapter XVII – Unwelcome Guests

As they struck out westwards, away from the city and its lamps, the light ahead of them became more and more obvious. Thousands of campfires across the plain between them and Ptanga. They had found the Narsian army. The sight caused them all to come to a standstill.

"I had no idea there could be so many of them." Teran spoke first. Whilst they were not able to see the soldiers themselves the number of campfires suggested a force at least twice the size of the entire joint Sambarian armies. Whilst armies could light extra fires at night in order to fool the opposing force, Teran thought this unlikely because the Narsians had no reason to expect unfriendly eyes to be prying on them.

"How have they been able to raise such a large army?" Banir asked, awe evident in his voice.

"We've never had a clear idea of how far to the south the lands of Narsos extend." Koran stated, also clearly effected by the size of the army, "Evidently it is much larger than we ever realized. We've never been able to secure maps for the region south of the capital, Nars, and none of our traders have been welcomed there. Now we know it is because they wanted to hide their potential from us, so we would consider them less of a threat."

"What has changed now, I wonder?" Offered Xantila, "If Narsos has the potential for this size of army why have they decided to only muster against us now? What has changed?" It was a good question, one that they

Child of Rydos

would have to postpone finding an answer to for the time being.

"We need to somehow make it around this army without being spotted, or pass through quickly enough that they can't keep up with us." Koran said.

"Both options seem quite unlikely." Teran interjected, "But we should try to pass around them on their southern flank. They will be looking to the north, towards Hrunta as the direction the enemy is likely to come from. Hopefully they will not place a proper watch on their southern flank."

"I can try and pick us up some horses once we're past the army and looking back on its west flank. Best not to arouse suspicions until we're ready to run though." Banir offered.

"Seems like our only option." Teran responded, "We seem to be stumbling from one hopeless situation to another."

"Yet even so we stumble closer to home with every step." Xantila said sagely. It was as good a plan as any so they began to make their way around the army. It was slow progress, keeping low to the ground so as not to be spotted. Teran's assessment that their sentry posting to the south would be thinner turned out to be correct. The sentries were also, stupidly, carrying torches, which helped them see a few feet into the darkness, but effectively blinded them to any more subtle movements beyond.

"We seem to be in luck." Banir whispered, "I suppose that they're looking out for large platoons of soldiers marching on their location and have no reason to look for a small number sneaking around their camp." The others nodded in agreement.

Unwelcome Guests

"Daybreak is going to rear its head before we make it around the encampment at this rate." Xantila broke the bad news. Koran swore, knowing Xantila's assessment to be true.

"We can't make it past this army in the daytime without drawing attention to ourselves and we're obviously not Narsian, I doubt we'd fare well." Teran said and continued, "Let's split up and look for somewhere we can hide for the day until night falls again. It's our best option." With a nod the group split up, focused on the task at hand of finding somewhere to camp down for the day. The local environment was not very conducive to their plans, however, as the land was mostly open, with few trees and hills to hide between. As dawn was beginning to threaten to break across the sky they regrouped.

"Did anyone find anything?" Teran asked, evident from the tone of his voice that he had not.

"No." Echoed Koran and Xantila at the same time.

"No…" Banir began, the tone of his voice revealing there was something more to his search.

"What is it, Ban?" Teran asked.

"Well I dismissed the idea at first, but I think it might be our only choice… I found an old burial mound. The tomb entrance hasn't been disturbed. If you're willing to be involved in desecration we could try hiding out there." Banir finished. The others all made a sign to ward off evil spirits. Teran looked up,

"Daylight is fast approaching. There are no other options. Take us there, Ban." Teran told him. Banir led them straight away to the gentle mound he had found, which had a stone lintel and door slab on its south side. "Elerin, forgive us for what we must do." Teran prayed

171

before pushing the bulk of his weight against the slab. It did not move. Signalling to the others to help, Teran leant his weight against the door again, this time joined by Koran, Xantila and Banir. At first nothing seemed to happen, but slowly there was a grinding sound and the slab inched imperceptibly inwards until there was enough of a gap for them to squeeze into the tomb. A thin ray of light now lit the tomb from the entranceway, showing this to be the vault of a single occupant. It did not look like it had been disturbed since it was first sealed. The air inside was stale, so they clustered near the doorway where fresh air was entering the tomb for the first time in what looked like centuries. They did not shut the door for fear of being unable to open it. They just hoped that no one would examine the tomb too closely and realize the door had been forced open and seek to investigate.

"The writing in here is High Narsian." Said Koran, "This tomb could be from the time of our first war with Narsos. Someone important I would guess given it is a lone burial in such a grand sarcophagus." Koran continued, looking at the intricately carved tomb itself.

"Let's pay our respects to the dead first." Teran said, "And then satisfy our scholarly thoughts later." A strange chill had come upon him since entering the tomb. Koran, suitably chastised by Teran, rejoined the others and the four of them sat down and each offered prayers to the gods of their homelands for the soul they had disturbed; Teran to Elerin, Koran to Grukan, Banir to Th'an and Xantila to the Mother spirit, who was the source of all life. Their prayers offered, Teran felt more relaxed. "We may as well all try and get some rest. We're not going anywhere until tomorrow night now." Teran suggested, then hearing Banir's stomach rumble, he continued, "I'm sorry we haven't got any food, we'll have to cope without sustenance for one day. I didn't think about it in our rush to escape."

"None of us did." Said Koran sadly.

"I'll take first watch." Offered Banir, "I'm too hungry to sleep right away." The others tried to lie down and make themselves comfortable.

A few hours passed uneventfully. Banir had not seen any movement on the south side of the barrow mound through the crack in the open door by the time Koran rose to relieve him.

"Try and get some sleep now." Koran offered and Banir, suddenly in need of the rest, nodded gratefully and tried to find comfortable spot to lie down. Comfortable being a relative word when one was considering sleeping on the stone floor of a tomb. Koran stood watch by the door as Banir drifted off.

After a while, when it was obvious that no one was approaching the burial mound Koran's curiosity got the better of him and he started to inspect the tomb. He felt irresistibly drawn towards the sarcophagus, but his methodical nature got the better of this desire and he started from the outskirts of the tomb, inspecting the walls and floor before making his way to the sarcophagus itself. The outer parts of the tomb were completely bare, giving neither a clue as to the person who lay in this tomb nor the story of his or her life.

The sarcophagus was a different matter, as Koran had already observed. It was intricately carved with runes that Koran recognized as High Narsian, a language not spoken for nearly five hundred years. Koran was skilled in linguistics and had studied the old tongues in order to read the old histories and documents collected in the libraries in Ariss.

"Agathan, brother of the dark path, soldier of Khaen. Resting until called." Koran read aloud. He thought it was an odd epitaph. There was much more writing on the sarcophagus, but he suddenly lost interest in reading any more. It did not occur to him that his intense interest and sudden apathy were at all peculiar. It had been a long day and he was exhausted. He fought the urge he had to sleep, knowing it was his turn to watch, but could not help himself. He slumped down next to the sarcophagus and drifted off into a deep, yet troubled sleep.

Fog rolled in across the water in a thick bank. It was broken only by the trees on the water's edge which caused it to eddy and swirl, giving brief, tantalizing glimpses into the distance. Koran stumbled through the trees, looking for the others. He did not remember how he had gotten here and he could feel a slow terror building inside him. As he stumbled onwards, not remembering what his goal was, he would sometimes see a shadowy figure out of the corner of his eye, but whenever he tried to focus on it, it was gone. He felt tired and exhausted. He could not remember how long he had been stumbling around. He tripped over a tree root and fell on his face. Raising his head, he spat leaves out of his mouth and tried to lift himself up, but he found he could not muster the energy. He knew he had to go on, had to get out of these woods, so he slowly dragged his body along the ground.

Eventually he found his way to the lake. The fog was clearing here and in the midst of the lake stood the shadowy figure, staring directly at him, piercing red eyes glowing in the darkness. He reached the edge of the gently lapping water and fell face down into. The icy cold water lapped against his ears and covered his nose, preventing him from breathing. As he fell there he noticed two others who had just reached the lake. He thought he recognized them and that he should know their names, but he could not manage to recall them.

Teran had wondered through the fog-filled forest the sense of unease growing upon him. He knew that this was wrong. When he had reached the lake, he saw the others there and he knew their names, though it felt like he had to wade through mental fog to recall them. He looked at them each in turn and remembered their names. Xantila. Banir. Koran. They had all fallen into the lake. Teran knew that he should rush to help them out of the water, but he did not.

"This is wrong." Teran stated calmly, but with conviction and the scene before them melted away. They were still in the barrow mound, though it was now dark outside. The others were slumped around the sarcophagus, whilst Teran was still standing. Their skin was pallid. Hovering over the sarcophagus was the ghostly figure from the lake vision. Its diffuse glow lighting the tomb, here it seemed almost solid, as if it was gaining strength and substance. Teran knew that he had to get them all out of the tomb right away. "Wake up!" He shouted to his slumbering friends, shaking Xantila, who happened to be the nearest. The others did not wake, but Xantila stirred at his touch. This action brought the ghost's attention fully on to Teran. "Xan, wake the others and get out of here!" Teran shouted as the spectral figure advanced towards him.

Teran could feel himself weakening under the spectre's gaze, his will to action being drained from him, but he forced himself to focus. Xantila reached Koran and Banir and her touch wakened them as Teran's touch had her. They were confused as they came to, but they sensed Xantila's urgency and so focused themselves. Xantila looked back towards Teran, he seemed to be flagging and the ghost was nearly upon him.

"Let's get out of here!" Xantila said, pushing Koran and Banir towards the door. Xantila, herself, darted towards Teran and, grabbing him by the arm, pulled him towards the door and the fresh air.

They ran out of the tomb as fast as their legs would carry them. Outside it was growing dark, they had obviously slept away at least a day under the influence of the spirit in the tomb. As they passed under the door lintel they started to feel their energy return to them, as if their life force had been drained from them, but was now being restored. An unholy scream reverberated from the tomb, Teran turned to look behind to see if the ghostly spirit was following them. He could see a pair of red eyes peering out from the doorway, but it was not pursuing them. Perhaps it was confined to its tomb. Then Teran's eyes were drawn upwards to the lintel itself and he stopped in his tracks and swore. Carved into the lintel, burning fiercely with energy, was the snake and sword emblem, which had plagued them since they entered Azin forest. What did it mean?

The screeching of the spirit was causing a stir in the distant army encampment and Teran could see torches bobbing towards them.

"We need to be away. Now!" He called to the others

as they continued to run. "Xan, can you obliterate our tracks at all before those soldiers get here?"

"Yes." She said simply as she slowed slightly to fall behind the others in order to focus on masking their tracks. She did not have time to do a good job, but hopefully in the dark her crude masking would not be discovered.

They still needed horses to get to Ptanga, but they needed to get away from the tomb which was drawing the attention of the Narsians to them. Teran hoped that if there were any magicians in the army that they were focused on the spectre itself and not using their powers to search for who had disturbed the tomb. They made their way further west and north again, skirting around the army whose attention was now focused both northward and to the tomb site in the south. The cries from the tomb had not subsided as they made their way around the camp through the night. Whilst disturbing, they were thankful for the continued screeching because it meant the distraction was ongoing.

When they had made their way sufficiently far around the army encampment so that they were ready to strike westwards again towards Ptanga, they paused. Their route had been tense, but uneventful.

"Some horses would be really helpful about now." Koran said.

"Do we risk it?" Teran asked the others, "We seem to have been lucky to have escaped notice so far. Stealing horses would certainly draw attention to us, but the journey will be slow without them."

"If there are magicians in the army and they are able to communicate with that ghost they might be able to find our trail and give chase." Xantila suggested.

Child of Rydos

"I'm good," said Banir, "But I won't be able to steal horses and not have them notice eventually. At best, we'll have until daybreak." There was silence amongst them whilst they contemplated their options.

"Do it." Teran said to Banir, "Take Xantila to help." Banir looked like he was about to object to the company out of habit when Teran cut across him, "You can't manage four horses by yourself and if you get into difficulty you might find Xan's skills useful."

"Don't worry, I agree." Banir said quickly, "I'm just so used to operating by myself that I find myself objecting automatically. Xantila is a stealthy mover too, so I doubt the two of us will raise alarm in the camp. At least until after we've grabbed the horses that is…" With that, Banir and Xantila made their way towards the edge of the encampment whilst there was still a little cover of darkness left to cover their actions.

About thirty minutes had passed, when Banir and Xantila came flying at high speed towards them.

"Quick, ride!" Shouted Banir as he and Xantila threw reigns for the two spare mounts to Teran and Koran. Behind them Teran could see there were soldiers in pursuit. "Wasn't quite enough distraction in the camp. We were caught when one of the horses started making a fuss about being taken out of the stable at night." Banir filled them in. Koran and Teran wasted no time, they leapt into their saddles and raced after Xantila and Banir.

"I assume they're on horseback too?" Koran asked as they sped through the night.

"Yes," Grinned Banir, "But they're probably being slowed slightly by the bumpy ride..."

"Banir damaged the rest of the tackle beyond repair."

Xantila filled in, "The soldiers in pursuit didn't have time to grab tackle from another stabling yard if they wanted to keep up with us."

"Good work!" Koran shouted back, joining in with Banir's grin. They continued racing across the open land throughout the night. Slowly they could see that their pursuers were falling behind. They were pushing the horses hard, but the other option was not desirable.

Chapter XVIII – Swift Sails

Teran and his companions had been riding hard all night and for the better part of the day. It raised a few eyebrows when they passed people on the road, but no one tried to intervene or question them. They were all exhausted and hungry, but they did not yet dare to stop. Teran was thinking about when it might be safe for them to pause for food when suddenly he was thrown head-over-heals from his horse as it stumbled and fell. Teran rolled sideways, narrowly missing being crushed by the falling horse. There was a crack of bone and the horse screamed. The others pulled up their horses mid-gallop and cantered around to rejoin Teran.

Teran staggered to his feet, holding his head, more out of shock than injury. He swore as it looked at the state of his mount. They had not yet had an opportunity to procure any weapons. He started looking around for a stone with which to put the horse out of its misery when Banir handed him a dagger. Teran did not ask where Banir had found it. Instead he focused on the task at hand and rapidly put the horse down by opening its throat.

"I guess we're stopping here briefly." Said Teran, "I shouldn't have let us push the horses so hard. I don't think we're going to have many other opportunities to eat, so I think we should butcher the horse for its meat."

Within short order they had butchered the horse and used its skin to create a makeshift bag for the meat. They would cook the meat later, rather than pause in the middle of the day to light a fire. Teran doubled up with Banir and they slowed the pace of the horses to give them a bit more rest. They still had another day's journey before they would be able to reach the town of Ptanga and who knew what they would find there.

A day and a half of hard riding later, or at least as much as their tired steeds could manage with Teran and Banir sharing, they found themselves approaching the walls of Ptanga. They had managed to pause overnight, cook some of their horsemeat and rest, but the journey was still filled with tension. They could see other campfires on the horizon behind them and they suspected they were being followed. If their pursuers had realized they were Sambarian they had probably guessed their approximate direction of travel, despite losing them. Whilst no one had caught up with them, they still feared this pursuit and so the ride that day had not been easy going. Their only advantage was that they had reached Ptanga first.

They passed through the gates and into the city without much trouble.

"We need to make our way to The Pearl Fisher. It is a tavern on the waterfront." Teran told the others, "I should be able to find our contacts there." They made their way to *The Pearl Fisher*. It was a shabby looking establishment, which took up a large portion of the dockside. The waterside tavern was heaving with business, with people pouring in and out of the doors continuously. Sailors, it seemed, like to get as much drink as possible whilst they were on land and their duties allowed. The inside of the establishment was no surprise. It looked like it had seen better days. The

Child of Rydos

furniture was worn and had signs of occasional heavy repair and the décor was outdated and faded, but the place smelled relatively clean. Teran went to straight to the barman on duty to see if they could procure rooms.

"I can give you one room to share and put an extra cot in there so that it can sleep all four of you. No other space." The barman said, not particularly interested in being helpful.

"That'll be fine." Teran said, "Can you put it on Loren's tab?" He continued, using the secret code word that his father had established. The barman raised his eyebrows, but nodded as he kept cleaning the mug he was clasping through a towel.

"You can wait in the back room whilst we're getting your room ready." The barman said, nodding towards a door at the back of the bar. Not quite sure what to expect they made their way to the door.

On passing through the door they found themselves in a small room with plain dusty walls and exposed wood floorboards. There was no natural light. All the light in the room was supplied by a single lamp which burned on a table set in the middle of the room which was surrounded by chairs. Across the other side of the room there was a second door.

"I guess we wait here." Koran said, pulling out a chair and sitting down.

"Let's just hope we haven't made a mistake." Teran responded and they waited.

They did not have to wait long. Within about ten or so minutes they heard someone turning the handle on the door opposite the one through which they had entered. A short man with dark, curly hair entered, his complexion marking him as Narsian. This was further confirmed when the man spoke and revealed a thick Narsian accent.

"You are agents from Rydos?" He asked. Teran tensed, worried, but responded in the affirmative,

"We need return passage to Cheros." Was Teran's response.

"You've run into trouble here in Narsos?" The man asked.

"We'd prefer to leave as soon as possible." Teran confirmed.

"It can be arranged." The man responded.

"I…" Teran began.

"No, don't tell me any more. The less I know the better." He continued, "Don't worry about fees for staying here, they will be covered. Come with me, we have a much better suite of rooms for you where you can stay out of trouble until your passage can be arranged." With this the man opened the door through which he had entered and beckoned them to follow. He led them up a staircase that was obviously used by the staff of the establishment, rather than the guests. He led them along a first-floor corridor which was obviously also only used by the staff. "The original owner of this establishment liked the idea of his tavern operating like a grand house where the staff were not seen." The man confirmed. At the end of the corridor he opened a door which led to a palatial suite of rooms which included a shared lounge. "I will make sure some food is sent up for you." The man said as he left them, closing the door behind them.

"Looks like we're here for a while then." Said Koran, flopping into a chair.

Child of Rydos

"Let's hope we can take that man at his word and he isn't ratting us out to the Narsian authorities as we speak." Xantila said.

"There isn't any proof that we've done anything wrong, so hopefully we'll be okay." Teran suggested.

The hours passed by. They had been served two meals in their suite before the unnamed man returned with tidings for them.

"Seems like you've been causing some trouble for the army gathered near I'sos." Was all he said, as he nonchalantly entered the room and sat down with them. The others did not say anything in return. Looking at Banir and Xantila, he continued, "People matching your descriptions were spotted stealing four horses and are wanted for that theft, the destruction of army property, the illegal freeing of slaves and the desecration of an ancient tomb." The man sounded amused, if anything.

"I can explain…" Began Teran.

"No. Don't. I told you before, the less I know the better. You must have the bad luck of resembling some trouble-makers and thieves." The man responded, "Besides, it is unlikely that anyone noticed you arriving here. We have so many clientele."

"Can you still help us gain passage to Cheros?" Koran asked, getting to the point.

"Yes." The man confirmed, "But it'll be difficult. The Sailor's Daughter is ready to sail and can take you, but the port had been closed."

"Closed?" Teran asked in concern.

"A few hours after you reached the city an army squadron rode into town and demanded the port be closed until further notice. They're looking for four people, but only have crude descriptions."

"How will we leave?" Xantila asked.

"The Sailor's Daughter will run the blockaded port. She's fast. Hopefully she'll outrun any pursuers. If you can make it as far as the Ptanga reef you will be safe. The Sailor's Daughter has a Rydosian crew and navigator, so you'll be able to clear the reef, unlike your pursuers. Once she is free of Ptanga and she has delivered her cargo to Cheros she'll make for the port of Rydos where she'll undergo a refit and become a new ship and lose the reputation she'll gain here tonight."

"We leave tonight?" Teran asked.

"Yes. We'll have to smuggle you out of the tavern. We'll hide you in barrels which contained Narsian fire wine until recently and hope no one checks too carefully." With that concluding remark their host left them once again to make arrangements and they were left to their own thoughts and discussions.

As evening fell there was a knock at the servants' entrance and Koran rose to let the caller enter. It was a different man from the one who had dealt with them earlier. Teran recognized him as the barman they had first dealt with.

"Follow me." He said, leaving the room through the servants' door again.

"Don't like wasting words do they?" Banir whispered to Koran under his breath. They followed the barman along the corridor and down the stairs again. This time they descended an extra flight and found themselves in a cellar. There were four open barrels there.

"Get in." The barman confirmed. The companions clambered into their unusual carriages. "The barrels need to be sealed in order for the lids not to fall off. This could be a bumpy ride for you, but it should be safe. Oh, and there should be enough air for that not to become a problem..." With this the barman lifted on the lids of the barrels and nailed them shut.

After the banging stopped, they heard the barman call out for some help and they guessed that some other bar staff had joined them. The barrels were leaned onto their sides and rolled along. Then there was the sound of ropes being lashed around the barrels and the sensation of being hoisted into the air. Teran wondered if they knew what their cargo was. He assumed not by the way in which they were jostled around as they were rolled towards the quayside, if the sounds outside were anything to go by. They would all have more than a few bruises to show from this dubious mode of transport. After a while they were hoisted upwards again and swung through the air before being finally lowered to a flat surface. Then they were left. All that could be felt was the gentle bob and sway of a ship at anchor.

Time seemed to pass very slowly inside the sensory deprived environment of the barrels. Teran began to worry about running out of air, but he managed to think through the situation logically so that he did not begin to hyperventilate. The air in the barrel was not stale or changing feel, so fresh air must be making its way in to the barrel. The barman probably had not sealed the lids properly on purpose to allow them to continue breathing no matter how long their sojourn. Either that or it simply had not been long enough yet for them to become deprived of air. How long did it take to suffocate in a barrel anyway?

After what seemed like an age, Teran, accustomed as he was to life on a ship by growing up on Rydos, sensed a change in motion of the ship, indicating that they had cast off. Their speed picked up rapidly and from the shouts Teran could hear he guessed their flight had already been noticed. He hoped surprise would aid their flight enabling them to break past any Narsian ships which had been given guard duty of the port. Teran could hear the shouts of the first mate giving orders to the crew to trim the sails to the wind for maximum speed. Time continued to pass and still their speed continued to grow. Teran took this as a good sign. They had not been stopped yet.

The minutes and seconds trickled on. Eventually Teran heard what sounded like a crowbar being applied to the nails in the wood above his head. The lid of the barrel was lifted off and bright sunlight flooded in to assualt his dark-adjusted eyes. After a few moments, his sight adjusted and he could see sailors helping Koran, Xantila and Banir out of their respective barrels. A sailor dressed more finely than the rest and less well suited for manual work on the ship came and stood before them.

"I'm Yan. I'm the captain of the Sailor's Daughter." He told them, "We managed to pass the ships guarding the harbour before they could block us. They're in pursuit, but we have a head start on them. We're making for the Ptanga reef. If we make it there without being caught we'll be safe."

"Thank you, Yan. To both you and your crew." Teran said on behalf of them all.

"It sounds like you've had a rough journey so far, if the report I've been given is true. Rest for now. We've got a full complement of crew so you'd only get in the way and slow us if you tried to help. Gregory will show you to your cabin." Yan responded, indicating one of the sailors with him and giving the companions leave to rest.

Teran, Xantila, Banir and Koran each had a bed in a four-bunk cabin. They had been resting for a little over a turn of the hourglass, the most reliable way to measure the passage of time at sea despite the rolling of the ship causing the sand flow to fluctuate, when there came a knock at the cabin door. Banir leapt down from his top bunk to answer the door and the captain entered. The captain looked at Banir and Xantila and their slightly pale complexions and said,

"First time at sea?" They both nodded miserably. "You'll probably get used to it and the sickness will wear off." The captain continued, "Unless you're unlucky. Now, to the matter at hand, follow me to the deck." They left their cabin and followed the captain to the aft of the ship and climbed to the poop deck. The captain pointed towards the horizon. Teran, Xantila, Koran and Banir squinted in the direction he had indicated.

"Another ship following us?" Xantila asked, making out a smudge on the horizon with her keen eyes.

"Aye," Captain Yan responded, "And it is gaining on us. Slowly, but she's still gaining. Those tubs guarding the port gave up pursuit but they obviously had a clipper or two which they've sent in pursuit."

"Will it catch up with us?" Teran asked the captain.

"Hard to say at this point. We should make the Ptanga reef just before dusk. No way they'll be able to follow us in there, especially in darkness. Too much chance of foundering." The captain responded, "The

Sailor's Daughter is a fast ship, but they're definitely gaining. I would have said that we were the fastest ship in port, but the proof I was wrong is gaining on us as we speak. It's almost as if unnatural agency aids their flight towards us. Only time will tell. Thought you should know." With that the captain left them to their own thoughts and returned to the business liaising with the first mate about encouraging the crew to their tasks.

Throughout the day the smudge on the horizon grew larger and larger. Teran had stayed on the poop deck, transfixed by the pursuit. Banir's seasickness had grown steadily worse and he had spent most of the time after lunch with his head over the side of the ship. The reef was fast approaching but so was the other ship. The sails of the other ship were full to straining, catching wind which did not seem available to their own sails. Teran could make out the crew of the other ship now. In the midst of the deck stood a robed figure who appeared to be chanting.

"That magician is aiding their flight towards us." Koran said, who had just rejoined Teran at the side of the ship.

"If they catch us, we're in trouble. Hopefully the magician will be too exhausted from aiding their pursuit to join the fight, but the deck of that ship is teeming with more than sailors." Teran responded, pointing out the soldiers that stood on deck.

"I don't like the odds either. We'd better make it to the reef in time then." Responded Koran.

The ship grew inexorably closer until Teran was sure that he could see the whites of their eyes. He could hear various shouts and commands coming from the other ship as they eagerly prepared to try and board the *Sailor's Daughter*. Suddenly the *Sailor's Daughter* took a sharp turn in the water towards starboard, slowing down, and then bearing to port. The pursuing ship kept on a straight course towards them, gaining even faster since their ship had slowed. The *Sailor's Daughter* had slowed dramatically now and was turning towards port and starboard frequently and seemingly erratically. Teran could see the excitement on the other ship as it closed in on them. The pursuers threw grappling hooks some of which caught on the ship, causing both ships to be twisted off their current courses as they became interlocked.

"Cut those ropes before they drag us further off course!" Shouted Captain Yan and sailors jumped to his command. "Keep us on course, you dogs!" The captain shouted again, urgency evident in his voice.

"What's going on?" Banir, who was having a brief interlude in his regime of nausea, asked Teran and Koran.

"We've reached the Ptanga reef." Teran answered, "That's why we're following such a complex course through the waters. We can't afford to be taken off course by the other ship either."

"So, we're out of danger?" Asked Banir.

"Not quite yet." Responded Koran, "We need to get deeper into the reef and away from the other ship to be completely safe." The pursuers were throwing more grappling hooks now and linking the two ships again.

"We need to help cut those ropes again. The captain is going to need the crew focused on navigating us through the reef." Teran told Koran and Banir, so they dove to business, helping the sailors cut lose the grappling hooks, as more continued to sail across the gap separating the two ships. Xantila had been watching the course of the ship through the water, admiring the navigational skill of the sailors. The only sign of the dangerous reef was the gentle breaking and swirling of water over the hidden obstructions beneath. Her revery was broken as she noticed that help was needed and so she joined Teran and others in cutting themselves loose from the other ship.

With the extra hands to help they managed to free themselves from their pursuers and continued their complex course heading. Their pursuers were still trying to bear directly down upon them. Suddenly there was the sound of a violent crack; the sound of wood splintering. The shouting and calls from their pursuers changed in urgency and focus as their ship lurched peculiarly. The ship had finally hit the reef hidden beneath the waves and it had rended a hole in their hull. The sudden lurch as the ship took in water disturbed the reverie of the magician, who stopped chanting and looked at his surroundings, as if seeing them for the first time. The sails of the ship slackened as the air caught in them was no longer supplemented magically. The distance between the two ships began to grow again.

As the *Sailor's Daughter*, slowly gained ground through the reef and away from their pursuers they could see the panic in the men on the other ship. The rend in the side of the ship must have been large because the ship was beginning to sink. It was unlikely the whole ship would be lost until a storm came along and dislodged it from the reef to float freely back out to sea, or unless the sailors foolishly did this themselves. If they were lucky they might be rescued by another ship before the ship

Child of Rydos

was completely destroyed or before they ran out of provisions. They would get no assistance from a ship under the Rydosian flag though, as they jealously guarded the secret of the use of the reefs from the Narsians. They could see the fury of the magician as he stormed about on the deck of the other ship shouting at the captain, crew and soldiers without discrimination.

Teran and his companions were safe now. They would reach Cheros within the next two days and be able to report their findings there. As Teran contemplated all this, his thoughts were drawn to the companions who they started out their journey with as he wondered if they had made it to Korrath safely, whether they would be reunited there, and whether they had already begun to move the Sambarian forces towards Cheros.

Chapter XIX – Reunion

Morning light was spilling across the plains stretched between Cheros and the forest of Narsos. As it did so it reflected off the armour and weapons of hundreds of soldiers camped in tents across the plain who were rising with the day's beginning, breakfasting and seeing to the duties their officers had posted for the day. In Cheros itself, all the inns in the town had been requisitioned by the army for the higher-ranking officers to sleep in and to provide space for the many meetings occurring to organize the finer details of the planned push into Narsos.

The *Piebald Pony* was one such inn in the common room of which the heads of state from across Sambar now gathered. The room itself had been stripped of its usual furniture and instead a large table was placed in the middle, which was blanketed with maps of the region, such as the Sambarians possessed. Around the edges of the room were comfortable chairs for the conference. On the bar, there were various refreshments for the gathered dignitaries and generals to enjoy. The barman was absent from the room as it was a private conference. Teran, Koran, Xantila and Banir's ship had sailed into the harbour at Cheros early that morning. They had immediately been brought through the town to join the meeting in the inn's common room. When they entered the room they found their earlier companions as well as the assembled rulers of Sambar.

"You made it back safely then." Olin said in his gruff

voice, though a smile broke out across his face. Teloran and Temac both leapt up as they saw the others enter and rushed to embrace them. Relief evident on their faces.

"What happened to your leg?" Koran asked Olin as he looked towards him and realized the reason he was staying seated.

"Long story involving a lost frostling. Will fill you in later." Olin replied and the others looked at him in disbelief.

"And who is this new companion you picked up after you ditched us?" Teloran asked looking towards Banir.

"Oh, that's also a long story." Teran answered, "Let me introduce Banir. We picked him up in Baxen. He's got certain skills which have proved very useful on our journey." He finished mysteriously.

"What sort of skills?" Asked Teloran.

"I'm a thief." Banir answered for himself, causing concerned looks from the gathered nobles in the room who all instinctively reached to pat themselves where their money pouches were. Banir laughed in response, "Don't worry, your belongings are all quite safe. Teran made me promise not to pilfer things from any of you." King Tlanic of Laconia looked scandalized by the remark, but Olin just laughed in response, breaking the slight tension in the room.

"I can see why you like this one, Teran." Olin said, "Good entertainment value." Teran saw his brother, Seban, across the room and raced across to embrace him.

"It's so good to see you again, my brother." Teran said to Seban.

"I was so worried about you. I prayed to Elerin every

day that you were gone." Seban responded, who was not used to being completely separated from his brother for such a long period.

"How are mother and Loren?" Teran asked his brother.

"Beran has seen them most recently, but I believe they are well. They are still adjusting to life without Father, as we all are." Seban returned. Beran, swordsmaster of Rydos, approached Teran at this point.

"I can confirm His Majesty's words. Your mother and sister are indeed both well." Beran informed Teran. Teran embraced Beran as well, whose tutelage he had grown up under.

Teran brought his focus back to the room and to the task at hand. It was good to catch up with friends and family, but this was not the time. More urgent matters demanded his attention. They needed to go to war. He noticed King Arran in the room and spoke to him to bring the room to focus.

"It is good to see you again, Your Majesty." Teran said to Arran. "I presume that you've brought Conclave up to date on the events in Arinach when we last saw each other."

"Yes, thank you Teran." King Arran responded, "Conclave are aware of all those events. There have been other events though, which your travelling companions are better placed to bring you up to speed with." Teran, Koran and Xantila looked towards Olin, Temac and Teloran.

"We had an interesting journey to Korrath once we left you at Tellac." Teloran began.

"As I mentioned earlier, we were attacked by a frostling. It was on the border between Hrunta and

Arinach. I broke my leg during the battle." Olin continued after Teloran had spoken, then he filled them in on the details of their journey to Korrath and the full details of the battle with the frostling.

"But what was a frostling doing on the Hruntan border?" Xantila asked.

"What is a frostling?" Added Banir.

"Fearsome beasts of living ice that live on the northern ice land wastes, which cause my people no end of trouble." Rhan Orin answered.

"We've no idea how the frostling reached the Hruntan border." Temac continued, "We assume it must have been another magical attack on us."

"We also had further magical attacks, but not quite as mysterious. We know we provoked our antagonists." Teran responded. The gathered Conclave muttered in interest, but Olin continued.

"Let us finish our part of the tale first, otherwise, we might miss an important bit of information." Olin chided.

"Okay, okay." Teran responded, pretending irritation, but the warmth could be heard in his voice.

"We were stationed with the troops gathered around Korrath once we reached the city to report. We discovered a Narsian spy who was poisoning the water supply." Olin continued.

"If Olin hadn't found the spy when he did many more lives would have been lost." King Teslas added at this moment, "Hrunta is very grateful for his diligence and observance."

"You've stationed all the troops from the armies of Sambar along the southern border with Narsos now?" Koran asked.

"Yes." King Gethas of Gerak contributed, "It's a long border spread from here to T'emar in Arinach and beyond. We have no idea where the Narsians will strike so we've had to spread ourselves thinly. We can't afford to leave any parts of the border unprotected." Teran looked towards Koran, Xantila and Banir, the concern evident in all their faces. Teran spoke on their behalf.

"I don't think that is a good idea. We had a horrendous journey into Narsos and out again, which we'll fill you in on. We saw their army. It is colossal. If we split our forces thinly we'll be overwhelmed. I think we have no choice but to concentrate our defensive positions and if that leads to losing land we'll have to accept it in the short term until we can reclaim it." Teran spoke confidently and concernedly. The room responded with lots of grumbling about this plan.

"There is more." Koran interjected loudly over the discontent voices, "Their army is most certainly aided by magicians with all sorts of magic well beyond our understanding. You already know about the events in Arinach, but hear the details of our journey after we left King Arran." With this the room quieted again. They may have been upset by Teran's words, but they were not stupid or rude. They had sent these people on this mission specifically for this sort of reconnaissance because they valued their skills and opinions.

"We left Arin and made straight for T'emar near the border with Narsos, but our first trouble reached us before we'd even left Arinach." Teran began, "Agachen, the magician who had manipulated King Arran, accosted us on the road. He used magic to paralyze us as would have called fire out of thin air to burn us all if Xantila hadn't been able to counteract his magic."

Child of Rydos

"The Rangers have magic?" King Tlanic of Laconia asked, both surprised and discomforted.

"Maybe with the help of the Rangers of Azin we will be able to fight the magic that Narsos will throw at us?" Teslas of Hrunta suggested before Xantila had the opportunity to interrupt their musings.

"I am sure the Rangers will be willing to help fight this enemy as their influence affects us all. We are not the magicians you suppose us to be, though." Xantila disappointed them, "Our gifts stem from an affinity with nature and are not at all in the same league as the magic that magicians, like Agachen and the others we met, wield. It was only because he was not expecting it that I was able to make any difference at all to the encounter with Agachen." She explained.

"After we scared off Agachen, we continued into Narsos." Teran continued the story. "It was then that our trouble really started. We were captured by slavers and marched to I'sos. Banir helped us escape and we took flight towards Ptanga."

"I sense there are a lot more details to this story." King Gethas commented.

"A lot more," His son, Koran, agreed, "But they aren't relevant to our current discussion."

"We encountered the Narsian army in the fields west of I'sos. There were at least a thousand camp fires at night." Teran continued.

"That many?" King Arran asked in concern. Teran and his companions nodded.

"Under the cover of night, we skirted around the army. We took refuge over night in a tomb." Teran said.

"That was horrible." Banir interjected. The gathered crowd looked intent upon the story.

"We were attacked by the ghost of a dead soldier whose tomb we had camped in. His spirit or body had obviously been ensorceled at some point in the past." Koran explained.

"We escaped." Teran said, "But in the process, we caught the attention of the army. We stole some horses to reach Ptanga, with the Narsian army in pursuit. In Ptanga we used father's contacts, Seban, to secure passage by ship to Cheros."

"That was fun." Koran commented, "We were chased by a ship whose pursuit was aided by magic. If we hadn't reached the Ptanga reef when we did we would have been captured." The gathered company sat in silence considering the report.

"Do you have a firm idea of how many magicians the Narsian army has supporting them and of their ability?" King Gethas asked them.

"No." Teran answered, "But if we take account of all the strange incidents that have happened and of the direct attacks we received I think we need to take this very seriously. We have to ask the Mystics of Laconia for help." King Tlanic snorted in response to Teran's suggestion.

"I doubt the Mystics will help us. I'm not sure we can trust them either." Tlanic said.

"I don't think we have much choice." King Gethas said after some consideration, "We cannot afford *not* to ask for their help."

"But after they abandoned us after the last war five hundred years ago, can we really trust them now?" King Tlanic asked.

"That's our history, but I'm not sure we should trust it fully." Koran interjected, "I've read a lot of our history

Child of Rydos

from Am Bære's time and precisely what caused the Mystics to abandon us and head into seclusion is not clear. Whatever the reason though, we need their help."

"I am willing to lead a small envoy to plead for their assistance." Offered Teran.

"Does everyone agree?" King Gethas asked. There was a general assent.

"I will take Koran, Xantila and Banir with me again, if they and Conclave will agree." Teran requested.

"Agreed." King Gethas confirmed and the others nodded in assent.

"If we pass through Azin Heart again on our journey northwards I will enlist the aid of the Rangers to come south and join the fray." Xantila offered.

"Good. All the support we can muster will be much welcome. Now we need to discuss our plans for forging southwards to fight the Narsian army." Rhan Orin refocused the discussion.

"We focus our troops into two main forces. One forging southwards from here in Cheros and the other gathered around T'emar. We try and take the fight to them, before they invade our lands in force." King Arran suggested.

"I don't like the idea of leaving parts of our border unguarded, but given the reports we've received, I'm not sure we have much choice." King Teslas offered his opinion into the discussion.

"Since Arran's and Teslas' people are most affected by this decision, since they are both agreed, shall the rest of Conclave concur with their position?" King Gethas asked. This caused an erruption of mummering and discussion, but eventually it was agreed as the only viable option.

Reunion

"Until we've established a foothold in Narsos we should maintain two bases of operation. One here and one in T'emac." Rhan Orin suggested, "Olin can remain here to manage this centre, because his broken leg incapacitates him. We need to establish who will support each base of operations and who will lead troops on the ground."

"Stay here and miss the action?" Olin spluttered angrily, "You must be joking father." Orin look at Olin with a fierce stare.

"Don't be foolish, Olin. You still need to heal or you'll be no use to us. You can join us further south once we've established a foothold in Narsos. You may even be healed enough to lead some of the action by then." Orin told his son.

"I think it makes sense if the Laconians support Arinach as our lands are directly north of theirs." King Tlanic suggested.

"Yes. And Gerak will support Hrunta." King Gethas agreed.

"Because of the lay of the forest land and the location of the Narsian army, I think it more likely that the Narsians will attack Hrunta first, so we Ruors will lend our forces to the Hruntan effort, but be ready to change tack if fortunes should change." Rhan Orin commented.

"I guess that leaves the Rydosians." King Seban commented at last, after all the others had spoken, "I suggest that we'll take the battle to the sea and try and secure the port of Ptanga. We already have some agents there who might help us make the port and take the city. Then we have a secure base in Narsos from which to supply the army with speed using the shipping lanes."

"This seems like as sound a plan as we can muster for

now." King Gethas suggested, "Let's get some rest today and tomorrow we can set our plans in motion." Conclave agreed the matter and then was formally closed. The rest of the evening was spent in a more relaxed manner with friends and relatives catching up with each other and sharing stories. The impending war and the unknown danger of the magicians of Narsos cast a sombre note across the evening's gentle relaxation though and created an edge to conversation. When eventually the gathered crowd did retire for the night, sleep was hard won and the cruel morning came all too soon.

Chapter XX – Gorilla Warfare

Conclave put their plans into action the very next morning. Whilst the Sambarians did not muster their forces with alacrity, for they had little to no cheeriness about the prospect of the forthcoming war with the Narsians, they were speedy and efficient once the decision for a preemptive strike had been made. In this they, unknowingly, echoed the actions of their ancestors five hundred years previously who had also taken the fight to Narsos upon the rumours of war.

Teran, Xantila, Koran and Banir, freshly provisioned with horses, equipment and food had forged northwards. King Arran had returned with his retinue towards Arinach. He was accompanied by King Tlanic, who had sent runners to his troops still stationed near Azin to instruct them to move camp to T'emar. King Teslas began to move his troops southwards towards the border with Narsos. Gethas and Orin whose troops, already on the move southwards, were still far to the north, sent runners to update them and encourage them to speed their journey to the Narsian border. The Rydosians fleet, rather than prepare immediately for an attack on the city of Ptanga sent the majority of their ships northwards to carry the Gerakan and Ruor troops more swiftly southwards than they would manage on foot. The remainder of their ships were sent to patrol the waters near Ptanga to keep an eye on the disputed waters there.

Within a few days, the first of the Hruntan troops

were ready to make their way into the forest that separated Narsos from Hrunta. The forest was too thick with trees for the Hruntan troops to move through it in formation and on horseback, so the vanguard of their army made their way on foot through the trees, sending scouts ahead. The horses were, for the meantime, being looked after with the baggage train which followed at a more stately pace behind the front line of the advance.

The advance was a slow process. Behind the frontline troops, a strip of the forest was being cleared in order to allow the easier movement of reserve troops and supplies. The first day of movements was uneventful for the main army, but the scouts had a number of encounters with the same beasts that had attacked Teran and his companions. The scouts and the army were invading their territory and upsetting their pattern of life, which caused the animals to become aggressive. The scouts had to work more closely together than they usually would in the open landscape in order to not be hurt by these upset animals which, they had learned from locals living near the edge of the forest on the Hruntan side, were called gorillas.

The first night had fallen since their foray into the forest and the army was camped in a dispersed pattern, as the trees would allow. A large guard was set because it was difficult to see the approach of any potential hostiles given the reduced visibility in the woodland. The scouts had all returned and Teslas, Gethas, Orin and Temac had gathered to discuss the advance so far. Kiesan, General of Gerak's army, was still with the Gerakan troops further north, as were the other aides, and Olin had been left behind in Cheros for the time being, despite his vocal complaints.

"So far everything has gone as expected." Teslas said to the others, in the dim light of the oil lamp which was lighting the inside of the command tent.

"Well, except for those gorillas slowing the advance of our scouts." Temac commented to his brother.

"Yes, but they, at least, don't seem to have anything to do with Narsos or their magicians. They're just native animals to the forest." Teslas countered his brother.

"Do we continue much the same tomorrow, as planned?" Gethas asked the others.

"Yes," Orin responded, as the others nodded, "And each slow day of advance in the forest here at least brings our reserve forces from the north closer to hand." Finished the Rhan, reflecting how worried they all were about the reported size of the Narsian army and the current thin spread of the Sambarian troops. Despite the relative ease of their march southwards so far, the night brought little rest to those in command as they thought about all that was to come. The troops also found rest difficult, surrounded by the unfamiliar noises of the forest, not to mention their elevated adrenalin levels that accompanied the knowledge that they really were going to war with Narsos again.

The soldiers rose early the next morning, efficiently broke camp, and the army continued forging southwards, hoping to get clear through the forest and establish a foothold in Narsos, which they could fortify and supply easily. They had plenty of wood for constructing fortifications as they had been keeping everything they had collected as they opened a clear path for the supply train behind them to follow the army southwards. Today, though, was to be very different from the previous one.

The sun was shining through the leaves and all was suspiciously silent as Ferin, one of the Hruntan scouts, crept forward.

"I hate this forest." He thought to himself, "It feels creepy and it is far too difficult to scout easily and full of those annoying gorillas." There were other scouts both to his left and his right, just keeping within earshot of each other. Ferin heard a noise to his right like the snapping of wood underfoot, breaking the silence, and turned to berate his companion. What he saw made him freeze momentarily, as the scout's body slumped to the floor, his head having been caved in by another man wielding a club, who now had his eyes fixed on Ferin. Ferin spun to his left to see the scout there fall to the ground, an arrow having sprouted from his chest. Ferin swore and spun northwards and ran as fast as his legs would carry him back to the vanguard of the Hruntan force. They had found the Narsians and they were a lot further north than had been expected.

Ferin felt one arrow, and then another, whiz past his head and still he kept running. His legs ached with the exertion. Aching and pain were good. It meant he was still alive. He did not look back, but focused on the path ahead, not wanting to trip, whilst in flight over the uneven terrain. Eventually he could see the vanguard ahead of him, but he did not slow. He did not trust that the Narsians had not pursued him fearlessly right into the Hruntan army.

Temac saw Ferin racing towards their front line and recognized him as one of the Hruntan scouts. He knew something was wrong, so ordered the front line both to expect attack and to make a space for Ferin to pass through. No attack came immediately, but Ferin sped through the opening in the front line before it closed behind him. He did not stop until he was sure he was far enough behind the front line to be out of the range of enemy arrows. Temac caught up with Ferin as he was bending over, trying to catch his breath.

"Report." Ordered Temac, cutting straight to the chase.

"Nar…sian scouts… no more than … half a … mile away." Ferin reported, needing to take deep breaths as he spoke. Temac swore.

"That means the Narsian army has already mobilized northwards towards Hrunta, since Teran's group encountered them." Temac responded.

"I would guess that the army is not far behind. The Narsian scouts were very keen not to leave any of us alive." Ferin continued, having regained some of his composure.

"Things are going to get messy rather shortly then." Temac said, "The forest is no place for a clean battle. Go and report your story to my brother and the other commanders, they are back there discussing the organization of the supplies, I believe." Temac ordered, waving in a general manner towards a cluster of officers slightly further north, "I'll report this news to the front and make sure that we're ready for an attack."

Orders were given and the vanguard formed up, progressing very slowly now through the forest, expecting attack at any moment. Scouts were still being sent in advance, but they were keeping closer together and closer to the friendly line. Still any advance notice of the Narsian front was better than none. When the first skirmish came, it came quickly and it was fierce. The Hruntans outnumbered the Narsians, indicating clearly that they were not encountering the full force that Teran and his companions had seen near I'sos. The Narsians, more used to the forest and more used to fighting on the ground than the Hruntans, were easily able to hold their own. The day descended into relative chaos. In the midst of the trees it was difficult to maintain a strong line and the fighting quickly became messy, with small groups from opposing sides attacking each other as opportunity arose. There was no clear advantage for either the Hruntans or the Narsians and as night descended, causing both sides to retreat. No ground had been gained or lost since the fighting first commenced.

As darkness fell and the fighting lessened as troops withdrew for the night, the Hruntans regrouped and secured their lines. King Teslas met with Orin, Gethas and Temac to discuss the fighting so far and tactics for the dawn, which would inevitably bring further fighting.

"I hate all this close fighting!" Exclaimed Teslas, slamming his, recently removed, gloves down on the table. "These forests are only fit for gorillas. I can't wait until we can do battle on the open plains."

"I know what you mean." Temac agreed with his brother.

"You're both too used to fighting on horseback." Orin commented.

"You can't tell me that you think this sort of fighting is easy." Teslas countered.

"No. Skirmishing like this, not knowing what side an attack is going to come from, is no one's idea of a good battle." Orin said, pacifyingly.

"How long do you think until we get any substantial reinforcements from the north?" Teslas asked Gethas and Orin.

"Difficult to say." Responded Gethas, "Armies move much more slowly than individuals, so probably at least a week before the advanced guard manages to join us. Perhaps less if the Rydosian ships can bring some reinforcements sooner."

"Without greater numbers, I don't think we're going to be able to advance much further south." Temac commented, "Neither force seems to have the clear advantage at the moment."

"I was hoping we'd get further south before we encountered the Narsian army." Gethas said, "When Teran gave his report, it didn't sound like they had mobilized their army yet."

"I don't think they've mobilized their whole force." Added Orin, "At least, if they have then they haven't sent them all north into this part of the forest, if Teran's report of their numbers is correct."

"His report will be accurate." Temac commented, "Teran is not prone to exaggeration. He has a clear head upon his shoulders for one who is relatively young."

"I agree with Temac's assessment of Teran." Said Gethas, who had known Teran from a young age when he had played with his own son, Koran, when court occasions brought the families together.

"We have to assume then, that Teran's excursion into Narsos is what has stirred the hornets' nest and brought these troops northwards." Teslas surmised.

"That would seem likely." Gethas agreed.

"All we can do then, is continue the fight and hope that our reinforcements arrive before any of theirs do, allowing us to gain a hold on the plains south of this gorilla-infested forest." Orin stating aloud what they all knew.

"One thing to be thankful for." Temac interjected, "Is that this advance party seems not to have brought any magicians with them."

"Yes, something to be thankful for, I suppose." Gethas said darkly.

"Or is it possible that their magical ability has been exaggerated?" Teslas asked.

"The experiences of my companions and of Teran's companions were real enough and not exaggerated." Temac was quick to respond, irritated by the implication that their experiences were false or ill-reported.

"Indeed." Gethas said, trying to prevent any further argument, "We must assume they have their own reasons for not using magic yet." There was little more to say that evening. Further discussion would not give any more advantage, but more sleep would. They retired in order to have clear heads for the fighting the morning would inevitably bring.

Arran, Tlanic and their retinues made good time across country from Cheros, through the Hruntan plains via Baxen to T'emar where they joined the bulk of the Arinachian army. They had encountered no trouble travelling across Sambarian lands. Under normal circumstances they would not have expected any, but everything had been far from normal in recent weeks and months and it was a relief when they reached the relative safety of T'emar and the Arinachian army. It would still be some time before the Laconian forces were able to join the Arinachians, but delay was not advisable, so the Arinachian army had advanced southwards towards I'sos.

The eastern advance was a lot easier than the western advance. The route between T'emar and I'sos had become a regular trade route, which meant that a path through the forest had already been cleared for traders. Though it was not wide enough for the full Arinachian army, without enlargement, it was a good start and much easier than making their way through dense, unmanaged forestland. There also had very few encounters with the native gorillas because, having become used to the regular traders using the route, the naturally shy creatures avoided the road.

The disadvantage of such an easy route southwards into Narsos was that it was similarly easy for any Narsian troops trying to invade northwards. On the second day of their march southwards along the traders' road their scouts met an advance party from the Narsian army and the battle was joined. The fighting here was much more ordered as the clear road allowed a much more established line of defense. At the edges of the road, where the forest threw thicker, fighting was more haphazard, but the Arinachian forces held their own against the Narsians. It was evident that, here also, the Narsians had not committed the full might of their forces. They did not seem to have expected to encounter the Arinachians so far south and during the course of the day were slowly beaten back southwards by the superior numbers of the Arinachians forces.

As night fell the Narsians retreated back from the frontline of the Arinachian forces, though they remained in view, almost as if they were goading the Arinachians to attempt a night-time attack. Arran ordered a watch kept and got his reserves to build a palisade back from the front line in order to protect the bulk of the army

Child of Rydos

and to form a defensive position if the Narsians managed to beat them back northwards on the following day. He hoped it would not be needed but he was a cautious man by nature and wanted to make their position as defensible as possible. He knew that the fight, now joined, would be long and any victory would be hard-won.

Chapter XXI – Northern Run

Teran, Koran, Xantila and Banir had left Cheros at first light, the day after Conclave had met. They headed northwards towards Quin, where they would cross the River Hrun before striking northeast towards Qatar and on through Azin forest, towards Yellath and into the mountains where they hoped they could find the mystics. They were well provisioned with supplies and being on horseback one again was a pleasant change to either having to make their way on foot, or by sea. The weather was warm and the sky clear as they set out and if they had not had such urgent business it would have been a pleasant journey. They had been given papers by each of the heads of state, which would enable them to requisition further supplies, including fresh mounts, to aid their journey. As such they rode at a speed which might be considered reckless, not worrying about whether they wore out the horses, knowing they would be able to procure new mounts if necessary.

At the speed they were travelling the journey was hard, but it meant that they made good time. They encountered very few people on the road because the majority of the Hruntans, being nomadic, had moved to the lands to the south in order to support the army. King Teslas had told them that those with young children and the more vulnerable or aged members of the population had migrated northwards, away from danger, over the River Hrun to the lands between Quin and the Gerakan border, so they would expect to meet the Hruntans only after they had passed into the northern parts of the country.

They rode into the town of Quin late into the evening of their second day of travel. They had made the journey in record time, but the horses were completely exhausted. Indeed, it was possible that the horses would never recover. They would be able to get new horses in Quin and they would get the best available thanks to their paper warrants from King Teslas, but the obvious ill treatment of their mounts would win them no favour amongst the Hruntans living in Quin. Most people were in their homes by the time of night they reached the town, but those who were still out and about in the streets were indeed casting scowls towards anyone who would overwork horses as they had. In order to avoid any further attention, they made their way to the first inn that they could find, which turned out to be *The Nomad's Head*.

As they brought their horses into the stable yard they could see it was clean and well-appointed, which served to raise their hopes of the comfort they might find inside after a night on the road and two days hard riding. They gave their horses to the ostler, who looked less than impressed, but took their coin and stabled the horses whilst the companions went inside. The inside of the inn was not a disappointment. The common room was spacious and clean with well-oiled tables and matching wooden chairs. The room was busy with evening drinkers, though not so packed that they were not able to find a table. The kitchen had closed for the evening, but there was still a little stew left which the inn keeper had his wife heat up for the travellers, providing them with good ale to wash it down with too. They finished their food then retired for the evening. As most of the drinkers in the common room were locals there was plenty of space for the night and Teran, Xantila, Koran and Banir had their pick of rooms to choose from.

By the time the sun broke over the horizon the next morning, Teran and his companions were already on the road again. They had risen whilst it was still dark and managed to acquire fresh horses from the ostler. He probably would not have sold them new mounts, given Hruntan pride over their horses and the obvious poor way their previous mounts had been treated, but the papers they had from King Teslas brooked no argument. They had left the town through the north gate and reached the ford across the river. The River Hrun was extremely wide at this point as its flow slowed and split into a broad delta before the waters spilled into the Great Western Sea. As they forged into the shallowest point of the river, which was used as a ford, they began to hear a strange noise coming from the east.

"What is that noise?" Asked Banir, the first of the companions to notice the noise, cocking his head as though to hear better. They paused in their tracks to consider the noise, which they could all now hear. That turned out to be a mistake. As they looked eastwards and upstream they suddenly saw what was causing the noise.

"What on earth?!" Exclaimed Koran.

"Ride as hard as you can. Come on!" Shouted Xantila, as a huge surge of water pulsed down the river towards them. They urged their horses, which needed little encouragement, into a dead run towards the opposite bank of the river and dry land. The river was broad, though, and the water surge was moving towards

Child of Rydos

them with unnatural speed, seeming to gain momentum.

Teran was in the lead on his mount and barely reached the opposite bank in time, he could feel the splash of water against him as the surge approached. Panting for breath he turned around in his saddle, hoping his companions were behind him. He saw that Xantila and Koran were literally just behind him, mounted on their horses and drawing deep breaths, just as he was, but Banir was still crossing the ford. The surge was nearly upon him; he was not going to make it. There was nothing that Teran, Koran and Xantila could do, except watch in horror as the water bore down upon Banir. They could see from the look in his eyes that he knew it too.

Just as the first wave of the surge was about to hit Banir and his horse, Banir, loosing his feet from his stirrups, drew his feet up on to the saddle. With a mighty push of his legs, he leapt from the horse's back towards the shore line. The water hit him as he did, obscuring the scene before Teran, Koran and Xantila in a confusion of waves and spray.

When the surge passed Banir and his horse were no longer visible in the ford. Teran, the colour drained from his face, darted forward to see if he could discover what had become of him.

"Banir?" Teran cried out, "Banir?" There was no response. Teran looked down stream and saw, by the riverbank, a tree, the large roots of which broke through the ground, gnarled and twisted, and into the nearby water. Tangled amongst the roots there lay Banir. "Xan, Koran, come quickly!" Teran shouted to them as he leapt off his horse and ran down stream to where Banir's body lay.

Reaching Banir's body, Teran shook it and called his name, but there was no response. Koran caught up with Teran and together they lifted his body away from the water's edge and laid him on the dry ground.

"He's not breathing." Said Teran, having pressed his ear to Banir's mouth to listen for the slightest signs life. Teran, having grown up in a seafaring nation, albeit in a position of privilege, was familiar with the effects of drowning and knew that there might still be some hope. He opened Banir's mouth and turned his head to one side, to let water in the nose and mouth trickle out. Then he turned Banir's head back, pinched his nose and proceeded to breath deep breaths into Banir's lungs using his own. It seemed to make little difference. Teran paused in his actions to see if Banir had begun to breathe by himself, then pinched his nose again and continued to breathe air into Banir's lungs. Koran and Xantila were not sure how to help and so stood by, looking on anxiously over Teran and the prone boy.

Time seemed to slow as Teran continued giving breaths to Banir. It did not seem to be working. Tears welled in Teran's eyes and he was on the verge of giving up when suddenly Banir coughed, water spurting from his mouth.

"Banir, are you okay?" Teran asked, the concern evident in his voice. Banir could not respond as he was still coughing up water and taking deep breaths, but he managed a weak smile. "I think he'll be all right now, once he has recovered from the water on his lungs." Teran told the others, who were looking on in amazement at the scene, sure that Teran must have performed some magic to bring Banir back from the verge of death. "It's not magic." Teran said, catching the look in their eyes, "Any sailor worth his salt would be able to do the same to a half-drowned comrade. You just have to encourage the lungs to work again so that they can throw out the water in them and draw in fresh air." Banir was coming back to his senses again now and was slowly sitting up.

"Thank you, Teran." He said, "I thought I was a goner there for sure." Teran, embarrassed by the attention, just smiled.

"He did manage to lose your horse though." Koran commented, trying to bring some levity to the situation.

"I don't think I could have resuscitated a horse, even if it hadn't been swept away in the surge." Teran said in rejoinder.

"Being a horse down is going to slow us." Banir said.

"Yes," Said Teran, "But I don't fancy crossing the ford again to buy another one in Quin. I've never experienced anything like that surge before. Something about it did not seem natural."

"We can always try picking up a horse from the Hruntans who have come north of the river, away from the impending war in the south." Xantila suggested.

"A sensible idea, I think, Xan." Agreed Koran, "I agree with you Teran. There was definitely something unnatural about that surge. I've never heard of anything like it happening before in this river and it hasn't been raining enough for a water build up like that."

"The source of the River Hrun is in the forests of Narsos." Teran commented, "I think we can assume that someone is turning their magical attention on us again. Somehow they must know the purpose of our journey and be trying to prevent us from reaching the mystics to enlist their help."

"I don't know how they could possibly know all that and be tracking us, whilst being so far away." Xantila said, "But I cannot think of a better explanation either." Unsettled by the river's surge and by the result of their discussion the companions set to the road again. Teran lifted Banir onto his own horse, so that they would ride doubled up. Banir was small and relatively lightweight, an advantage to his chosen profession of being a thief, so the two of them did not overburden Teran's horse too much. Nonetheless, the companions had to set a slightly slower pace as they travelled north towards Qatar.

It had taken Teran, Koran, Xantila and Banir three days to reach Qatar. They had, luckily, passed a Hruntan camp around midday of their first day out of Quin. Thus, they had been able to stop for a good lunch and also to purchase a new mount for Banir, so that he and Teran did not have to continue to ride doubled up, slowing their progress. Their stay in Qatar was uneventful. They stayed in an inn of no particular noteworthiness for the night before leaving Qatar and finally striking northeastwards towards Azin forest and Laconia.

Evening was beginning to fall on their first day beyond Qatar. The companions were looking for somewhere suitable to camp which would be relatively sheltered from the wind and also easy to defend if necessary. Koran had been scouting ahead and was just returning to the group. He had a smile on his face, so the others presumed that he had found a suitable place for their camp. As he approached them his smile fell from his face.

"What's wrong?" Banir asked.

"Look!" Koran said, pointing behind them. Banir, Teran and Xantila turned in their saddles to see what had concerned Koran.

"That's not possible!" Teran said in alarm.

"Who wasn't paying attention to our rear?" Koran asked.

"No, I mean it isn't possible. They were not there a moment ago." Teran responded. Bearing down upon the four companions was a platoon of what looked like Narsian cavalry.

"Ride!" Shouted Koran, knocking them out of revere and spurring them into action. There was no time to think now, action was required. They could not hope to defeat a platoon of soldiers; their only hope was to ride as hard as possible for Azin forest and hope for the aid of the Rangers again.

The chase was on, but the companions were able to maintain their lead on the soldiers. The forest was some distance away. This was going to be a long pursuit, as long as none of their horses threw a shoe or became exhausted, in which case it would be much, much shorter. Darkness descended completely and the only light to guide their way was that of the stars, for the moon was barely past new. They could no longer see their pursuers, but they knew they were not safe yet because they could hear the sound of the soldiers riding hard to catch them.

Suddenly they could feel trees around them as they plunged under the boughs at the edge of Azin forest. It was dark and they had to slow to avoid plowing straight into a tree. Thankfully their pursuers would also have to slow once they reached the forest too. They continued to make their way blindly through the trees, branches slapping against their faces. They could hear the crash of the soldiers close behind and their panic began to rise in their throats even more. Their pursuers were being more reckless than they were and not caring if some of them rode hard into a tree and so were gradually gaining on them.

The companions were being outflanked and they now had no choice by to try and stand and fight if they wanted to keep their lives. At a signal from Teran they pulled back on their reigns and drew their swords. Banir and Koran, who had been bringing up the rear, swiveled around to meet the attack head on. Xantila and Teran turned to their sides to meet those who had been trying to outflank them. Within moments the soldiers were upon them. The dense forest made it difficult for their assailants to swarm them at once, which enabled them to make a semblance of a stand against the superior force. They were not facing ill-equipped local brigands though, but trained soldiers and Banir, in particular, was no seasoned soldier.

Banir let out a cry as a thrust from his assailant passed through his guard and scored a hit on his left arm. The shout caused Teran to turn, overcoming his martial training, ill-advisedly responding to a companion in need when he himself was under heavy attack. The turn nearly caused Teran to lose his head as his attacker took advantage of his distraction. Teran knew that the end was near for him and his companions unless they were lucky again and a Ranger scouting party was in this region of the forest.

"Hold out just a little longer." Xantila shouted to the others, "Help is on its way."

"How can you possibly know?" Koran asked.

"The forest. I can feel it now that I am close to home again. My people approach." Xantila answered, simply. Thankfully, they did not have to wait long for Xantila's words to be proved true.

"Drop you weapons!" A voice shouted from the shadows. The Narsian soldiers did not respond to the command, they simply grinned and renewed their attack on the companions with increased ferocity. The Rangers did not wait any longer. Their arrows flew through the air and the Narsian troops were quickly felled. When those who were attacking the companions died, the remaining Narsian troops stepped forward to take up the offensive. The Rangers had little choice but to kill all the attackers.

"It seems your new friends, Xan, bring trouble with them into our home again." The Ranger who had spoken before said to Xantila.

"It is good to see you too, Janis." Answered Xantila, smiling at her old friend as the Rangers came out of the shadows to embrace Xantila and meet her companions.

"Are you okay, Banir?" Teran asked him, coming over to inspect his injury.

"It is just a light wound, I think." Banir said, putting on a brave face.

"Kala, here, has some skill with healing, let her look at the boy." Janis said, indicating another of the Rangers, realizing Teran's anxiety over Banir's injury. Kala came over to treat Banir immediately, a slight frown of concern on her face.

"You will be okay." Kala said to Banir after a short while of examining him, the frown vanishing from her face. She drew a liquid phial from her backpack and poured it in Banir's wound. "This will help keep the wound from infection." She said before drawing bandages from the same bag and beginning to wrap them around Banir's arm.

Once Teran could see that Banir would be fine he turned his mind to other matters.

"We need to examine these bodies." Teran said, "We need to know if they are real Narsian soldiers and if there is any indication of how they made it this far north." Koran, Xantila and Teran began to move amongst the dead soldiers, checking their bodies. It took some time to search all the bodies. The Rangers split into two groups. The first group dug a mass grave, not wanting to leave the bodies to rot above ground. The second group went to search for a suitable place to camp for the remainder of the night that was not too far off, but not immediately next to the site of the fight.

"They are all normal soldiers, no unusual identifying marks, definitely of Narsian descent though." Koran said, looking up from the search to talk to the others.

"These are the same." Xantila responded to Koran's comments, with this short report on the bodies she had examined, "There is no indication how they got here."

"Come and look at this one." Teran said, waving the others over to him. "This one is different to the others. He looks like the other soldiers on the surface, but under his armour he is dressed like those mysterious ambushers we encountered last time we were in Azin forest. And look at this." Teran twisted the dead man's arm to reveal the underside. On his forearm was the mark of the sword and serpent that those first ambushers had been tattooed with. The mark that had followed them ever since they first set out from Ariss.

"Interesting." Koran commented, "Different from the first ambush, but related."

"I think we can assume that some magic spirited these soldiers from the south to pursue us into Azin forest." Teran added, "And that this man was the one in charge."

"It is unlikely that they managed to break through defenses in the south and ride so blatantly this far north without notice." Xantila agreed.

"More magic?" Banir asked, shuffling up to the others, his treatment having been finished for the time being and not wanting to miss out on any of the discussion, "I think it is safe to assume that somehow we are being tracked." The others looked at him sharply with concern as he continued, "How else would we be constantly running into magical trouble without there being reports across Sambar of rampant magical activity?"

"A very apt point." Teran conceded.

"The real question is *why* are we being followed?" Banir continued. The others had no clear answer to that question. How could the enemy possibly know the companions' intentions and how could they have known from so early on in their travels, well before they broke across the border and travelled first into Arinach and then into Narsos itself.

"Are you ready to leave this site and come and get some food and rest for the evening?" Janis approached and asked them, breaking them out of their reverie.

"Food?" Banir asked, "Sounds good." Causing the other companions to smile and to collect themselves and join the Rangers at their evening camp.

Chapter XXII – Serfdom is not an Option

The next morning came all too soon. Teran, Xantila, Koran and Banir had slept well, but it had been late before they had finally been able to rest and they had a long journey over the next two days to reach Azin Heart. After they had breakfasted and broken camp the Rangers led them on foot through the forest. After a while, Teran began to feel the strange tingling sensation he had felt at the back of his neck the last time he had been led by the Rangers to their home. Again he thought it best not to mention the sensation, though he had grown to know and trust Xantila in the intervening time. He was not sure of the reason for his reticence, but he fixed his eyes firmly forward, as if unattentive to his surroundings, and allowed himself to be led onwards, Banir to his right and Koran to his left. Xantila was just ahead of them. She walked as if not quite sure whether to remain with her travelling companions or with her people, caught between the two.

As they walked on, Teran perceived Banir slowly coming closer to him, as if by chance, but Teran suspected that was a cultivated act. His suspicions were confirmed when Banir whispered to him.

"I think there is magic at play here." Banir whispered through the side of his mouth to Teran.

"Tingling at the back of the neck?" Teran whispered back. Banir nodded his head almost imperceptibly. "Don't worry. I believe it is the Rangers' magic. They don't like people knowing where they live. I think it easier if we don't let them catch on we know. I doubt we'd be able to find Azin Heart again without their help anyway." Teran continued. Banir nodded again and slowly moved slightly away from Teran. Teran subtly looked around. He did not think that any of the Rangers, including Xantila, had noticed their exchange. He took a subtle look at Koran. Koran seemed to be in the same trance that he had been the last time the Rangers took them to their home. It was interesting that neither himself nor Banir seemed to be affected by the Rangers' magic as Koran, and presumably most people, were.

The day wore on. They did not stop for lunch. Instead, the Rangers passed them travel rations to eat on the move. As on their first journey through Azin forest, they camped in the midst of the forest that night, before continuing in the same manner the following day. They walked all that day and evening fell before they finally reached Azin Heart. They were again taken to the great tree and the council chamber where the wise one, Xera, waited for them, with many other senior Rangers.

"It is good to see you again." Xera smiled to Teran and Koran, "And to meet your new companion."

"Banir, my lady." Said Banir, introducing himself and instinctively bowing. Xantila came forward and embrased Xera.

"Mother." She said simply.

"It is good to see you too, my child." Xera responded, smiling even more. Xera then clapped her hands and Rangers brought in a veritable banquet of forest foods, from berries and nuts, to deer and game. "I thought you might be hungry after such a long day's journey."

"Thank you, Xera, we are indeed hungry!" Teran responded and they sat to eat. The conversation continued over dinner.

"Tell me, what news do you have from the south? I sense a growing unease there." Xera asked Teran. Thus, Teran, found himself again reporting on all their activities. Koran, Banir and Xantila only jumped in with further detail when it seemed Teran might miss some point or other. Xera listened attentively whilst they spoke, only interrupting occasionally when she wanted clarification about particular parts of the story. Once Teran had brought Xera up to the present day, she turned to her daughter, Xantila, and asked,

"You have spent time with the Sambarians. What is your opinion?"

"This danger to the south will affect us all, if the Narsians invade and have freedom to roam all the lands up to the borders of Azin. Our skills alone will not be able to protect us. We should send what aid we can to help them resist the threat from Narsos." Xantila gave her expert opinion. Xera nodded.

"I agree with you my daughter," Xera said, "But I must leave this decision to the council of Rangers. I am their guide, but not their ruler." Then Xera turned to Teran, "You have a long journey ahead of you still, if you plan to entreat the Laconian Mystics for help. Sleep here tonight and continue on your journey tomorrow, refreshed. Xantila will continue with you. The council will meet tonight and you will know our decision by the morning, so that you may be on your way with that knowledge in your hearts."

"Thank you, Xera." Teran responded, bowing low to

the ground.

"Xantila will take you to a place where you can all rest." Xera said, dismissing the party as those on the council of Rangers began to discuss what part they would play in war between the Sambarian nations and Narsos.

Xantila woke the other three, who had been sharing a large room, in the morning. She was already dressed and it looked like she had been out hunting for game in the pre-dawn darkness from the equipment she had strapped to her. Koran gave her a look.

"What?" She asked, "I miss my life here. Thought I'd get a quick fix before we continued our journey north and east."

"Life with these two not adventurous enough for you, Xan?" Banir asked her and she laughed in return.

"It's a good time for us to rise and be on our way. Breakfast is waiting for you just outside." Xantila said.

"Do you know what the council decided?" Koran asked her.

"They will help, of course. They would be foolish to bury their heads in the sand and ignore the threat. We have a much better chance of repelling the Narsians if we work together." Xantila told Koran.

"When will they send a party southwards?" Banir asked.

"Janis has already left with a company at first light this morning. We don't wait around once we've decided to act." Xantila responded, proud of her fellow Rangers. Teran, Koran and Banir dressed and breakfasted and it was barely past the first hour in the morning when the companions set out from Azin heart, mounted again upon their horses. As they left the Ranger city, Xantila spoke to them.

"Make sure you focus on following me. If you don't you may get lost. The forest protects the location of Azin heart."

"I had suspected it might." Teran responded and Xantila looked at him in surprise.

"I think you are more sensitive to magic than you let on." She said. Teran shrugged in response, not sure of what more to say. They rode on in silence for some time as Xantila led them to the north, away from the centre of the forest and towards Dael.

It was the evening of the following day before they reached the edge of the forest and entered into mainland Laconia. Teran had expected that they would have to camp under the stars again, but it was obvious that the land right to the edge of the forest was farmed and in the near distance he could see the smoke from a farmhouse chimney.

"It looks like we might be in luck for a proper bed again this evening." Teran commented to his companions, pointing towards the rising smoke in the evening light.

"There are farmsteads scattered throughout Laconia, so we'll probably be in luck most nights. Assuming that they're willing to put up four strangers for the night." Koran told Teran. Teran looked everyone up and down.

"Well we do look a little rag-tag. Hopefully they'll at least let us sleep in their barn. I'm sure the extra income will be welcome." Teran suggested.

"Speak for yourself." Koran retorted, a grin breaking out across his face.

As they approached the farmstead they were met a

little way down the track from the house by a man they presumed to be the farmer.

"Can I help you?" He asked, obviously slightly wary of the four strangers approaching his home.

"May we stay here tonight?" Koran asked the man.

"You've come from the forest?" The man asked, looking suspicious. It was obvious he was uneasy about the forest and its inhabitants, although he lived at its edge.

"We can pay you. Especially if you could also throw in some food." Teran told the man.

"Pay?" The man seemed surprised that they had planned to offer him money for their board and lodgings. "Well, you can probably stay in the barn. We've some ham my wife has just baked too that you can have for supper." He replied, looking somewhat mollified. The man led them to the barn. There was room for the horses to be stabled below and a ladder led to a roof space, which was obviously used frequently by visitors staying at the farm. The man stood there looking expectantly at Teran, who realized he was waiting for money to change hands before any further hospitality was offered. Teran gave him a generous amount of money to pay for their food and lodgings at which he was obviously pleased. "I'll bring you your food out here for you to eat. You can make a fire just outside the barn if you want to warm yourselves for a while." The man said before leaving them to go inside the house with his earnings.

"Friendly chap, isn't he." Banir commented to his back as he left them.

"Many people are wary of the forest and those who travel within it." Xantila said, "We like it that way. It means we are not disturbed unnecessarily." They made a fire, as the farmer had suggested, and were sitting there chatting when the man returned with the promised ham and they ate and retired for the night.

Their journey through Laconia to Yellath took three and a half days on horseback. Their first night they stayed in the small town of Dael and the next two nights at farmsteads before reaching the ancient city of Yellath. They experienced no further attacks like the one that had chased them into Azin forest a few days previously. In fact, they interacted with very few people at all, as when they passed people in the fields they would run and hide from their attention. The friendliest welcomes they received were from timid, yet inquisitive herds of sheep.

"Why do the people all run and hide from us?" Banir had asked Koran as they were riding, "I don't think we're that imposing."

"The Laconian Kingdom operates using an ancient system which is only slightly better than slavery. Serfs are allotted land to farm and in return are given the protection of the lord of the manor." Koran answered.

"That doesn't sound so bad." Banir repsonded.

"It is okay if you have a good and honest land owner who protects you, but many of the lords take advantage of it, giving minimal protection and demanded great dues." Koran continued.

"It is no wonder that they avoid anyone on horseback. They probably think we've come to extort more money or produce from them." Teran added to the conversation.

Child of Rydos

"That also explains the reluctance of our first host upon meeting us." Banir said astutely, "It wasn't just that we came from the forest, he probably thought we'd demand his food and lodgings for no compensation in return."

"A good point, Ban." Xantila commented. She obviously found serfdom as distasteful as the others did.

"When will the Laconians do away with this system and adopt a farer one?" Banir asked.

"I don't know, Ban." Koran answered, "The other nations in Sambar have petitioned King Tlanic, and his father before him, many times about the issue, but, as yet, they have been unmoved."

"I think Tlanic worries about losing the support of his lords if he distrupts their income and lifestyle too much." Teran contributed to the discussion.

"We will have to resume this political conservation another time." Xantila said, "The Yellath city guards approach and I think we should try and make a good impression." With that comment, their conversation dropped off whilst they introduced themselves to the city guard.

The companions found themselves being hosted by the Lord Mayor of the city of Yellath who was named Gustus. He was evidently a well-fed man of late years, who was used to a life of comfort; fed on the fat of Laconia and protected from life on the borders by the other nations of Sambar. He was tedious company, constantly simpering and fawning over such illustrious guests as the heir apparent to Gerak and the heir presumptive to Rydos. He paid Xantila and Banir less attention, but still fawned upon them, assuming they must be important to travel in such company. The only small advantage to his behavior was that they were not required to say much, other than to graciously thank him for his continued, over-the-top praise. Teran and Koran were long-used to statecraft and able to cope with the Lord Mayor's attitude and Xantila was of great patience, being used to the hunt. Banir, though, was a different matter. Although he was used to patience when waiting to take a mark, this idiot was irritating him beyond belief. Eventually it got too much and he spoke out.

"How can you sit here fawning over us, whilst your people live practically in slavery?" Banir asked Gustus heatedly. Gustus looked confused,

"Has my hospitality been lacking? I don't understand what you're talking about." Teran and Koran both glared at Banir, warning in their eyes. Banir plowed on, unheeding,

"All your wealth and hospitality is built upon the hard work of others." Banir responded.

"All that you have received is of my own table. From my own farms, which my own workers have produced. It is all fairly garnered." Gustus countered, obviously concerned and hurt by Banir's words.

"We've met the workers you talk of. They hardly have free lives." Banir continued.

"They have fair lives. They are protected for what they produce and they are freemen. No slavery is allowed anywhere throughout the nations of Sambar." Gustus now responded with a note of challenge in his voice.

"Forgive our companion." Teran now interjected, putting a hand on Banir's shoulder, "He is young and not used to travelling. He has not yet developed an understanding and appreciation for different cultures and how they operate."

"Well..." Gustus responded, obviously flustered by the whole exchange, "I suppose we must forgive those who are young when they speak unknowingly out of turn." The meeting continued, though Gustus was somewhat less enthusiastic about his guests than he had been earlier in the evening. Their conversation turned towards their goal of enlisting the aid of the Mystics.

"Can you tell us anything about how to find the Mystics of Laconia?" Teran asked Gustus.

"Not much is known of them. They do not interact with the general populace, but there is a pass to the north, up through the foothills into the mountains which is believed to lead to their home." Gustus answered Teran.

"It must be an ancient pass if it leads to the Mystics' home." Koran commented.

"It is," Gustus answered, "At least five hundred years old, but it is not the original home of the Mystics. Our ancient records reveal that they used to live here in the city of Yellath in the time of Am Bære." Teran and Koran looked surprised at this.

"I had not heard that piece of history before." Koran told Gustus.

"It is not well known. It is not a secret, but it was only realized recently when we uncovered an ancient archive during some excavations for some new building works." Gustus responded.

"That is interesting." Teran said, "Was there any more information which might help us find the Mystics, or the details of their reason for leaving here?"

"No." Gustus shook his head, "There were some old

parchments and books, but they are written in a language and script which is not intelligible to us. We have stored them in the city library."

"Do you have plans for those parchments and books?" Teran asked Gustus.

"Why? I told you we can't read them." Gustus asked, plerplexed and wary.

"We need to enlist the aid the Mystics if we hope to win the war to the south." Teran began, "If we do not, them I am certain the Narsians will have the upper hand and it will not be very long before they forge on as far north as Yellath itself."

"What does that have to do with the artifacts we found?" Gustus asked.

"If they belong to the Mystics from a time when they lived in the city here, as you suggest, then perhaps they would welcome them as a gift, encouraging them to be more sympathetic to our plight. I understand that they have little genuine concern for the nations of Sambar." Teran responded. Teran's companions were impressed with Teran's improvised plan and the upfront way he approached Gustus with the idea.

"Hmm..." Gustus mulled over the idea in his head, "I suppose the documents are of less value to us than they would be the Mystics. There is little love lost on them here in Yellath because they keep themselves so separate from the rest of Laconia, but I do not think that they are enemies, so I cannot see what harm could come from giving them at least some of what we have found. I know King Tlanic is campaigning in the south with the armies of Laconia and would value any assistance we can bring. I will make sure you're furnished with a selection of the material which we have archived." There were two things evident to Teran based on Gustus' reflection. Firstly, that he was agreeing to Teran's plan because it would, in all likelihood, raise his standing in the eyes of the King. Secondly, that they had found a lot more material belonging to the ancient Mystics than had been indicated at first and that he was only willing to part with a small fraction of the total.

"I think we must retire for the night to be well rested for our continued journey tomorrow." Koran interjected at this point in the conversation as Banir stifled a large yawn, reflecting how he himself felt.

"Yes, thank you for your hospitality, Mayor Gustus." Xantila paid her respects to the mayor. Gustus seemed pleased by the attention, though Xantila's companions, who knew her rather better than Gustus did, could tell that the mayor's company was not on her list of most enjoyable evenings. A sentiment they all shared. Still good food, warm comfortable beds and washing facilities with warm water, such as Gustus was offering them, were not to be sniffed at.

Chapter XXIII – Foothold

The forest warfare between the Sambarians and the Narsians dragged on. In the west, day by day, the Hruntans gained skill in fighting on foot and amongst the trees, but the Narsian reinforcements were arriving more quickly than the reinforcements from Gerak and Ruorland. In the east, the palisade that King Arran had ordered built enabled the Arinachians to hold their position, but again, the weight of Narsians surging northward towards their outpost prevented them from making any progress towards the south. Until the Laconians arrived, Arran had no chance of beating back the Narsian advance. The silver lining was that though two weeks had passed since the fighting began in earnest, there had been no attacks of a magical nature, which the Sambarians would have been ill-equipped to combat. They were neither able to account for this lack of magic nor reconcile it with the reports of magic issued by Teran and his travelling companions.

Night had fallen in the Sambarian encampment in the west and Gethas, Orin, Teslas and Temac were conducting the end of day debriefing, as had quickly become their custom during this war. They sat by an evening campfire, one of many set in the artificial clearing created by the logging undertaken by the Hruntan forces when they were not fighting the Narsians.

"We just need to hold out for one more day." Gethas said to the others, brandishing a report in his hand. "My runners tell me that the Rydosian ships have brought a sizeable number of our Gerakan and Ruor troops here to the south and that they are even now making their way across the final leagues between the coast and our position to bolster our numbers here." Orin looked pleased, whilst Teslas and Temac looked relieved, though still troubled.

"Are we going to manage to hold out that long?" Teslas asked, "The Narsians very nearly swept over us today and our troops are utterly exhausted as we've had to commit all our reserves in order to maintain our position."

"Send messengers throughout the camp tonight, letting the troops here know of the help which should arrive on the morrow." Orin advised, "That way they will rest better tonight and fight with renewed vigour when the sun rises, knowing that soon they will have the help that they need." Teslas nodded, whilst listening to Orin's advise.

"Yes," Teslas responded, "I think that is a good idea. Gethas, you are certain that the reinforcements will be arriving tomorrow? We cannot afford to give the troops false hope."

"I have no reason to doubt these reports." Gethas told Teslas, "In either case, Orin's advice is sound. If our reinforcements do not arrive by tomorrow we will be forced to retreat from this position anyway, so it cannot hurt to motivate our troops." Advice undertaken, Teslas called in a messenger to spread the news throughout the camp of the reinforcements set to arrive. Meanwhile, the kings set to discussing the strategy they would use for tomorrow's warfare, which would enable them to hold their position and rest the troops as much as possible whilst waiting for their reinforcements to arrive.

Dawn had barely broken the next morning when the Narsians struck the western defenses. Teslas' men were ready for the attack though; the Narsians had been attacking earlier and earlier each day and stayed fighting longer and longer until night had truly fallen. They were obviously confident that they had the superior numbers and this would allow them to win, so they were unconcerned with losing men to the additional injuries inevitably acquired when attempting warfare at night. At first the Hruntan forces were able to hold their own, but as the day wore on and the sun rose in the sky, they began to tire and the Narsians seemed to have a near endless supply of fresh faced troops to attack the Hruntan position.

By early afternoon the Narsians had pushed the Hruntans tightly back towards the position of their encampment. The fighting was fierce and bloody and the only thing that had reduced the Hruntan casualties earlier in the day was the difficulty the Narsian archers were having in finding marks amongst the trees. The Hruntan troops had been fighting courageously, but now their strength and resolve were failing. They were simply too exhausted. The Hruntan line waivered and was about to break under the onslaught when a cacophony of horns sounded in the forests around them. The confusion of sounds and what it heralded caused the Narsian advance to slow, allowing the Hruntans to secure their line. It was in the moment that the Narsians slowed their advance that the Hruntans realized it was Sambarian horn calls that were echoing

Child of Rydos

through the forest. The reinforcements had arrived.

"What is that third horn call?" Orin asked no one in particular as he strained to pick out the call of the Ruors and the Gerakans. Temac supplied the answer.

"It is little wonder if you don't recognize it. I'd wager it has been a long time since most Sambarians heard that call and lived to tell the tale. We heard that sound when we first entered Azin Heart. The Rangers have come to support us too. Teran, Koran, Xantila and Banir must have managed to enlist their assistance on their journey north." Temac answered Orin, before turning his attention, once again, to the battle at hand.

The echoes of the horns were still resounding in the air when the Gerakans, Ruors and Rangers joined the fray. The Narsians, not prepared to fight the greater force, were taken by surprise and were beaten back away from the Hruntan defensive position. The Rangers, in particular, were an unstoppable force, seemingly at one with the forest, dealing death through a flight of arrows or a knife to whomsoever stood in their way and melting away in to the trees before the Narisans could retaliate.

By the time that night fell that day, the fighting had been pushed significantly further south towards the Narsian plains. New temporary fortifications were being constructed and the forest cleared again behind the combined Sambarian lines and the weary Hruntans were given the opportunity for a true rest whilst the fresh faced Gerakans and Ruors were set to work. Gerak's Field General, Kiesan, who had arrived with the troops from the north was overseeing the construction work. Flint, Gerak's head of intelligence was busy instructing the scouts from the combined armies to infiltrate beyond the enemy lines and learn what they could about the Narsian numbers and their plans for the next attack.

The remaining officers and leaders were gathered to discuss tomorrow's action. Olin was amongst them, having travelled down with the baggage train of the reinforcing armies. He was still not healed enough to join in the fighting, but he yearned for action and was tired of sitting well behind the front lines, unaware of what was happening to his countrymen. Now all the armies had converged, he joined the united force and intended to offer his services as a tactician until he was healed enough to fight. They were currently in conversation with Janis, who was leading the company of Rangers.

"Will you continue to fight with us as we forge our way south?" Gethas asked Janis, "I'm sure Flint could find lots of uses for the forest skills your people have." Gethas suggested, thinking of how Flint could use their skill at stealth. Janis paused and thought a while.

"We work better alone and using our own methods." Janis responded, "I don't think you need our assistance in forcing your way deeper into Narsian territory and we prefer working in the woodlands. We will make our way eastwards as you fight southwards. We'll clear the forest of stray Narsians between here and your eastern armies, making sure you're not routed from behind." There was a generally nod of approval from the gathered assembly.

"How large a force will your company be able to combat as it sweeps from west to east?" Teslas asked.

"Being outnumbered should not be an issue. The Narsians will not know we are there until it is too late for them to raise arms against us. If we find a force more substantial than we can handle we can send word back to your forces here as you'll need to stop them from invading Hruntan or Arinachian lands." Janis responded.

"That sounds like a fair deal." Olin interjected and grinned, "We wouldn't want you to have all the fun now would we?" There was a smattering of laughter around the room. War was a serious business, but relief was sometimes needed to cope with the horrors and stresses it could bring. "Do you have any news of my friends who were travelling north? I assume Xantila asked Xera to aid us in our war here?" Olin continued after order restored itself.

"Yes, we entertained Teran, Koran and Banir at Azin heart again as Xantila passed through with them on the way to seek the Mystics of Laconia." Janis informed Olin.

"Good, so their quest to seek magical aid progresses well." Temac commented.

"Not that we've seemed to need to combat any magic…" Teslas said to no one in particular.

"You may not have faced magic here, but the Narsians are using it and want to stop your friends' quest." Janis told the gathered assembly, "They were attacked at the ford at Quin and chased into Azin forest again." Temac and Olin both moved forward towards the edge of the seats as Janis was talking. They had both experienced the affects of this sort of magic and wanted to see an end of it in their lands.

The Rangers were as good as their word. Over the coming days they swept through the forest, moving steadily eastwards. There were small companies of Narsians scouting through the forest, which were easy pickings for the Rangers. At no point did the Rangers encounter any major resistance to their movements. The principal Narsian forces were engaged with the Sambarian advances and most of those the Rangers encountered were either small scouting groups or deserters.

By the time the Rangers had advanced through the forest from the west to the eastward position of the Arinachian forces they too had received reinforcement from the Laconians and had been able to push their advance southwards through the great forest and into the plains of Narsos. Janis went to find the command position to report to King Arran and King Tlanic about their efforts to clear the forest. He found them with Teloran directing the construction of new defensive palisades now that the combined Arinachian and Laconian forces had a foothold on the Narsian plains just north of the Narsian walled city of I'sos.

"Your Majesties," Janis began, bowing to them both, "I am Janis, commander of this company of Rangers. We have come from your western front, clearing the forest of unwanted Narsians on the way to lend our aid to your position because between the Hruntans, Gerakans, Ruors and the Rydosian fleet there are not many Narsians left for us to play with in the west." King Arran grinned at Janis' comment.

"Commander Janis, you are most welcome here and I'm sure we can find plenty of Narsians for your Rangers to harry." Arran began, "Do you know how things fare on the western front?"

"When we left them, Your Majesty, they were still fighting the Narsians in the forest, but the battle was going well. I expect they have managed to gain a foothold on the plains by now, just as you have." Janis confirmed.

"We should send some scouts and messengers to find out and report our success so far too." Arran commented, mostly to himself, rather than to Janis.

"A few of my men can do that if you desire, Your Majesty. If they move through the forest's edge no Narsian they encounter will ever see them." Janis offered.

"Thank you, Janis. I will give you some papers to pass to the commanders." King Arran said gratefully.

"Janis, do your troops need rest or are you ready for a bit more fun already?" Teloran interjected at that moment, his focus taken momentarily from the fortifications being established.

"What did you have in mind?" Janis asked, bemused. King Tlanic answered on his nephew's behalf,

"We want to establish these fortifications as quickly as possible. The portion of the Narsian army encamped around I'sos knows what we are up to. They will want to slow us or prevent us from doing so. If your men are able to hold the attention of the Narsians for a while that will free up more of our troops to establish the ground works." King Tlanic elaborated. Janis' grin widened even more.

"I'm absolutely sure we can arrange an appropriate distraction for the Narsians." Janis answered.

"I think you're going to be very useful to have around." King Arran observed dryly.

Chapter XXIV – Ptanga put down

The sun was rising over the western encampment of the combined Sambarian forces. With the armies of Hrunta, Gerak and Ruor working together it had been possible for them push back the Narsian advance and they now had finally cleared a path through the great forest and were established on the edges of the Narsian plains between Ptanga and I'sos. If the whole Narsian army had come upon them at once, events would not have passed so well, but their attention had been drawn simultaneously eastwards and westwards and they had obviously not committed the full strength of their armies, if Teran's reports of the numbers of their forces were accurate. Whilst it concerned Gethas, Teslas and Orin that they were unable to account for the tactics the Narsians were employing they were thankful that it allowed them to push them back into Narsos.

Established on the edge of the plains, the Sambarians began to fortify their position using wood from the surrounding forest, creating earthworks and a palisade to ensure they could hold back the superior strength of the Narsian force if it came upon their position all at once. The main Narsian force was gathered further away, nearer to I'sos. The Narsian army in the west seemed to be holding its position, not trying to push the Sambarians back unless they themselves ventured deeper into Narsos.

The Hruntans, Gerakans and Ruors had fought their way southwards through the forests of Narsos, but the

Child of Rydos

Rydosians who had initially aided the Gerakans and Ruors to more quickly join the fray by ferrying them to Cheros had not been idle since. The Rydosian fleet had sailed through the Ptanga reef and laid siege to the city from the sea. Even when undertaken by an experienced navy, a sea to land assault is never an easy tactic to employ. The assaulting force can retreat swiftly, but any loss of a ship will lead to significant losses of life. The defending force must just keep the attackers from landing significant numbers inside the city. Nor is a sea assault an easy attack to achieve by stealth unless one is aided by thick sea fog. The Rydosians though, had agents inside Ptanga. The connections and networks that Lysan, the old King of Rydos, had set up in Ptanga were loyal to Rydos and they worked to aid them during the siege. Before the Ptangans could launch their own fleet or catapults in response to the Rydosian assault their agents within Ptanga ruined the ships' sails and sabotaged the firing mechanisms on the catapults.

The assault was still far from easy for the Rydosians. The Ptangan archers were still able to rain fire arrows through the sky on to the Rydosian ships. Then, there was the issue of the Narsian magicians inside Ptanga. There did not seem to be many magicians stationed in Ptanga, but a few were enough to wreak havoc on the Rydosian assault. Aside from throwing fireballs into the midst of the ships, they sent magic to play with the emotions of the attackers, confusing them each time they attempted to advance and instilling them with fear. Whilst the Rydosians had no direct way to counteract the work of the magicians, they were expecting the attacks. They doused the flames from the arrows and the fireballs as soon as they hit the ships. As for the emotional manipulation created by the magicians, that was harder to combat. It meant that the Rydosians had to fight against themselves as well as against the Ptangans.

The success of the Rydosian assault hinged upon two things, the support the Rydosians had within the walls of Ptanga, and the fact that the reach of the Ptangan magicians was limited. The magicians could neither cast fire into the ships anchored well outside the port, nor influence the emotions of the sailors on those farther ships. This allowed the admirals directing the attack to keep their wits and rely upon the discipline of the Rydosian sailors who were in the depths of the fray to not be overwhelmed by the magical onslaught. The strength of the agents within Ptanga were that they operated independently from the naval assault, without need for direction. This made it difficult for the Ptangans themselves to know how to combat the threat as the enemy cells inside their walls were not communicating with each other or with the Rydosian navy and they were each operating as they saw fit, making their attacks difficult to predict.

The assault on Ptanga lasted for a week. The Rydosians had managed to blockade the port, but they found themselves unable to break fully through the Ptangan defenses and invade the city whilst the magicians still held sway over their troops. The Rydosian admirals had gathered in the stateroom on *The Dolphin*, the flagship of the fleet, to discuss their current progress and the options available to them.

"Its been a week and we're not getting anywhere!" Admiral Errid exclaimed, slamming his fist down on the table around which the admirals and senior captains of the fleet were gathered.

"We're all very aware of that Errid, but what do you suggest?" Admiral Ahram asked, "You know as well as the rest of us that if we commit the full force of the navy against the city, we risk the magicians decimating our forces. We need a way to eliminate that threat before we can make any real progress."

"If the Sambarian forces to east could work their way here we could blockade the city on both sides and starve them out." Captain Marc suggested.

"The last report we had from the western encampment suggests that they won't be coming to aid us any time soon." Ahram answered, "And in any case, we don't have the time to commit to a siege to starve the Ptangans out."

"If only we had a way of communicating with our agents inside the city…" Errid suggested.

"Yes, they might be able to help eliminate the magical threat." Marc agreed enthusiastically.

"Yes, they are our best hope at this stage, but we cannot rely upon them." Ahram answered, "Their only security against discovery is their independence, which comes from the fact that we cannot contact them. We have no way of enlisting their aid, we just have to hope they are thinking along the same lines as we are and see our trouble." The conversation continued along much the same lines and progressed onto what little they *could* do, assuming that the magical threat continued.

Luckily for the Rydosian fleet, the agents working inside Ptanga had seen how the fleet was struggling because of the magic being used against them. Once the first cell decided to try and turn assassin and remove one of the magicians, the other cells caught on to the idea and turned assassin as well. One by one they picked off the magicians within the walls. A number of the magicians died before they fully realized the threat within their own walls, but the last few became incredibly cautious and many of the agents died in their attempts to assassinate the remaining magicians. The Ptangans loyal to Narsos had eventually sent riders to the main Narsian army for reinforcements, but no help arrived. It was too late to turn the tide of this battle and the main Narsian troops were already engaged elsewhere.

As soon as the magicians were either dead or preoccupied with protecting their own skins, the Rydosian assault advanced rapidly. Within the day, the port was over-run and the sailors were fighting skirmishes through the streets with the Ptangan city guards. The city was designed to be easy to defend against an invader from across the plains and not for conflict within the city. Consequently, the city's defenses were not effective in preventing the Rydosians from taking over from inside the walls. The skirmishes were bloody, but the Rydosians outnumbered the Ptangan forces, so the eventual outcome was inevitable. The remaining magicians did not go down without a fight either. Their magic, powerful when directed against one or two people, could not protect them from a simultaneous attack from many, but they chose to literally go down in flames, creating explosions that decimated parts of the city and killed invader and civilian alike. It was not enough. Eventually the Rydosians were able to raise their flag over the city gates and claim the city as their own. Once the town was secure, the admirals leading the invasion set up a headquarters in the house of the former governor of the city. From this base, they were able to manage the city and also its civilian inhabitants. After the magicians and Narsian military had either been killed or driven from the city, the local populace was more than willing to submit to Rydosian occupation. They had no great love for the rest of their Narsian cousins and knew the wealth that alliance with Rydos could bring. The spy cells that had been operating in the city came forward and met with the admirals and through their conversation much was learnt about the strange tactics of the Narsian forces. They did not come all at once, nor indeed overtly, preferring to continue to keep their identities as hidden as possible, but each reported to Captain Marc, who was a known contact to them, being a member of the Rydosian intelligence as well as a sea captain. Marc was able to collate the information he gleaned before presenting it to the other admirals and forwarding it in a report to King Seban.

"It is no wonder we could not fathom the depths of the Narsian tactics." Marc reported to the admirals one evening, "It seems the magicians were the one directing the defense efforts of the city, not the generals, and it won't surprise you to learn that they had their own particular agenda."

"And what was that?" Asked Admiral Ahram, raising one eyebrow.

"From what our spy cells working inside the city have gleaned, the magicians expected the city to fall, but they wanted to purposefully drag out the fighting as long as possible." Marc paused briefly before continuing, "It seems they are waiting for some sort of sign, or they are searching for some sort of totem, but they need more time to find it."

"A peculiar superstition. This information may well help the other Sambarians in developing their tactics against the Narsian threat." Errid said.

"I am also not a man prone to superstitious belief, but I also did not put much store in the power of magic before witnessing so much of it here." Admiral Ahram stated evenly, "We should not dismiss the importance of this thing the Narsians seem to be searching for. Include it in the report to King Seban, he can decide how to inform the other rulers." Captain Marc nodded to these orders and took his leave to pen his report.

Securing the port of Ptanga meant that the Sambarian forces, at least to the west, could be provisioned more easily and resources and troops exchanged more quickly via sea routes than they would have been able to if they had been limited to the routes established over land. Despite this and the foothold that the Sambarians had created in Narsos, their advance had stalled. When the Narsians attacked the Sambarian camps they did so without the use of magic and always without the full might of their armies, so the Sambarians were able to hold their positions. Whenever the Sambarians tried to advance further into the plain, they would feel the full force of the Narsian magicians and their troops would melt away before the pressures and fears created through the magicians' magical manipulation of the minds of those who opposed them. This created much discussion in the Sambarian camp.

"It doesn't make any sense!" Gethas exclaimed, slamming his fist down on the table around which he and the other sovereigns of the western part of Sambar

Child of Rydos

sat with their closest advisors discussing the state of the conflict with Narsos. "This stalemate is so frustrating."

"I agree that little of the tactics that the Narsians are using against us seem to make sense. But, we must be thankful that we are able to hold our position here at least. If we were to suffer magical attack here the Narsians would doubtless be able to drive us back into Hrunta and probably occupy the lands permanently. We still have no way to combat their magic." General Kiesan responded.

"Perhap something stops them." Olin suggested.

"What do you mean?" Orin asked his son.

"Well, they seem to freely use their magic against us on the plain, but although on my earlier journeys with Teran and the others across Sambar we experienced the affects of magic sometimes, they don't see to be using it on us here. It seems perhaps something prevents them." Olin answered. The others looked thoughtful, considering Olin idea.

"It makes sense," Temac commented, "If there was something that made it harder for them to use magic against us within the lands of Sambar itself, it would explain why we have been able to hold position here. Though not why you and I, Olin, experienced magical attacks within Sambar…"

"I don't think we'll have answers until Teran returns, hopefully with the Mystics alongside him to assist us." Teslas contributed.

"And what do you make of this report from Ptanga about the tactics there? That the Narsians were looking for some sort of sign or totem." Temac added.

"It paints an unsettling picture." Gethas said darkly, "I think we're going to have to hold out here and wait for the Mystics before we get any real answers."

"At least it gives us time to bed in the supply routes and the defenses here." Kiesan reflected, ever thinking towards tactical advantage.

Chapter XXV – Mountain Mystics

Teran, Koran, Xantila and Banir climbed through the foothills and up into the mountains north of Yellath. The first day out of Yellath had not been hard because the path was well defined and led past hamlets and farmsteads. There had been many people on the road and even more sheep in the hills. It was after that first day when things got more complex. The obvious path they had been following slowly disappeared and finding the correct track up into the mountains became more like guess work. Teran, Koran and Banir were more thankful than ever to have someone with Xantila's skills in tracking and path-finding and those skills were being tested to the full. It would not have surprised her if the path they were trying to follow had not been used for nearly five hundred years. Xantila was amongst the best trackers and path-finders that the Rangers could boast of, but the close attention to detail that was required to keep to their path was a slow business which took time and energy. It would have been much easier if she had a second, or even a third, skilled tracker to work with as she scouted for the path. It was further complicated by the fact some of the trails were used by the local population who worked in the mines in the mountains, so the most obviously travelled paths were not necessarily the lead they required.

Teran chaffed at the slow progress they were making now, compared to their earlier flight. He did not blame Xantila though; he knew that what they were asking of her was difficult and exhausting. He just hoped they were on the right track and had not accidentally started following some grazing sheep's trail. It was half way through their third day on the road north when they finally found solid proof that they were on the right track and it came in the form of a way marker. Xantila had found a path which led steeply out of the foothills and into the mountains. It was a narrow track, almost unnoticeable if you did not know what you were looking for. Teran would have assumed it was nothing more than an animal track except that carved into the rock nearby, covered by a growth of moss, until Xantila had pushed it aside, was the symbol of an eye.

"That looks like one of the devices which are drawn on these manuscripts." Koran said, pointing to the carving and then waving generally to the papers that the Mayor of Yellath had given them as a peace offering for the Mystics.

"Indeed." Teran breathed a sigh of relief, "It means we're on the right track."

"Don't you trust my path finding skills?" Xantila asked Teran, tongue in cheek.

"No, it's not that Xan." Teran replied quickly, "I think you've been doing an incredible job. It's just been so difficult; I was sure we must be on the wrong track. We haven't exactly had the best luck on our travels."

"I was just teasing you, Teran." Xantila responded to his apology, "It looks like we're about to start climbing in earnest now, so our journey should be a bit quicker. There are likely to be fewer options for where the path leads now we're leaving these muddy foothills and climbing up rock and stone."

"I, for one, will be pleased not to have to squelch

through mud for a while." Banir butted in, who had got mud inside his boots on more than one occasion when dismounting from his horse. Koran looked at the path ahead.

"It looks like we should be able to continue with our mounts. At least for a while." Koran said, "Though I wouldn't be surprised if we have to turn them loose eventually. The path would only have to get a little more restricted and steep for it to be too difficult for our horses to manage."

"Yes," Teran sighed, "I'm not sure why I assumed this journey northwards was going to be easier than our previous one east and south." Teran trudged forward and the other companions followed him along the marked track leading up the mountain. There were frequent clefts in the rock and openings which looked like caves. They did not pause to explore each of these because it would have wasted their time, but they all felt uneasy about what could be hiding in any one of the openings in the mountains.

Evening fell and the companions began to look for a suitable place to rest of the night. Just as it was beginning to be too dark to travel much further the path leveled out and widened a little there was also an entrance to a cave. Banir, being the smallest, went in to explore the cave. He returned a short time later.

"It is not much of a cave, there are no passages leading further into the mountains. But there should be enough room for us and the horses to rest away from the elements." Banir confirmed, so they set up camp for the night, using wood and provisions that they had carried with them to light a small fire and eat something before getting some rest.

The next day they found that they had to leave the horses behind. They set the horses free, but also left some provisions for them to feed on, hoping that this might entice the horses to remain there until their return southwards. The only path that led away from their campsite was finally too steep and narrow for the horses to manage. It was more of a scramble than a climb, over loose rock and shingle. After a while the climb leveled out into a path again and they had no choice but to continue on foot.

Occasionally the track would split and they would have to choose a path to take. There were no further way markers and they had to rely on Xantila's experience of what looked like the more likely path. When all else failed they just chose the path which caused them to climb more, leading them deeper into the mountains. Eventually they reached a place where the trail leveled out again and broadened enough for them to stand abreast. Then, abruptly, the trail seemed to finish, bringing the companions up short.

"We must have chosen the wrong trail." Banir said glumly, imagining the climb back down the mountain until they could choose another route.

"I suppose we must have. I am sorry." Xantila said, feeling responsible for the wrong turn since she had been leading the company.

"It is hardly your fault, Xan." Koran responded, warmly, "This mountain terrain is unfamiliar to us all and we would have likely been completely lost if it hadn't been for your skill. It's just going to take us a little longer to find the route to the Mystics home than we had hoped." Koran, Xantila and Banir turned to make their way back down to path to the last point where it diverged.

"Wait." Teran said, his eyes fixed in the direction they had been climbing, "Something is not right here."

"What do you mean?" Koran asked.

"I'm not sure," Teran responded, "It's just a feeling." And with that Teran sat on the ground, cross-legged, staring forward.

"We haven't got time for this, Teran." Koran said irritably.

"Just wait, Kor, I'm not trying to waste our time. I just need to concentrate. There is something out of place." Teran entreated his friend. "Can none of you feel it?" He asked. Koran shook his head, still irritated, but Banir and Xantila tried to see if they could focus on what Teran was talking about.

"There's…" Xantila began.

"… something." Banir finished for her, tilting his head to one side. Teran sat in silence, eyes fixed forward still. After some time, he rose from where he sat.

"Join hands and follow me." Teran asked his friends and companions.

"What? Why?" Koran asked.

"Please." Teran entreated and they did as he asked as he stepped forward.

"There is no way…" Koran began, but Teran led them forward despite the lack of any path. Suddenly their perspective shifted and they were standing on a clear path leading further up the mountain. They looked back and could see the place where they had been standing, but now the path was obvious.

"I'd say we're still on the right path." Teran commented. "The Mystics clearly desire to minimize the number of guests they have to entertain."

"Magical concealment of the path?" Koran asked.

"It must have been." Banir said, a little in awe.

"Well spotted, Teran." Xantila said. Taking the lead once again as they continued their climb.

As they climbed further, they began to notice a foul smell assaulting their nostrils. The more they climbed the stronger the smell became until it was almost overwhelming. The trail broadened again and plateaued against a large cliff face in the mountain. There was a huge opening in the face of the cliff. It was the only way forward and the smell seemed to be emanating from there.

"What on earth is that horrid smell?" Banir asked, gagging.

"I've never smelled anything like it in my life." Xantila responded. Teran and Koran nodded in agreement with her.

"It looks like we've got little choice but to soldier on though." Koran said.

"I don't like it." Banir responded, "Nothing good could create such a foul smell." As they slowly approached the mouth of the cave they could see the bones of various animals, picked clean, piled around the entrance. A low growling moan reached their ears. "What was that?" Banir asked.

"Shh!" Xantila cautioned, waving her hand in a gesture to say that they should quietly back away from the cave. As they were following her command, the growling crescendoed to a roar and there was a rush of foul air towards them from the mouth of the cave as something surged forth from its concealment in the

259

shadows.

A beast of truly epic proportions emerged from the cave, its roar threatening to split their eardrums in its intensity. It swung a giant arm, like a club, sending the four travellers flying through the air to land on their backs, some distance off, stunned by the impact of the blow. As the beast stood in the open air now, it straightened to its full height. Banir, dazed and confused, thought it was possibly tall enough to be classified as a small mountain in its own right. Though it was shaped like a man, it was the height of at least twenty. It looked like it was made of living rock and it had eyes which glowed deep red. It was hard to tell what level of intelligence it possessed as, though it seemed fully away of its surroundings and of these intruders, it uttered only growls and roars from its mouth, nothing which could be recognized as speech in any language. Its evil, red eyes were fixed on the companions and it started to slowly step towards them; each step like an avalanche of rocks upon the mountainside.

"Wha… What is that thing?" Banir stammered fear in his voice, which was felt equally by all the companions.

"I've never seen or heard of a beast like this." Xantila responded, slowly getting to her feet and helping the others up.

"It looks like a titan." Koran said.

"But they are a fairy tale…" Banir said, regaining some of his composure, "Aren't they?"

"Perhaps we're looking at the evidence that they are not simply fairy tales…" Koran responded, his voice breaking slightly, belying the fear hidden under his calmly composed features.

"The mountain makers are a myth. Surely…" Xantila said, though her voice began to lack conviction in the face of the beast before them.

"The titans are a myth." Teran said with some conviction, though his senses reeled from both from the physical assault which had sent them flying, the foul smell invading his nostrils, and the mental assault of the fear welling up inside him. Looking at the others he could tell they were sharing his difficulty.

Something else was pressing against Teran's senses too, but so overwhelmed were his faculties that it took him a while to notice and even longer to identify what it was. After what seemed like an age of internal battling, but cannot have been all that long as neither his companions nor the beast had moved in that time, Teran spoke,

"This *is* a titan. Titans *are* a myth. *This* is an illusion." Teran forced each sentence out a word at a time, as if the speaking of them was a hard-won battle. As he spoke the confidence in his voice grew and he gained control over the onslaught against his senses, though he could still feel the assault.

"What?" Koran asked, as if dazed and confused. He and the others still seemed intently focused on the beast, whose presence was now not bothering Teran. Teran repeated what he had just said. He could see it seeping into, and slowly registering in, the consciousness of each of the others.

"What do you mean?" Banir asked eventually, turning to look at Teran.

"Just like the absent path earlier, this is another illusion created by the Mystics to keep visitors away." Teran answered.

Child of Rydos

"How can that be?" Koran asked, "A blow from that thing sent us all flying."

"I didn't say it couldn't hurt us. It is magic, after all." Teran responded.

"It doesn't appear to be moving now that we're ignoring it." Xantila noticed.

"I think the magic works by feeding on our fear. If we control our thoughts and voice the truth it seems it ceases to have power over us." Teran continued.

"What do we do now then?" Banir asked, "It's still guarding the way forward."

"Follow me." Teran said, striding forward towards the beast. The others thought perhaps he had gone a little crazy, but they reluctantly followed him. As Teran strode into the space occupied by the titan it shimmered like a mirage and suddenly they stood not before an open cave, but a huge pair of iron doors, highly decorated with runes and images representing the four elemental spirits of water, earth, air and fire. In front of the closed doors stood a lone figure, robed in a brown, cowled habit and wielding a staff, which looked to be made of an engraved black metal. Teran thought that he could detect a look of surprise, but the cowl obscured the face too much to be certain. If there was surprise, it was not evident in the voice that spoke,

"Who are you and why do you seek the home of the Mystics?" A man's voice issued from the cowl.

"I am Teran, son of Lysan and brother to King Seban of Rydos." Teran answered for himself, then introduced the others in turn, "This is Koran, son of King Gethas of Gerak; Xantila of the Rangers of Azin forest; and Banir, a citizen of Baxen in Arinach."

"You keep a peculiar combination of travelling

companions, Teran of Rydos." The man responded, looking intrigued, "And again, why do you seek our home?"

"We need your help." Koran answered, stepping forward, "We are at war again with Narsos and without your help we fear we will suffer great loses and possibly even lose our lands to Narsos."

"We have no desire or need to aid the warmongering descents of Am Bære. We know your family's history and the apple never falls far from the tree." The man answered derisively.

"We are not warmongers." Teran answered hotly, confused by the veiled accusation that was being made, "You supported us in the last war until you abandoned us to retreat to your insular lives here. Without your help, the Narsian magicians will freely weave their magic across Sambar, creating chaos and fear."

"Despite what you believe, we never abandoned our duty. We have continued to protect these lands from magical incursion these last five hundred years, though we had plenty of reason to abandon you to your own fates. The Narsian magicians have no power within the lands of Sambar." The gatekeeper said.

"Their magic has plagued us every step of our journey through Sambar. It is why we entered the lands of Narsos to see what they were planning and why we have travelled here to enlist your help." Koran informed the man evenly. This time Teran definitely detected a look of concern cross the man's face. His eyes grew distant for a time, as if he was having an internal monologue with himself, then he looked at them intently.

"You had better come in and explain your journey

and experience in more detail to the gathered assembly." The man said, then drawing back the cowl of his habit to reveal a lean middle-aged face, with golden eyes and a shock of blond hair, he said, "My name is Elvan. I am the gatekeeper of Kuellath, the new Yellath, home of the Mystics." And with that he spun around and wrapped his staff on the great doors which swung silently open in response, revealing a wide neatly paved road leading into the mountain. Interesting, thought Teran, that what the mayor of Yellath had said about their town once being the home of the Mystics seemed to be true.

Chapter XXVI – Mystical Assembly

The passage into the mountain had led through a long tunnel to open out into a lush and green valley, surrounded on every side by steep impenetrable cliffs. The path from the mountain led down, by a winding path, to a small walled city of elegant spires and bridges built across the banks of a river, which ran down from the mountains. It was a city to rival any to be found in the nations of Sambar and its position was extremely defensible due to its isolation. Teran supposed that the Mystics must use their abilities, somehow, to keep the weather in the valley more suitable to gentle living than one would expect for a home nestled in the northern ranges. This city must be Kuellath, to which the companions were being brought by Elvan.

Upon arrival in the city itself the companions were taken directly to a great amphitheatre, evidently used for large gatherings of the people. They were walked to the centre of the amphitheatre, where there stood another robed Mystic, a gold chain hung around his neck, marking him for some particular office.

"This is Ylorac, High Magician of Kuellath, our leader." Elvan said by way of introduction. The companions bowed towards Ylorac, who responded with a nod of the head.

"I am Teran…" Teran began, but Ylorac cut him off,

"Your introduction will not be necessary, we are all aware of the introductions you made of yourselves to the gatekeeper." Ylorac stated, not in an attempt to be curt, but in order to save time, "You will explain the events you alluded to at the gate in front of the High Council." Ylorac waved his arm expansively and the companions, looking up, could see that the lower tiers of the amphitheatre were filling with robed people, each wore a chain similar to Ylorac's, though less ornate. In the higher tiers people dressed in ordinary clothing were filling some of the seats. "All meetings of the council are open and transparent. We are a people who are truly democratic in how we govern ourselves."

"First, your Highness…" Teran began.

"Ylorac will do." Ylorac responded.

"Ylorac. We have secured a gift from the archives of Yellath. In a recent excavation, they discovered a previously unknown store of ancient manuscripts that they believe date from the time you lived in the city. We have brought a sample from that archive as a gift for your people." Teran told the leader of the Mystics, presenting him with the parcel of papers that they had brought with them to the mountains. Ylorac inspected them.

"These are written in High Larcon, the ancient language of our people, and are authentic." Ylorac confirmed for the gathered assembly, "And you say there are more of these papers?"

"Yes," Teran answered, "A great deal more." A whisper swept up through the amphitheatre. *The ancient library. The lost arts.* Teran caught the excited mood. "I am sure that King Tlanic could be appealed to for the return to you of what is obviously part of your ancient heritage."

"At what cost? We have kept ourselves separate from your people for nearly five hundred years for good reason. A betrayal of trust is hard to overcome." Ylorac asked, before continuing without waiting for a response, "Why do you seek our assistance now?" Teran thought it best to answer the immediate question first rather than tease out and expose the obvious injury that stood between the people of Sambar and the Mystics, so he began to tell their story. Each of the companions wove the part of the story with which they were most familiar. The Mystics interrupted at several points for the purpose of clarification or to highlight particular incidents they were interested or concerned about.

Teran spoke of the first call to Conclave and the news from Arinach and Narsos that had set them on their journey. He spoke of their ambush inside the borders of Azin forest. Xantila spoke of what she knew of the strange appearance of the ambushers, including their sword and snake tattoo, the emblem which seemed to follow them around on their journey. This caught the attention of the Mystics who asked lots of detailed questions about the nature of the Rangers magic and what they had detected in their realm. The Mystics looked increasingly concerned as they heard more, but they allowed the companions to continue their tale without too many interruptions. The storm in Tellac and the appearance of the frostling both provoked raised eyebrows, but few additional questions. When Teran began to speak of Agachen and his work in Arinach the Mystics grew particularly attentive, some leaning forward from where they sat as if straining to hear as much as possible.

All four of the companions were made to tell the Mystics of their interactions with Agachen each from their own point of view, until all possible questions and points of view had been exhausted. Teran finished by telling them of the conviction of Conclave to seek the help of the Mystics and of their experience at the ford and their second pursuit into Azin forest. When all had been told, the day had worn on and the companions were exhausted.

"Will you help us then?" Teran asked Ylorac bluntly, once their tale was finished.

"Much of what you have said is of great concern to us." Ylorac responded, "Despite what you may believe about having been abandoned by the Mystics, we have continued to watch over the lands of Sambar. Other magicians should not be able to work their magic in the lands of Sambar at all and certainly not without our notice. We should have already been aware of the incidents you bring to our attention, but we were not. We did feel the exchange between yourselves and Agachen when he attacked you in the wilderness, but we had not been aware of his subtle magic up until that point and we should have been able to detect it."

"What does that mean?" Koran asked.

"We do not know." Ylorac answered, "We need to confer on these matters. You have had a long and exhausting journey. Why not rest for a while and take refreshment? We will send for you again when we have had the opportunity to discuss these matters." Ylorac dismissed the companions. They nodded in return, seeing the audience was over and Elvan led them from the amphitheatre.

As Teran was leaving, Ylorac caught his arm and whispered to him, "There is more. There is something about you. Something that allowed you to break Agachen's defenses. It is also what allowed you to see through our defenses, which you should not have been able to do. Who are you?" Ylorac concluded, eirely echoing Agachen's words to him in their confrontation in the countryside of Arinach. Teran though was just perplexed by the exchange as he did not know to what Ylorac referred. Ylorac could see this in Teran's face and let him follow his companions to the rooms where they would rest.

Elvan had brought them to a spacious chamber, which had a balcony that commanded beautiful views across the valley from the city; in the light of the late afternoon, the sun nearing the horizon cast beautiful shades of red and orange across it. In the centre of the room was a table laden with as much food as they could possibly desire. Scattered around the room were cushions and day beds as well as chairs for reclining on. This room was obviously designed to facilitate waiting in comfort and the companions made full use of it after their strenuous trek into the mountains, depositing themselves around the room, picking from the food at the table and engaging in idle conversation.

Teran sat by himself, whilst he, Koran, Xantila and Banir waited. He had chosen a seat to recline in that commanded a good view of the valley over the edge of the balcony and there he allowed his thoughts to become introspective. Ylorac's final comment to him, out of earshot of the others, was fixed in his mind. Instead of having his thoughts fixed on the war and what lay ahead, as his companions supposed, instead he was reflecting again on his experiences with Agachen and of the journey into the mountains to reach this stronghold and homestead of the Mystics. There was something different about him; he knew it. If he was honest with himself, he had known it ever since he was a young boy, but had never been able to articulate it. He knew he had perception that others lacked. At first, he had assumed it was simply that he held a greater attention to detail than most other people, but it was more than this, and his recent experiences proved it. Teran mulled these thoughts over and over in his head, but this did not gain him any great, new insight. He remained unable to answer the simple question that Ylorac had set him, except in the most mundane and prosaic terms, *who are you?*

Eventually, after a considerable wait, the only interruption being when a maid entered to light some candles and oil lamps as the afternoon drew on to evening and the evening into night-time, there was a knock at the door of their chambers and Elvan entered with Ylorac and another, unnamed, Mystic. Obviously, they were not required to return to the assembly. The companions all paused in what they were doing and gave Ylorac their full attention.

"You call us the Laconian Mystics, but we have another name for ourselves." Ylorac began, "We are the Yash-tu, in our ancient tongue. It means the watchers. We have watched and guarded over these lands a long time, as I told you at the assembly, though you have not been aware of it. The snake and sword emblem you spoke of earlier is the symbol of the brotherhood of the dark path, a group who follow the dark God Khaen."

"I had not heard of Khaen before we read the inscription above the tomb in Narsos." Koran commented.

"I would be surprised if you had." Yloric answered, "His followers are very secretive and knowledge of him has, for the most part, thankfully disappeared from the lands of Sambar, which we protect."

"This means you will help us?" Banir asked in the silence of Ylorac's pause, the question that was burning on all the companions' minds. Banir looked embarrassed at his presumptive outburst almost as soon as he is made it.

"Yes, young one, the Yash-tu will respond to Sambar's call for aid. This use of magic within the borders of Sambar is of great concern to us and we would know more." Ylorac answered and then turned to the unnamed man who had entered with him and Elvan, "This is Ylornic, my son. He will lead a company of our people southwards with you to the borders of the great forest and into Narsos to help you combat the magic which works against you and to discover more about its source if possible." Ylornic bowed to the companions upon his introduction,

"I hope we will be able to work together well." Ylornic simply said.

"Thank you, Ylorac, Ylornic." Terans responded with relief, "We are in desperate need of your aid and it is clear that there lies more in the past between our peoples than I realized. Thank you for seeing beyond this to our common need. If you have any concern or questions at any point about our actions against Narsos or interactions with you, please come and talk to me directly and I will try and ensure these concerns are addressed. We respect your people and the help you now offer us in free will." Teran finished, utilizing all his skill in diplomacy to engage the Mystics.

Child of Rydos

"Come and dine with us, if you are not already too repleat with food, we haven't eaten during the deliberations of the council, so are hungry despite the late hour." Ylornic offered to the companions, "We will not be able to set off before tomorrow and it would be good for us to grow more accustomed to each other."

"More food?" Banir asked, his face lighting up, as only those who are young and able to have few concerns outside their own preservation and desire can achieve.

"Thank you, Ylornic, we shall certainly take you up on your offer." Koran answered for the companions. Banir's stomach chose to rumble at that moment, as if punctuating the invitation, and causing the others to chortle and his embarrassment to deepen.

The companions rose early the next day to break their fast. They had discussed Conclave's plans with Ylorac and Ylornic over dinner the previous night. The opportunity to explore the Yash-tu's falling out with the nations of Sambar had not arisen and the companions were just pleased to be able to enlist their help now. It had been agreed that two small companies of the Mystics would accompany them to Narsos, one to work on the western front and one of the eastern front. They were provisioned with supplies and new horses and assured that the mounts they had abandoned would be reclaimed and housed in some of the city stables and put to good use. There was apparently a tunnel that would lead them on a quicker route out of the mountains back into Laconia. They would ride as a joint company as far as Korrath and then split into two companies there, one heading south-west and the other south-east. Koran would travel with the Mystics riding east, to affirm their credentials to the Sambarian army when they reached the eastern front and Teran, Xantila and Banir would return to the main position on the western front.

Chapter XXVII – Northern Support

The stalemate between the Narsians and the two Sambarian fronts on the edge of the forest of Narsos had continued for now for three weeks. The Sambarians had stopped making forays beyond their defences because it usually led to a loss of many soldiers without being able to push their foothold any further into the lands of Narsos. Instead, they worked at building their defensive position and responded into any Narsian attacks, though these too had grown rare. They were still unable to fathom the tactics of the Narsians and why they were not using magic upon the Sambarians' foothold positions, but were using it in the open plains. The Rangers had continued to roam back and forth between the eastern and western encampments, picking off any groups of Narsians who attempted to travel into Sambarians lands by skirted around the encampments. As of yet, the Narsians had not attempted to send a large force between the two Sambarian footholds into Sambarian lands. Given their superior numbers, which fresh scouts had now corroborated and compared to Teran's initial report, the finest tactical minds amongst the Sambarian nations were at a loss as to understand why the Narsians were holding out.

Overnight the Narsian tactics changed. The number of attacks against the Sambarian footholds dropped off. This was of little comfort to Gethas and the other commanders because it meant that the Narsians were sure to try a new tactic shortly, one which the

Sambarians may not be prepared for. The western commanders of Gerak, Hrunta and Ruorland were meeting in their forward command tent to discuss what should be done. The Rangers has recently returned from their latest sweep across the forest between the two Sambarian fronts and so Janis had also joined their deliberations.

"Why now?" Asked Olin, "What has changed?"

"Nothing as far as I can see," Responded Temac, looking over the rough maps strewn on the table before them, "But little of the Narsian tactics so far has made particular sense, so we can take little comfort in this, event if it has resulted in a much-needed break for our troops."

"We need to send out some scouts to find out what those slippery Narsians are up to." Suggested Kiesan to the gathered commanders.

"Let me send some of my men. They might be able to infiltrate behind enemy lines a little more easily than the regular scouts." Gerakan Intelligence officer, Flint, suggested.

"Agreed." Gethas responded and the others nodded in assent.

"The Rangers will join you in your scouting efforts. We could use a new challenge to encourage us to keep our arrow tips sharpened." Janis assented on behalf of his people.

"Thank you." Gethas answered on behalf of the Sambarians. Kiesan and Janis left the tent immediately to commission their scouts on their new mission deeper into enemy territory. The remaining commanders continued to discuss what the Narsians might have in store for them, whilst Olin took to penning an update to

Child of Rydos

be delivered to the eastern front.

It took a couple of days for the scouts Janis and Kiesan had sent to return to the Sambarian encampment with tidings of the Narsians. Those tidings were not comforting.

"It seems that the Narsians are finally responding to the fact that they have not been able to overwhelm our position here." Kiesan reported to the gathered commanders, "They are consolidating and amassing a large force which is, even now, moving towards our western pallisade here."

"Are their numbers too great for our fortifications to cope with?" Temac asked Kiesan and Janis who were reporting their scouts' findings.

"It will be bloody." Janis responded, "There will be no way to fight such a large force without losing many of our own, but it is possible that we'll be able to hold this position." Gethas swore,

"Holding our position is not good enough." He exclaimed angrily, "We need to push down into Narsos and end this war. Otherwise they'll bleed us dry one slow cut at a time." There was silence throughout the tent as the others gathered together thought about how to respond. They agreed with Gethas, they too were frustrated by the lack of progress in this war, which had been forced upon them, but there remained the huge elephant in the room. Finally, Olin spoke,

"What about their magic, which they use on us every time we venture further south?" He asked. He was not particularly making a jibe at Gethas for a lack of thought, but more asking the question, which he knew the whole room was pondering, the sharp end of which he had personal experience of.

"I just don't see that we have much choice." Gethas concluded, "We'll eventually lose this battle if we don't forge further into Narsian territory and decapitate this attack at its source. We don't have the resources to maintain this position indefinitely, we need to supress the Narsians, or ultimately we'll lose this war anyway." It was a gloomy prognosis, but true. Silence stretched out before them, an unwelcome and morbid companion to their thoughts. Into that silence no-one spoke, for not one of them could think of what could be said. The facts were before them and they had already, over and over again, exhausted themselves with offering up ideas, none of which provided a realistic solution to their troubles. As the silence continued, growing increasingly oppressive, a call rang across the camp, diverting their attention. A runner entered the tent to report.

"Your Majesties and Sirs," The runner began, bowing low as he entered the tent, "Teran, Xantila and Banir have returned from the north. They bring with them the Laconian Mystics." Hope sparked in the eyes of the gathered commanders.

"Thank Ranek. Show us to them, at once." King Gethas commanded, rising to his feet with excitement as the rest followed suit, "This may be a much-needed answer to our prayer to the gods."

Teran and his companions had gathered at the camp muster point and awaited the arrival of the camp commanders to report. As Gethas approached them with the other commanders he did a quick tally in his head. Teran had brought fifty of these Mystics from the north. Would it be enough?

"Report." Gethas commanded Teran, noting his son was not with them. Teran obviously noticed Gethas' concern, as he included word of Koran almost immediately in his report.

"Your Majesty, Your Majesties," Teran began, bowing to them each in turn, "We return successfully from our mission to gain additional support from the Mystics of Laconia. We split the company in two at Korrath and Koran led that half towards the eastern front, so he could vouch for the company to King Arran and King Tlanic." Teran paused briefly for a breath, at which point Ylornic stepped forward, obviously wanting to speak, Teran nodded his head, almost imperceptibly, and introduced him, "Your Majesties, may I introduce Ylornic, leader of this company, son of Ylorac, the leader of the Yash-tu, whom we call the Mystics."

"Your Majesties," Ylornic spoke clearly, bowing to them, to show that he recognised their authority, "My father has bid me support you in any way we are able against the magics of the Narsians. We are not an aggressive people, so will not be much used to you in hand-to-hand combat, but we are skilled at magical defence and subterfuge."

"I'll say you are." Piped up Banir, interrupting Ylornic and earning himself a frown from Teran, "We didn't have an easy job finding you..." Banir's comments faded away and a subtle blush came to his cheeks as he realised he'd spoken out of turn, unused to such formal proceedings. King Temac spoke next,

"Though you live within the borders of the nations of Sambar, you are an independent people. Will you truly recognise our authority and aid us in this struggle?" He asked. He did not sound concerned, as much as curious about the Yash-tu and the part they intended to play.

"The mayor of Yellath has offered us a link to our

historic past of great interested to us." Ylornic answered truthfully, "But we would have continued to come to your aid in any case. A growth in strength in the magicians of Narsos serves us no more than it serves you."

"That is the second time you have referenced your pre-existing support for us," Rhan Orin spoke gruffly, a scowl upon his face, "Tell us, what support have you been thus far?" Teran shook his head, as if hoping it would cut off Orin's words, before he jumped in and spoke on Ylornic's behalf, not wanting to upset what seemed like a fragile alliance.

"The Yash-tu use their influence to suppress the Narsian magic within the borders of Sambar. It is why they have not been successful in bringing magic to bear upon your encampment here, though obviously the magic does sometimes get through, as Olin, Temac, Xantila, Banir and myself know only too well." Teran responded with chagrin.

"That explains a lot." Gethas commented, looking at the other commanders. Ylornic then spoke on his own behalf,

"Your ancestor, Am Bære, made a deal with us, when he swept through the northern reaches uniting disparate tribes under his banner to form what became the Kingdom of the father of the nations. In the old dialect, S'Am Bære, and over the hundreds of years since then, Sambar. He allowed us our autonomy if we would protect his lands from magical incursion. We lived for a time in peace with the Sambarians, until we were betrayed. We are a faithful people and we have kept our oath with those who are oath-breakers. To protect ourselves we retreated deeper into the mountains to live without interference, but our sacred duty we have always upheld and so we are here today." Silence followed Ylornic's speech, which all nearby had craned to hear. Ylornic spoke as if these events, which happened in the mists of time had happened yesterday. He spoke of history which was forgotten to the Sambarians, yet was obviously still recalled vividly by his own people. It was difficult for the Sambarians to know how to respond.

"Thank you for your honest words and for your continued help." Gethas responded smoothly, "Is there any way we can compensate your people to repair the rift between us?" Ylornic paused to consider Gethas' words thoughtfully,

"There is nothing you can give to repair the past. The, already promised, restoration to us of the archive found at Yellath is a great gift, revealing your good intent. The past is behind us, let us leave it there and each work towards a new future built on trust instead."

"Yes, let us look towards the future." Gethas answered on behalf of all those gathered, "Your men must need some rest after the long journey southwards and we were just discussing our immediate plans due to some new intelligence on the Narsians' movements. Why don't you join our discussion whilst your men set up camp?"

"A good idea." Ylornic agreed and the assembled dignitaries dispersed to head back towards the command tent, where maps and refreshments could aid their diliberations. "My men?" Ylornic queried.

"I'll have a sergeant show them where they may most easily set up camp. We can show you where they are stationed after this initial briefing." General Kiesan offered, nodding to the nearest sergeant, who took up the order immediately.

"Thank you." Ylornic said gratefully. As they walked to the command tent, Teran stepped in alongside Olin and Temac, closely followed by Xantila and Banir.

"What is the news from the eastern front, as I've just sent Koran there?" He asked.

The eastern front was considerably nearer the Narsian front line than the western front was. This was particularly true since the Rydosians had captured Ptanga, whilst the city of I'sos remained a Narsian stronghold where their principal force was gathered. Nonetheless, the tactics that the Narsians had brought to bear against the Sambarians in the east was a near mirror image of their tactics further west and were equally confusing to Arran, Tlanic and Teloran, as they were to the commanders from Gerak, Ruorland and Hrunta. The arrival of Koran with a company of Mystics, followed the next day by a missive from the western front with an update on their plans to push the attack deeper into enemy territory and towards I'sos gave a much-needed boost to morale.

In order to support their cousins in the west, with the help of the Yash-tu, they planned also to make a push towards I'sos, ensuring that the Narsians would have to continue to divide their attention between two fronts and hopefully increasing the likelihood of success for the Sambarian campaign. The sense that they were finally bringing the fight to the Narsians, rather than responding to attacks sent upon them, created a great sense of eagerness and anticipation, which masked the fear they all felt about being confronted directly with Narsian magic, irrespective of the help from the Yash-tu.

Child of Rydos

"At last an open field on which to do honest battle!" Teloran had exclaimed to the gathered armies of the east before they marched further south and west, which was met with a roar of approval.

Chapter XXVIII – Nars Opens

Ten days of the bloodiest fighting any of them had ever experienced, with many losses on each side, saw the Sambarian forces pushing the Narsian armies back towards I'sos where they had their main staging area. Once the Hruntans, Gerakans and Ruors had pushed further south than Ptanga, the Rydosian troops stationed there had sallied out to join the army, giving their forces a needed boost in numbers. The Yash-tu had been as good as their word and had prevented any Narsian magic from halting their advance. Still, the Narsian tactics continued to confuse the combined commanders of the Sambarian forces. The Narsians had used their superior numbers to ill effect and, given their forces. The Sambarians were more than a little surprised they had managed to get this far. They put their success down to the seeming inexperience of the Narsian commanders and troops to mount an effective attack or defense.

As the armies came together in the fields outside I'sos though, the Narsian army seemed to dig in and the Sambarian advance came up against fierce resistance.

"Looks like they've decided we've come far enough." Commented Temac to Teran and Xantila, as their companies took a brief respite from fighting on the front, being replaced by fresh Hruntan and Ruor troops. "I think... What..." Teran's response trailed off as he looked towards the fighting with horror. Magic like he had never experienced was suddenly unleashed from behind the Narsian lines, sending fiery missile after fiery missile swirling up into the sky to then rapidly snake straight into the Sambarian troops, scattering their defensive line. The Narsian troops surged forward, the only thing preventing a complete collapse of the Sambarian front being that the missiles killed any Narsian they hit too. Teran glanced towards where the Yash-tu were positioned. He thought he could see a look of surprise upon some of their faces, combined with intense concentration, beads of sweat trickling down across their foreheads and cheeks, as they chanted under their breath. Suddenly there was a shimmering in the sky and the missiles began to explode in mid-flight against some invisible barrier, rather than continuing their descent into the lines of soldiers. The chanting from the Yash-tu grew louder and more frenetic and a wave of counter missiles rose from their position to stream deep behind the Narsian front line.

"Looks like they over shot the mark." Temac commented.

"No, look." Answered Xantila, as the counter-missiles impacted on another invisible barrier, "I think their aiming to take out the source of the enemy magic. Is that... yes, Agachen is amongst them."

"You've got good eyes if you can see that far." Countered Temac.

"I'm a hunter and a Ranger." Xantila shrugged.

"I think our break is over." Teran sighed with the weariness of the seemingly endless battle, "We need to help secure the front line again whilst the magicians are occupied and try and press any advantage we can manage." The others nodded and called their company back to order to return to the front.

From that point onwards, it was obvious that two battles were being waged that day. It had always been a battle of muscle and steel, but there was now a second battle of forces, well beyond the comprehension of most, being fought. The signs of it were all around the soldiers though, as explosions of light, fire and wind erupted erratically around them. The effect of this was to greatly unsettle soldiers on both sides of the battle lines, making them edgy and prone to error of judgement. Time seemed to slow as the battle surged backward and forward as lines formed, were broken and reformed time and again. It was not long before commanders on each side had little knowledge of who was winning, or what was going on. The battle had a life and energy of its own. All their fortunes were lost to fate and all they could do now was offer prayers to whatever gods were listening and hope that they would survive the ordeal.

Teran stepped back from the front line, his chest heaving as his lungs drew in much needed air to combat his continued exertion. He looked up at the sky to see the passage of the sun in attempt to ascertain how much time had passed in this crazy battle. His ears burned as blood surged through his head and body, as his heart worked overtime to catch up with his actions. He could barely hear anything over the clash of steel, the explosion of magics and the shouts and screams of dying men. Suddenly he heard a thudding sound which rocked his body slightly. He looked down to see an arrow protruding from his chest, somehow piercing his chain mail, and a crimson stain of blood blossoming across his clothes from the shaft. His mouth formed an 'O' shape, but before a sound could escape he collapsed to the ground.

"Teran has been hit!" Xantila shouted above the din as she glanced back to his position, whilst dancing in and out of the front line dealing death to any Narsians who tried to slip past. "To me!" She shouted at Temac who was a little further down the line, as she ran back to Teran's body. Temac joined her shortly, the grin he wore from the exertion of battle fading fast as he saw Teran. "He's unconscious. We need to get him to a field medic, immediately." Xantila said with urgency in her voice as she and Temac bent to lift Teran and carry him away from the battle.

It felt exhilarating to be in a good and honest battle and to be on the back of a good and honest steed too, thought Teloran, as he prepared to lead another charge of Laconian knights' cavalry into enemy lines. This was how he knew best to fight. He had already led several charges against the enemy line and reformed as they retreated and he would charge again. With the Arinachian fighters they had now pushed the Narsians right back to the walls of I'sos. The eastern and western fronts of the Sambarian forces now stretched as one band, arcing across the landscape and closing off any northern advance the Narsians might attempt. Of course, after the exhilaration of these early battles it was all starting to go wrong. Magic was erupting everywhere and as Teloran looked around, he thought he might have to revise his estimation of this being a 'good and honest' battle any longer. The whole situation affronted his sense of a properly ordered world, according to the

Laconian mindset in which he had been raised. With a dark scowl upon his face, he shouted the order to charge, slamming down the visor on his battle armour and tipping his lance as his cavalry wheeled around and towards the battle front – an unstoppable stampede of sinew and muscle working in perfect union as the battle-trained mounts scythed into the Narsian front line of infantry, who were ill-equipped to repel a cavalry attack.

Nearby Orin and Olin, his wounds sufficiently healed, led the Ruors into battle, screaming obscenities as they waved their well-notched axes and charged at the enemy. The sight of the frenzied barbarians was enough to intimidate a courageous man, let alone a timid one as they felled foe after foe in front of them, as if they were felling timber to survive the northern winter frost. The Laconians wheeled their advance around, creating a pincer, forcing the Narsians to chose death from either side.

A stray magic missile sizzled through the air, causing confusion as soldiers from both sides leapt aside from the magical attack. Then an explosion sounded and a temporarily blinding light, which caused the Laconian advance to falter momentarily. Their horses, though battle hardened, were not used to magical intervention and this could still unnerve them. Teloran's horse reared in the confusion and he was thrown from his saddle. Olin, as his vision cleared, seeing his companion was missing, forged his way towards the spot where he could see the riderless horse. The frenzy of his attack increased as he focussed his mind on the task at hand and not a single man could stand against his fury as he made Teloran's position. Teloran was lying still on the ground. Orin, Olin's father, came right behind him and now took up a defensive position, allowing Olin to lift Teloran over his horse.

"I need to get him out of here." Olin stated, wasting no words. His father did not waste words either, nodding grimly as Olin took the saddle behind Teloran's prone body and charged with them out of the battle.

The battle was not going well for the Sambarians. Though they had pushed the Narsians back this far, the enemy still had superior numbers and that was beginning to tell on the increasingly exhausted northerners. The magical battle going on overhead seemed at an impasse, with troops from both sides being caught and killed in the cross-fire. Ultimately, numbers would tell and the Narsians would overwhelm the invaders. What happened next would remain forever etched in the memories of those who witnessed it and it would change the balance of power between the kingdoms for centuries to come.

An eardrum splitting rush of sound split the sky which became wreathed with flame. The flames contorted and swirled, all the while the sound continued. From the fire a shape emerged, a colossal thing made of of living flame. It lifted its head and from its beak sounded a piercing cry, which stunned everyone on the battlefield, bringing all the frenzied fighting to a brief stop. It beat its wings, sending down sheets of flame, as it rose higher into the sky. It appeared bird-like and graceful as soared high above the scene.

Then the firebird dove, swooping low to the ground, over the Narsian lines. As it passed through their ranks it left chaos in its wake, the stinking remains of charred bodies and blackened earth. When the Narsians realised it was attacking them, their resolve broke and they began to flee in terror. Still the firebird swooped again and again, causing complete devastation. The Narsian magicians tried to counter its attack, focussing all their magical will against the beast, but their magics seemed to have little effect, other than to make the beast notice them. It swerved mid-flight and bore down upon their position, wiping out the majority of their clustered magicians. Not a single flame from the firebird licked any of the Sambarians, its attack was purely focussed on the Narsians. Seeing this broke any remaining resolve amongst the Narsians and they were completely routed.

"Wha... what's going on?" Teran asked groggily, rubbing his eyes as he came to and trying to sit up from the position he was laying in, for which he was rewarded with a sharp pain in the chest.

"Lay back down!" Xantila said irritably, pushing Teran gently onto his back again, "You've been out cold. You took an arrow to the chest. Pierced straight through your armour somehow. You're lucky to be alive, you need to rest."

"What's happening in the battle?" Teran asked, unable to hide his frustration at being prevented for helping any further in the fighting.

"It wasn't going well for us. You got critically wounded. Teloran..." Xantila turned her head to the side. Teran followed her gaze, turning himself slightly whilst trying not to put tension across his chest. Teloran was lying near by, his plate armour had been removed and he was lying very still.

"Xan, Is he...?" Teran began.

"...Dead. Yes." Xantila finished the sentence for

him, sorrow in her eyes and in her voice. "One of the magical volleys startled his horse so that it threw him. He got trampled in the chaos, he died shortly after arriving here. Olin brought him in before returning to the fight."

"You said the battle isn't going well for us. Why didn't you return to the fight with Olin?" Teran asked.

"I said it *wasn't* going well. One extra bow or sword wasn't going to make enough of a difference and I wanted to make sure you would be okay. Olin preferred to return to the battlefield to vent his anger and sadness. I think he was moved by Teloran's death more than he would let on. You get to know people well when you travel a difficult road with them. I guess it makes them family." Teran nodded.

"We've managed to turn the tides of the battle in our favour then?"

"You wouldn't believe me if I told you." Xantila snorted, "It is nothing we've done, some damn magic the Yash-tu conjured up. I'd take you out of this tent to show you, if you could move." Teran caught the fact that there was a strain in Xantila's voice. She evidently did not like this magic and given what they had already both experienced together, this left Teran's mind running down all sorts of horrific imaginary avenues. Xantila could see Teran straining to know more, so she put him out of his misery, at least to the best of her descriptive ability.

"The sky is filled with living flame..." She began, "The Yash-tu have conjured a colossal firebird, its wreaking havoc amongst the Narsians and has wiped out their magicians." She was cut off from continuing by the entrance of Ylornic into the tent. Teran's face had dropped, incredulous at the description Xantila was giving.

"It's not a firebird," Ylornic contributed without fanfare, "They are small creatures. It must be a phoenix, a primordial spirit of fire. The Yash-tu didn't conjure it. Until a little while ago I thought the phoenix was a myth, extinct, or sealed from entering our world from the void." Ylornic halted in his speech and looked concerned that he'd spoken out of turn.

"You're not in control of it?!" Xantila exclaimed, "Why is it here then? Can you stop it before it runs out of Narsians and starts taking an interest in us?"

"I have my suspicions. That won't be necessary." Ylornic answered each question directly and without preamble.

"Why?" Teran asked. Ylornic let his gaze fall upon him.

"As quickly as it appeared, its fire went out. It is gone. It is only the remaining carnage from its presence, which we are left to deal with, which convinces me I didn't dream the whole episode."

"The magic that brought it here has been used up?" Xantila asked.

"Perhaps." Was all that Ylornic was willing to commit in answer to her question.

"What is happening on the battlefield now?" Teran asked, bringing them all to the present.

"The battle is over. The Narsians are waving a white flag and calling for terms." Ylornic answered, to which Teran and Xantila both breathed a sigh of relief, irrespective of the circumstances which had delivered it.

"Presumably, we're not going to let the Narsians know we didn't conjure that thing…" Teran conjected.

Epilogue

Kellor, who had been the commander of the Narsian armies, represented Narsos in the negotiations with the Sambarians over the terms of the Narsian surrender. He was of the Narsian imperial bloodline and so had authority to speak for the emperor in the capital of Nars. He met with Conclave to discuss those details. It seemed that Agachen had been the driving force behind the Narsian aggression and their peculiar tactics. Kellor had been commanding the forces, but had been answerable to Agachen. It transpired that Agachen's tactics had not impressed Kellor and had been the source of some heated arguments between them, but ultimately the emperor had given Agachen an imperial writ to lead the invasion as he saw fit, despite the fact he was a foreigner. The fact that Agachen was not of Narsian descent was a matter of intrigue, but Kellor could give no details as to his lineage. It seems that Agachen had ingratiated himself in the Imperial Court at Nars in a similar fashion to that which he had in Arin. These concerns were largely academic now. Agachen had been with the other Narsian magic users when they had been consumed by phoenix fire and so was assumed dead and would not have to answer to the emperor for his failure. Kellor would have that pleasure instead.

The Sambarians pushed their advantage in negotiations almost to breaking point. Northern Narsos from the great forest, right down to the Great Nars River was to become a protectorate of Sambar,

Epilogue

administrated out of I'sos. This was to create a region of open land under Sambarian control to make it more difficult for Narsos to infiltrate spies or troops into Hrunta and Arinach without notice. That land would be policed by Sambarian troops, made up from a mixture across all their standing armies, but under control of the adminstrator in I'sos. Narsian troops would not be allowed to bear arms anywhere in the protectorate. Slavery, which was legal in Narsos, was to be outlawed in the protectorate. An ambassador was also to be assigned from the Sambarian nations to be stationed permanently in Nars to act as a liaison between the empire and the Kingdoms of Sambar.

A disgruntled Temac was given the duty of administrator over the protectorate. He had been hoping to return home to the pastures of Hrunta, but instead found he was moving his family further south. He'd have to see if he could breed some good equine stock in these warmer climbs of Narsos. Flint was made ambassador in Nars, partially due to his existing extensive knowledge of Narsos and its language. Gethas chose not to share with Kellor that Flint had previously been the head of Gerakan Intelligence. Teran suspected that Koran would be taking over that role, at least for a time, once he returned home to Ariss.

After the negotiations between Kellor and Conclave had been finalised and Temac had made some initial decisions and set up a command structure as administrator, the majority of the Sambarian armies began their long treks home, excepting those seconded to the protectorate. The royal families of Sambar, rather than head immediately home, travelled with the

Laconians to their capital of Azin on the edge of the forest. Here a full state funeral was held for Teloran. It involved an honour guard of five hundred fully armoured Laconian knights on parade, dressed in ceremonial black plate armour – an intimidating, yet moving, sight. The general populace of the city was devastated at the loss of their crown prince. Teran was moderately surprised at the level of feeling, given Teloran's inability to fully sympathise with others. It obviously was not expected of him by the Laconian populace, who were weeping fully as much as Teloran's own family.

Immediately after the funeral service, King Tlanic held a ceremony, in the presence of the other rulers across Sambar, for the Yash-tu. He formally thanked them for their support in the conflict against the Narsians and gave them a formal written decree which entitled them to claim any and all materials discovered in Yellath relating to their former home and life there. He also offered to commission further excavations in the city, if they desired it, to fully uncover any other forgotten remains. Ylornic rose to receive the gift and to respond to Tlanic's offer.

"Our most sincere and humble thanks for your gift, Your Majesty." Ylornic said as he received the writ, bowing deeply, "We also offer again our condolences to your family and nation in their loss. I do not think we need to tear up half of Yellath looking for more of our history at this precise moment in time. It will take the assembly long enough to go through the materials you have already found, and offered to us, from our past." Ylornic then shifted himself and addressed his remarks to the gathered members of Conclave, "I have spoken with my father this morning. The Yash-tu assembly has decided to offer to each of the nations of Sambar, including the protectorate, a permanent member of the Yash-tu assembly to act as a liaison between our peoples. This is so we may never become so estranged again." There was a general murmur of surprise and discussion amongst all those listening to Ylornic's words. Both in the fact that he could communicate with his father instantly over long distances and also regarding the offer of the Yash-tu. Ylornic continued, "This will allow us to keep a closer eye on magics being cast within the Kingdoms, to avoid a repeat of our recent war. It will also allow you all instant communication with the assembly and between the other nations of Sambar, if you wish to use our abilities." Tlanic looked towards Gethas, who stepped forward to speak, looking at each of the other leaders who all nodded to him in turn.

"On behalf of Conclave, we accept your gracious offer." Gethas asserted. Teran did not get the impression that they had any real option in this offer, but having the Yash-tu closer at hand would undoubtedly be a good thing if they were the brunt of further magical attack from the south, not that this seemed likely in the aftermath of the phoenix event, as it was being called.

"Will you be sending a representative to live with the Rangers?" Xantila asked Ylornic. Ylornic looked at her,

"Would we find welcome in Azin heart, or find ourselves mysteriously lost on the way?" He asked with a quirk of his eyebrow.

"I could not say for sure. The magic of the forest is wild. It might not agree with your digestion." She responded honestly, yet with a little cheek.

Child of Rydos

"I think your people are safe from interference for now. You can always come to Azin to seek our help if required." Ylornic finished. Teran thought he heard Xantila mutter something under her breath, but did not think anyone else noticed.

Teran leaned against the bow of the ship, the spray from the ocean giving relief on this hot day, as he looked out towards the harbour of Rydos, which was finally coming into view. By Elerin, it was good to be home, he thought. He was looking forward to seeing his mother and sister again. Things would have a hope of settling back to normal now. As he was thinking this, he heard a sailor shout in annoyance and he glanced back to see Banir hastily apologising and backing away from a spilt slops bucket. No doubt he had been scampering about without paying attention to his surroundings again. Teran could not say for sure why he had let Banir stay with him. The boy had nowhere else to really call home and Teran had become used to his company, and so seemed to have adopted the boy on some level. Perhaps things would not be quite so settled with Banir there to make trouble.

Ylornic came to stand beside Teran at the ship's rail. Teran had initially been surprised that Ylornic would be the representative sent to Rydos, but after some consideration the surprise wore off. Teran was the first to speak,

"I know you're keeping an eye on me." He stated. Ylornic shrugged,

"You're worth keeping an eye on. You know you are different from most people. You have a natural aptitude."

Epilogue

"For magic?" Teran asked.

"If you want to call it that." Ylornic answered, "Or you could consider it being more in tune with reality and the natural world around you."

"You want me teach me to explore this aptitude?" Teran hedged a guess.

"It might be safer. If your ability grows wildly it could cause... trouble..." Ylornic was obviously holding back on his words.

"The Rydosians are not very fond of the idea of magic. I do not think it would go down very well to have one of the royal household practicing it." Teran stated.

"It doesn't have to be public knowledge." Ylornic suggested, "Also," He concluded, "Tell me if you have any violent dreams involving fire again." Teran looked at him, the surprise across his face revealing the truth of the suggestion.

Here ends the *Child of Rydos*.

Printed in Great Britain
by Amazon